Headstrong and Heartsick

"I am asking you to marry me, Catherine," Lord Coverdale declared, "though I cannot promise you mad and passionate love."

Catherine had no choice but to answer, "I cannot do so—and allow you to shoulder problems that are not of your making, my lord."

That, then, was that. Catherine had done what pride demanded. She clung to that belief until after the earl departed, and her aunt, Lady Clinton, quietly told her, "I hope you did not refuse him. For if you did you might just regret it for the rest of your life."

Normally Catherine never heeded the words of others. But now even she had to wonder: *How could doing something so right feel so terribly wrong?*

IRENE SAUNDERS, a native of Yorkshire, England, worked a number of years for the U.S. Air Force in London. A love of travel brought her to New York City, where she met her husband, Ray. She now lives in Port St. Lucie, Florida, dividing her time between writing, bookkeeping, gardening, needlepoint, and travel.

SIGNET REGENCY ROMANCE
COMING IN SEPTEMBER 1991

Carol Proctor
A Dashing Widow

Melinda McRae
An Unlikely Attraction

Emma Lange
The Unmanageable Miss Marlowe

Talk
of the
Town

~ *by* ~

Irene Saunders

Ⓞ
A SIGNET BOOK

SIGNET
Published by the Penguin Group
Penguin Books USA Inc., 375 Hudson Street,
New York, New York 10014, U.S.A.
Penguin Books Ltd, 27 Wrights Lane,
London W8 5TZ, England
Penguin Books Australia Ltd, Ringwood,
Victoria, Australia
Penguin Books Canada Ltd, 2801 John Street,
Markham, Ontario, Canada L3R, 1B4
Penguin Books (N.Z.) Ltd, 182-190 Wairau Road,
Auckland 10, New Zealand

Penguin Books Ltd, Registered Offices:
Harmondsworth, Middlesex, England

First published by Signet, an imprint of New American Library,
a division of Penguin Books USA Inc.

First Printing, August, 1991
10 9 8 7 6 5 4 3 2 1

BOOKS ARE AVAILABLE AT QUANTITY DISCOUNTS WHEN USED TO
PROMOTE PRODUCTS OR SERVICES. FOR INFORMATION PLEASE WRITE
TO PREMIUM MARKETING DIVISION, PENGUIN BOOKS USA INC.,
375 HUDSON STREET, NEW YORK, NEW YORK 10014.

Prologue

THE ANCIENT CARRIAGE bumped and bounced along the sadly neglected private road leading from Hayward House to the pike road. Overgrown branches slapped first one side and then the other, and Catherine Hayward shuddered at the thought that it might overturn. She glanced nervously across at Mark, her younger brother, who on entering the confined space had flung himself into the opposite corner and now slumped there, glaring angrily at the tips of his Hessians.

A light rain had begun to fall, and soon the decidedly unpleasant smell of wet leather began to permeate the confined space. The usually ruddy cheeks of Maggie, the young maid who was accompanying her mistress to London, were growing paler by the minute and Catherine began to envy her papa, who rode his stallion some distance ahead of the carriage. He was covered from head to toe in an almost waterproof cloak, and seemed completely oblivious to anything save the need to get them to London as quickly as possible so that he might take ship to Antwerp and thence to Brussels to help Wellington put a period to Napoleon's renewed ambitions.

"How can he expect me to get around in London without either a horse or a carriage, for I'd not be seen dead in this old rattletrap." Mark did not expect an answer and was surprised when Catherine responded.

"There's little need to worry, Mark, for I have the gravest of doubts that our conveyance will remain in one piece as far as London," she said tartly. "And if you mean to complain the entire way, you may suffer the same fate, for I've heard all I wish to hear on that head. You're not the only one who is put out by Papa's decision.''

"So I would assume from the way the two of you were going at it last evening after I went out for some air,'' Mark said snidely, ''and I'm sure you deserved the sound slap he gave you.''

She flushed. "I should not have spoken to him the way I did,'' she admitted, ''for I told him he'd already done more than enough for a mad king and a spendthrift prince, to say nothing of a country that despised the returning soldiers and cared nothing if they starved to death.''

"What difference does it make to you whether you spend a couple of months at home in Norfolk or in London?'' the young man asked in a surly tone.

"It doesn't, of course, for I'm still in mourning and will not be going about socially, but I'm worried about Papa. He had narrowly missed being killed when he came home wounded last time, and Mama told me he has scars all over his body. He's taken too many chances with his life already,'' Catherine told him, her eyes bright with unshed tears.

Mark reached over and patted her knee. "Don't take on so, Cathie,'' he said gently. "Papa knows how to take care of himself, and this time it will be over very quickly according to what everyone says. Did you bring any cards with you? I'll give you a game of piquet, if you like.''

Her face broke into a smile as she reached into the large bag at her side. Mark wasn't bad as youngsters went these days, she told herself. It was just that Mama had spoiled him terribly when Papa was away so long, and he'd grown far too accustomed to getting his own way.

Handing the cards to him, she took off her black bonnet and let her chestnut-colored hair fall softly about her shoulders. It was the identical color to her brother's, as were her blue eyes, and the casual observer might have thought them twins until he saw Mark's still boyish features. A closer look might also have revealed more character in Catherine's face than her additional two years would seem to warrant. They were approximately the same height now, but Mark was still growing, and in a year or two would be taller and would broaden out. As yet, however, he had the same slender build as his sister.

They played piquet most of the morning, not seriously, of course, for the sway of the coach frequently caused the cards to fall onto the floor, but it passed the time, and they were both surprised when the carriage slowed down and they heard their father's voice alongside them instructing the coachman about changing the horses.

Major Sir John Hayward was smiling as he opened the door, for he was happier now that he was drawing nearer to his goal. "I know that you packed a luncheon, Catherine," he said, "but let's leave it for later and get something warm in the inn after that chilly, wet ride. I've secured a private dining room for us."

This was indeed more than Catherine had expected, and she was glad to step down and enter the cozy warmth of the inn. Even in early June a blazing fire was a welcoming sight, and when a motherly woman came hurrying forward to take her father's cloak and set it to dry, Catherine felt better than she had all day.

"Does Aunt Genevieve live in the center of London, Papa, near the park?" she asked.

The major smiled a little ruefully. "I'm afraid not," he said with a shake of his head. "My sister was always a bit of a do-gooder, and when her husband died just a few years after they were wed, she bought a large house on the corner of Devonshire Place and Kennington Lane, just around the corner from Vauxhall Gardens. What she does is take in young country girls who come up to London, mistakenly thinking they can find work there more easily than in the country. Before they get themselves into serious trouble, she trains them as maids and such, and finds them positions."

Catherine's eyebrows rose. Now she realized why her Mama had always been reticent regarding Aunt Genevieve's unusual activities. She knew her to be only a couple of years younger than her papa, but she must be cut from a very different cloth.

"I'm sure she'll appreciate any help you can give her," her father continued, "and I'll expect you to keep an eye on Mark here, and make sure he keeps out of mischief. I don't want to come back and find him about to be deported, or worse."

The young man scowled, but knew better than to say anything, and Catherine wished her papa had been a little more tactful, for this was just the kind of remark to put Mark in a pelter and set him off on some wild escapade or other.

"I don't think you need worry in that regard, Papa," she said quietly. "Just do what you feel you have to do, and get back as quickly and safely as you can."

After a satisfying meal they resumed their journey, spending the night in an inn about a half day's ride from London. By the middle of the next day, after passing through an area of decrepit-looking warehouses and inhaling the stench of the River Thames, they were rattling over London Bridge toward their destination. Catherine was somewhat disappointed that they had merely skirted the city itself and completely missed the fashionable Mayfair section she had heard so much about, but her father was anxious to find out about his own transportation from here on, and had reminded her at breakfast that she would see all she wanted of London in the days ahead.

"I don't believe your aunt enters much into society herself these days, but she has a sister-in-law who never misses the Season. No doubt you'll have a chance to see some of the fashionable folk if she has a mind to take you for a ride in the park one day," he had suggested kindly.

Catherine had little hope of this, however, as she glanced down at what had once been a pretty but rather worn pale blue pelisse but which, together with most of her gowns, had been dyed black when her mama had passed on. Though the official mourning period would be over in a month or so, her meager funds would not permit so much as one new gown.

Aunt Genevieve was expecting them and hurried to the door as the carriage drew up. She was a small, plump lady, not at all like her brother in appearance, and her face wore a concerned expression which Catherine quickly realized had become habitual in her chosen work.

"Come along in, all of you, for luncheon is on the table and you'll not want it to get cold," Lady Clinton urged, as her brother left his horse in the hands of a groom and hurried up the steps.

Mark alighted from the carriage and glanced around at the shabby, smoke-blackened houses and the empty, dirt-strewn streets. He grinned sardonically at his sister and offered her his arm. "Welcome to London, Cathie. Though this is hardly Mayfair, I'm sure I'll find a way of getting there before long."

One

CATHERINE WAS FIRMLY convinced that she did not care for London, or at least what she had seen of it thus far, and she had, in fact, seen a great deal more in three weeks than most people did in a lifetime. In all honesty, however, she knew it was not so much London that she disliked as the terrible waiting to hear what had happened to her father in the horrendous battle that had taken place at Waterloo more than a week ago.

There had been dancing and celebrating in the streets of London, for Wellington had, of course, been victorious, though at the cost of a tremendous number of lives. But, with no word thus far as to whether their papa had survived, she had not had the heart to celebrate.

She sadly missed her chestnut mare and the daily rides she took around the estates at home. After the first few days, Catherine could no longer bear to sit in her aunt's house and listen for hours on end as Lady Clinton instructed her girls on household duties which she had been familiar with since early childhood. Instead, she had taken to walking miles alone each day.

She was an unusual sight as she came along Kennington Lane, not taking dainty, ladylike steps, but striding out, her head held high and her arms swinging, a healthy color in her cheeks, and a sparkle in her eyes despite her worries.

Today she was hungry, for she had been as far as Westminster Abbey, crossing over the Thames at the Westminster Bridge, and regretting that the new bridge being built near her aunt's house would not be completed for some years yet.

As she turned into Kennington Lane she paused to allow a curricle to pass, and could not help but notice how the driver, quite obviously a gentleman of means, turned and stared at her as though he had never seen a young woman taking a walk before.

The Earl of Coverdale was, in fact, wondering what a respectably, if not quite fashionably, dressed young woman was doing walking alone in the streets of London. He turned to look back once he had passed her and was even more surprised, for she did not have the look of a servant, even an upper-class one such as a governess.

As he continued on his way, however, he quite forgot her, for his thoughts dwelt on the interview he must have with the family of a fellow officer who had been less fortunate than himself at Waterloo. Major Sir John Hayward had been severely wounded, and the unpleasant duty of informing the major's family lay ahead, for chances of complete recovery were slim indeed.

A casual observer, seeing Coverdale's troubled face, might have thought him much older than his years, for he was possessed of an unusually strong sense of responsibility as far as his family and friends were concerned. He was tall and well-built, with broad shoulders, and at almost twenty-eight years of age, he was young to have risen to the rank of colonel. His black hair was almost hidden beneath his top hat, and was already showing traces of silver. He had not worn his uniform for today's call, because the fuss being made of soldiers newly returned from Waterloo caused him considerable embarrassment. Instead, he wore a deep blue morning coat, light blue knee breeches, and highly polished leather Hessians.

He had no difficulty in finding the house, one of the largest on the street. Despite its location, it was not unattractive, and had a small, well-kept garden in front and what appeared to be stables on the side opening onto Devonshire Place.

Leaving his tiger to walk his curricle, he stepped down and approached the front door, which was quickly opened by a maid, and a few minutes later he was shown into a neat but old-fashioned drawing room to await Lady Clinton's pleasure.

She did not keep him waiting long, but came bustling in while he was still standing looking at the painting of Lord Clinton which hung over the fireplace. As he swung around, he had to admit that he saw not the slightest resemblance between this lady and her brother, for she was small, plump, and rather bird-like, with graying hair, whereas the major was quite tall and gaunt.

"I am Lady Clinton, Sir John's sister, and I am sorry to say that neither of his children are at home at the moment. But perhaps that is as well if your news is not good," she suggested as he bowed over her hand. She tugged on a bellpull before sinking into a chair.

"Do sit down, my lord," she continued. "I expect my niece back at any moment, but I'm afraid I don't know when my nephew will return. May I offer you a glass of sherry?"

"Only if you will join me," Lord Coverdale agreed, and a few moments later a young maid hurried in and, responding to an inclination of her mistress's head, slowly and very carefully filled two glasses from the decanter on the sideboard and then served them.

He had not even reached for his glass, however, before he heard a commotion in the hall and, to his surprise, the young woman he had seen striding along the street came into the room. He rose at once and Lady Clinton introduced her niece, Miss Catherine Hayward.

"Are you come from Brussels?" Catherine asked, a tremble in her voice. "You have news of Papa?"

"Yes, Miss Hayward," he said, drawing forward a chair. Catherine looked as though she would have preferred to stand, but as he was waiting to seat her she had little option but to permit him to do so. Before resuming his own seat, he placed his untouched glass of wine into her hand.

"I have news, but I'm afraid it is not very good," he told her. "You see, he was still alive when I left, but very badly injured, and cannot be moved for some time."

"Is he expected to survive?" Catherine's voice was now no more than a husky whisper.

"He was holding his own when I left," Lord Coverdale said gently, "but he suffered both head and chest wounds, and I was told he had lost a vast amount of blood. He is in the care of some nuns just outside of Brussels, who will keep me informed of his progress.''

''Did you see what happened?'' Catherine asked sharply.

He shook his head. ''I'm afraid not, for I was with my own regiment in a different part of the battlefield. When it was all over I went looking for him. You see, we had met the night before. A ball was in progress and as neither of us had any wish to dance, we became acquainted over a glass of brandy.''

Catherine looked at him strangely. ''You mean to say that someone actually held a ball on the night before a battle?'' She sounded shocked.

''None of us knew just how close Napoleon was,'' Coverdale explained. ''As soon as orders came, we all left to report to our units, marching out of Brussels in formation.'' He paused, a remote look in his eyes as he recalled the event. ''When it rained heavily all night, most were sure we would win, for all of Wellington's victories on the Peninsula were preceded by heavy rains. The battlefield turned into a field of mud, however, and both armies were soaked to the skin and got little sleep before the fighting began.''

''Would it do any good if my brother and I were to go over there and endeavor to bring him back?'' Catherine's blue eyes were now wide with concern, but Coverdale shook his head.

''If that had been possible I would have brought him back myself, but I was told that to move him at all for the time being would kill him,'' he said, touched by her deep regard for her father. ''I will receive word at once if his condition should worsen, and take you over there myself, but it is my hope that he will continue to improve.''

''You must feel extremely fortunate to have come away from such a battle completely unscathed, my lord,'' Catherine suggested a little tartly, ''but I believe you said that you were in a less dangerous part of the battlefield.''

Coverdale frowned, resenting her remark. He saw no reason, however, to tell her that he had received a saber wound in the thigh, and had dragged himself around looking for her father before having his own injuries attended to. This was why it had taken him so long to make all the arrangements and then get back to England.

"I said I was in a different part, Miss Hayward, but there was not any one place at Waterloo either more or less dangerous than another. We were heavily outnumbered and fighting with raw recruits, and regulars who had not seen action for some time," he told her a little sternly.

"What did two hardened soldiers talk about on the eve of the battle? Women, I suppose," Catherine suggested, her voice sounding strange as she tried to hold back tears.

Her aunt looked shocked and was about to say something, but Lord Coverdale stopped her with a slight shake of his head.

"If either of us had wanted women we would have been in the ballroom or out on the terrace, for there were plenty there quite eager to be taken," he said with a grim smile. "Your father did most of the talking, telling me about your mother and how very much he missed her. And speaking of what he hoped to do for you and your brother when he returned to England."

"You mean if he returned to England, don't you?" Catherine asked, "for he must have known that he might not."

Coverdale did not really approve of this sharply spoken young lady who went striding out around London without so much as a maid in attendance. But he knew completely how she felt, for it had not been many years since his father had died, and he knew that he had been extremely difficult to live with until he came to terms with his loss.

"Soldiers always know that a battle might be their last, but it's considered unlucky to talk or even think about it until it happens," he told her softly. "Your father very much wanted your brother to go back and complete his studies at Cambridge, then return to the estates and help get them in shape. And he wanted you to stay in London and have a come-out—find a good man to marry, and give him a bunch of grandchildren to brighten his old age. He told me that you have too much love in you to let yourself wither into a frustrated old maid."

She turned away, swallowing hard and trying to blink away her tears, then impatiently brushed them aside with the back of her hand.

"As Mark was sent down from Cambridge for bad behavior," she said sharply, "I doubt if they would allow him to return."

"It can be arranged, I am sure, if he is willing to go back. At a guess I would say that half of the House of Lords was sent down from college at one time or another, and taken back if sufficiently penitent," Coverdale told her dryly. "I'd be glad to see if I could arrange it, in your father's absence. However, I still have to meet the young man. I'll try to come by tomorrow morning, if that will be convenient."

"I really could not say if Mark will be home this evening for me to give him your message, or if he will have made other arrangements for tomorrow," Catherine began, ignoring her aunt's questioning glance.

Lord Coverdale got carefully to his feet, for his injured thigh was inclined to stiffen when he sat for long. "I will take a chance on seeing him, and be here around eleven," he told her brusquely, then turned to Lady Clinton. "Thank you for receiving me, my lady, and I look forward to seeing you again tomorrow."

"I'll see you to the door," she said, "and offer my thanks for your kindness in bringing us news of my brother. I'm sure my niece would have done so had she not been too upset to remember her manners."

They were in the hall by now, and Lady Clinton, after glancing at her niece's face, had closed the drawing room door firmly behind her.

"Sir John spoke of a sister-in-law who might be willing to bring out your niece, once she is out of mourning," Lord Coverdale said. "I realize that the matter is a family one and would not usually be my affair, but it may be a month or two before your brother is able to return home, and even then he may not be in any condition to make arrangements."

"I understand, my lord," Lady Clinton said, "but at twenty, Catherine is already a little old, so the sooner something is done, the better it will be. However, once you meet him you will realize that the boy is in need of more help than my niece. I cannot keep him out of trouble, and neither can Catherine, so the best thing would be if you could get him back to Cambridge.

Perhaps after you've spoken to him we could talk further about the pair of them?''

Coverdale nodded. From the drawing room could be heard the faint sound of sobbing. "Go to her now. She's a brave young lady to have held off for so long, and I know that not being able to help makes it much harder to bear. I hope to see you tomorrow.''

She watched him limp slightly as he walked toward the door, and asked, "Did you get that at Waterloo?''

He turned and nodded, his eyes twinkling. "I'm afraid so, though your niece would have been most disappointed had I admitted to it. It's not permanent, for it was little more than a flesh wound, fortunately,'' he said quietly, before descending to his waiting curricle.

Catherine had a pink nose and red eyes when her aunt came back into the drawing room, but was quite composed once more, though she felt a little ashamed of herself. "Before you start to scold, Aunt Genevieve, I confess to being more than a little rude to Lord Coverdale. I think it was because Papa had been so badly wounded and he was completely unharmed.''

Lady Clinton nodded. "You're fortunate he is a gentleman, and a very understanding one at that, for Lord Coverdale *was* wounded. How he succeeded in finding John when he himself had a leg injury, I cannot imagine.''

Catherine's cheeks turned an even deeper pink than her nose. "Are you sure?'' she asked.

"Quite sure,'' her aunt said dryly. "He was favoring his right thigh, so it was probably a saber thrust. When I asked him, he said it was little more than a flesh wound, but his idea of little more, and mine, probably differ a great deal.''

Catherine frowned. "It was kind of him to come and tell us about Papa, but I'm afraid I got the feeling that he was more than prepared to take charge of us, and I quite resented it. After all, he is a complete stranger. Why should we do what he suggests?'' she asked a little angrily.

"Because your father asked him to help, and it is no doubt a comfort to my brother right now to know that he is keeping an eye on his children. You are both under age, you know, and

I do not pretend to have any control over either one of you,'' Lady Clinton said calmly as she walked toward the door. "And now I think I had better see what my girls are doing in the kitchen or we may have a burned roast for dinner. It was Betty's turn to cook the meat today."

Catherine sighed, then started to leave the drawing room also, but as she reached the door it swung open and her brother, Mark, came in.

"I say, Cathie, who was my aunt's visitor with the curricle and that bang-up pair of grays?" he asked. "I was itching to drive them, but me and Gordon had some business to conduct, and by the time I got back he was gone."

"What kind of business?" Catherine asked, frowning, for she did not at all like the young cit that her brother spent so much time with, but hoped that she was worrying needlessly.

"Nothing for females to be concerned with," her brother retorted. "I don't ask you what you do all day, and I don't expect you to try to put your nose into men's affairs."

She was about to make a sharp retort when she remembered that he still did not know about their father. "Come and sit down for a minute. I need to talk to you," she said, taking his arm and drawing him toward the large sofa.

Mark scowled. "If you're going to lecture me about what I do all day . . ." he began, then he noticed that she had been crying and abruptly joined her on the sofa, for tears were a rare occurrence indeed for Catherine.

"It's about Papa," she began, adding quickly as she caught the look of alarm in his eyes, "He's all right—or at least he's still alive—but he's been badly wounded and some nuns are looking after him in Brussels until he's well enough to be brought home."

"Can't we go and get him, Cathie? I have a little money. Gordon and I could go over there and bring him back, if you know where he is," Mark said, an urgency in his voice. "You nursed Mama, and if you took care of him here I know you'd have him right again in no time."

Catherine smiled sadly. This was almost the Mark she used to know, but she did not at all care for Gordon to have any part in this. "You know I would if I could, Mark, but apparently he's still not out of the woods yet, and can't be moved for maybe a month or more. The gentleman whose curricle was waiting outside was the Earl of Coverdale. He found Papa and took him to the nuns. I don't know what his rank in the army is, but it must be high for him to be able to get so much care for Papa." She sighed, relieved now that she had been able to tell him herself, for she had not wanted her aunt to do so.

"He's probably paying them well, and I'd like to repay him, for I have a little money put aside. I don't like to think of a stranger footing the bill," Mark said, trying to appear grown up.

"And just where did you get the money from? You said yourself that you had nothing when we first arrived here," Catherine said, frowning, for she suspected that he had not come by it honestly.

"Never you mind," Mark snapped. "I've learned a lot about London in the short time I've been here, and it's not at all difficult to make money, just as long as you know the right people."

Catherine's hopes that she had been mistaken about his activities faded at once, and she felt strongly that Lord Coverdale must not meet him and become suspicious, or her brother might not end up back at Cambridge, but in prison. Though she had formed her own very poor opinion of Mark's friend, Gordon Smith, on the one occasion when they had met, she knew better than to tell her brother so, for it would have made him all the more determined to continue the relationship.

"Well, so long as you're home tomorrow afternoon, you'll get your chance to meet him, for he said he would pay us a call then, in the hopes of seeing you," she lied, crossing her fingers beneath the folds of her gown.

"I'll make a point of being here, then, and I'll suggest he and I go for a ride so that we can talk in private, man to man," he said firmly.

Catherine grinned. "Don't try to bamboozle me. You've wanted an opportunity to see that curricle and pair a little closer since the moment you set eyes on it, haven't you? But suppose he should come on horseback instead?"

He paused and looked at her disbelievingly for a moment, for he realized that she really had hit upon the main reason he wanted to speak to their visitor.

"If he should, then I'll think of something," he bragged, "anything to get me out of this house of women for a while. Gordon calls it the nunnery, you know, and he's not far out at that. Do you know that when he tried to have a kiss and cuddle with one of aunt's girls, she actually slapped him and ran? He's not at all used to that kind of treatment, you know."

"You'd best not tell that to Aunt Genevieve, or she'll not allow him in the house again," Catherine warned.

She was secretly proud of her scheming to keep Mark and Coverdale apart, and even more so the next morning when her brother was up and out much earlier than usual. It was none too soon, for Lord Coverdale did not wait for the more conventional hour of eleven to call, but arrived at a half past ten, and Catherine received him herself in the drawing room, for her aunt was occupied at that time in instructing some of her trainees in the task of laundering.

"I'm so sorry, my lord," Catherine said, trying to look appropriately dismayed, "but my brother must have forgotten that I said you would be calling, and he left the house more than an hour ago."

Much to her surprise, Coverdale smiled. "You obviously have little influence upon the young man, my dear, and I must admit that my older sister could do little with me at that age, but I had strict parents to make sure I was aware of my responsibilities. Your brother has not been so fortunate in this regard."

Though in complete agreement with him for once, Catherine had no intention of letting him know it, so she said nothing and waited to find out what he meant to do now that his plans had been thwarted.

"I realize that you must enjoy exploring London on foot, but wondered if perhaps you might be free to take a drive with me and see a little more of this fascinating city, Miss Hayward?" Coverdale asked, smiling pleasantly. "An open carriage is an interesting and much less tiring means of viewing the sights."

Mark was not the only one who had longed to take a ride in that curricle, and though Catherine wished she could refuse, it was just too difficult, for she simply could not conceal her pleasure at the prospect. And once her face had revealed her eagerness, there was no possible way she could politely decline the invitation.

"If it would not inconvenience you, my lord, I would dearly love to ride in such an interesting conveyance. I have, of course, seen them about town, but never expected to ride in one so soon," she told him, for there was little use in dissembling.

His eyes twinkled in a way that made Catherine sure he had read her thoughts. "It will be my pleasure also," he murmured, "and I will wait here while you get your bonnet and perhaps a shawl."

Catherine glanced down at the gown she had made some time ago and had later dyed black, and realized with relief that, though outmoded, little of it would show if she arranged her good lace shawl over it, around her shoulders. Excusing herself, she hurried up to her bedchamber.

After leaving word for her aunt, she returned to the drawing room, still feeling a little self-conscious for she could well imagine the well-dressed ladies he was accustomed to escorting. Coverdale's smile of approval did much to restore her confidence, however, and she took the arm he offered and allowed him to escort her to the curricle.

Once they were comfortably settled, he took the reins and set off in the direction she had taken the day before, toward the Westminster Bridge, passing a surprising amount of either open land or land under cultivation before arriving at Bridge Road and crossing the Thames.

She had thought he meant to take her to Mayfair, though this was not the fashionable hour, but instead he turned on Parliament Street and proceeded at a slow pace. She was pleased that he pointed out the Privy Gardens on one side, and the Treasury, the Horse Guards' Parade, and the Admiralty on the other, for though she had been here before, she had not known what she was looking at.

As he swung left at Charing Cross, Coverdale asked, "Have you seen the Prince Regent's home, Carlton House, yet?"

Catherine's smile widened. "No, I haven't, for I was not quite sure where it was. Is it close by?"

"This is it, here on the left," he told her, gratified by her eagerness.

She secretly thought that it looked more like a museum than a home, with its imposing portico of Corinthian columns, but decided it was more tactful not to give this opinion.

"The prince chose Henry Holland as his architect. We'll pass Brooks's Club on St. James's Street, in a moment, which was one of Holland's earlier designs," Coverdale explained. "There was originally a muddle of buildings on the site of Carlton House, and I must say that he did an excellent job of remodeling and extending them. The portico was designed so that an entire carriage could be driven into it and its passengers alight without having to brave the elements.

"St. James's Street, which is at the end of Pall Mall, is a street where it is permissible for ladies to shop or drive by on a morning, accompanied, of course, but never on an afternoon. Only ladies of ill repute would be seen there at that hour of the day."

Catherine began to laugh. "I never heard of anything so ridiculous. Who makes rules of that sort?" she asked, a little scornfully.

"Certain ladies of the *ton* wield a vast amount of power, and it's really no laughing matter, my dear," he said quietly. As he spoke he turned into St. James's Square, and then left into King Street. "The building on our left now is Almack's, which you surely must have heard of."

"Of course," Catherine said happily. "Mama often spoke about going there when she was a young girl, and she always hoped that I would have the chance to go there, also, some day."

"Well, some of the people who make the rules of conduct of the *ton* are the ladies who run Almack's and decide who may be permitted to go there and who may not, and they can make or ruin a young lady's chances of a successful Season." He smiled at her look of scorn. "Don't take my word for it, my dear, but ask your aunt about it."

"I will, you may be sure. Have we been on the forbidden street yet?" Catherine asked with a grin.

"No," he said as he expertly turned the carriage around and

went back to Pall Mall. "We're coming to it next. Its bad reputation is due really to the behavior of the members of the men's clubs along it. Here now on the left is Brooks's, and almost at the end, on the right, is White's.

"Those are the two most popular men's clubs, and though there are many others, acceptance by one or the other is essential for a gentleman of the *ton*." He chuckled softly. "And now that I have confused you completely, I think that I had better take you back home and let Lady Clinton verify what I have told you. Perhaps, another day, you'll allow me to take you for a drive in the park? Do you ride, by the way?"

"Of course I ride," Catherine said quickly, "but Papa would not hear of our bringing mounts all the way to London, and I doubt if Aunt Genevieve would have room to stable them if we had done so," Catherine's voice held a note of sadness, for she dearly loved her mare, and missed riding.

"That is a shame," Coverdale agreed, "but perhaps your father felt that you would be going riding off on your own all the time, and getting into serious trouble."

There was a noticeable silence, then Catherine said, "I hope you do not mean to tell me that I could not take my mount out alone."

"I'm afraid I do," Coverdale said regretfully. "Please believe, however, that I did not make all these rules. I could find a suitable mount for you, though, if you would like to take an early-morning ride with me some time."

They continued in silence, Catherine considering the many pleasures which seemed to be forbidden in this city, and realizing that she had been rude to Coverdale.

Finally, she turned to him and, placing a hand on his arm, said, "I do beg your pardon, my lord, for being such poor company, and I'm only sorry that it was you who had to break the news to me about all these things I cannot do. If you would ask me again sometime to go for a drive or an early-morning ride, I would be happy to accept, and promise to behave with more propriety."

"I will hold you to that, my dear," he told her, smiling a little grimly, "and in the meantime, when would you suggest I might get a chance to meet with your brother?"

Catherine was embarrassed, for she really had not thought of what to do next to keep the two of them apart.

"He's always out in the evenings, though I really don't know where he goes," she said, adding, with eyes that twinkled, "Perhaps I could steal his shoes or, better still his cravats, to ensure that he remains in the house when you next visit?"

There was a glint in Coverdale's eyes that worried Catherine as he said, "Perhaps you could, or perhaps you could tell me why you would prefer that I not meet him."

She flushed. "I don't know what you mean, my lord," she said stiffly.

They had reached her aunt's house, and he stepped down to help her from the curricle. Reaching into his pocket, he produced his card. "When you have arranged a time and place that I can meet with your brother, I would appreciate your sending me word."

She slipped the card into her reticule and said quietly, "Thank you very much, my lord, for a lovely ride. I enjoyed every minute of it."

He bowed. "The pleasure was mine, my dear. I will wait to hear from you."

Mark returned to the house shortly before two o'clock, and by four o'clock he was not a little put out.

When Lady Clinton went to join her niece for tea in the drawing room she was quite surprised to see her nephew there also. She made no comment, however, but asked Catherine, "Did you have a pleasant drive this morning with Lord Coverdale, my dear? Where did you go?"

Mark's eyebrows rose. "You went for a drive with Lord Coverdale this morning, Catherine, yet you told me he would be here this afternoon? What kind of a game are you playing?" he asked, glaring at her.

Her cheeks took on a decidedly rosy hue. "There was, quite apparently, a misunderstanding," she said, looking carefully at the sandwich on her plate.

"But you knew I had come back specifically to meet him, yet you did not tell me you had already seen him and that he would not be returning. You don't want me to meet him, do you?'' he said suspiciously.

She got up. ''I don't believe I want tea today, Aunt Genevieve,'' she murmured. ''Will you excuse me, please?''

As she reached the door she was aware that Mark was right behind her and she continued through the house and into the back garden, for she knew she would have to give him an explanation, and preferred privacy to do so. He put his hand on her shoulder and swung her around.

''I repeat,'' he said, now quite furious, ''what kind of game are you playing, Cathie? You don't want me to meet Coverdale, do you?''

''Quite frankly, no, I don't. Because I don't know what you and your new friend, Gordon, are doing—where you're getting money from—and I have an awful feeling that he is leading you into something crooked,'' Catherine told him sharply. ''I have received the quite strong impression that Lord Coverdale is no more the kind of man to condone illegal activities than our papa would be, and he would not be as lenient as Papa.''

''You have no idea what you are talking about, Cathie,'' Mark said scornfully. ''Gordon knows his way around and is up to all the rigs. I've learned more in just the short time we've been in London than I learned all the time I lived in Norfolk. It's not the kind of thing they teach you at Cambridge, of course, but it's the only way to get along in the real world.''

''If that's the way you feel, then perhaps you had better have a talk with Lord Coverdale,'' Catherine snapped. ''If he approves of what you are doing, and how you are making that money you brag about, then I will feel a little less concerned about you. When do you want to see him?''

''As soon as I can,'' Mark said, angrily. ''Tomorrow afternoon, if that's all right with him, but I don't want you around when I'm with him, sticking your nose into things that don't concern you. As I told you before, I want a man-to-man talk with him.''

Catherine wanted to smile at the expressions her young brother used, but knew better than to do so. Lord Coverdale had seemed much more human today, save, of course, at the end, when he made it clear that he was fully aware of what she was doing. And though he didn't exactly threaten her, she was sure he would not bring a mount for her and take her riding, or drive her out in his curricle again, until she arranged for him to meet with Mark.

"What time do you want to see him?" she asked.

"Two o'clock would suit me," Mark told her. "And I'd prefer him to pick me up so we can talk somewhere away from this house."

"I'll send him a note and see what he says," Catherine promised. "And I know one thing for sure—you'll thoroughly enjoy watching him handle his horses."

"Are they real goers?" Mark asked, grinning now.

"They wanted to be," she told him, "but we were in traffic most of the time so he had to hold them back. It was fun, though, riding around for a change instead of wearing out my poor feet. He spoke of bringing a mount for me so that I could go riding in the park with him, and now I'm so glad I brought my riding habit with me."

Two

LADY CLINTON readily agreed that Catherine might send one of her girls with a message to Lord Coverdale in Grosvenor Square, and he arrived promptly at two o'clock the next day.

When Mark realized he was not going to get the ride in the curricle that he had so much looked forward to, his disappointment was only too obvious, to Catherine at least. But to their surprise, Coverdale particularly asked that both Catherine and Lady Clinton also be present at the meeting, and for the four of them the drawing room was the best place for the purpose.

"I've always found it much more satisfactory to speak with all concerned at the same time, for otherwise it is too easy to forget just exactly what occurred. We are all human, and much inclined to recall only the things in which we have a particular interest," Coverdale explained.

After he had carefully told them once more, for Mark's benefit, the condition Sir John was in when he left him in Belgium, Catherine was surprised to hear her brother speak up as though he had not been listening.

"I do not see any reason, sir, why I and a friend of mine cannot go to Brussels and bring Papa back here now. If Catherine took care of him, instead of a bunch of foreign nuns who have no feelings for him, and probably can't even speak English, I am sure that Papa would be on his feet again in no time at all," he asserted. "My sister is quite accustomed to nursing, my lord, for she took complete care of our mama for a number of years before she died."

"And no doubt she will look after your father also, when he

27

returns," Lord Coverdale said patiently, "but I thought I had explained that the doctors fear for his life if he is moved at the present time. Once I receive word that he may safely undertake the journey back to England, I will be glad to take you with me to get him. In the meantime, I must speak with you about your father's wish that you return to Cambridge to complete your studies there."

Mark scowled. "That's something I'd like to discuss with you privately, sir," he said, "for I'm not at all sure that they would permit me to resume my studies."

It was Coverdale's turn to frown, and Catherine also looked up in surprise, for she had not understood at the time that the prank her brother had been sent down for was such a grave one. She said nothing, however, but listened intently while Coverdale said quietly to Mark, "Then by all means let's talk about it, for I do have a certain amount of influence there, and it would do no harm to try."

It appeared that this was not quite what Mark had in mind, and he said suddenly, "The thing I cannot understand is what our affairs have to do with you, my lord. To the best of my knowledge you are not a relative, even a distant one, so why should you need to concern yourself in matters strictly to do with our family?"

Although Catherine now appreciated the help Coverdale seemed prepared to give her brother, she too had wondered why he would put himself out in this way, and waited with considerable interest to hear his response.

"Your father and I talked a great deal the night before the battle," he began gravely, "for it turned out that, though our positions were not exactly the same, we shared some of the problems that could arise if we were badly injured or killed in the battle the following day.

"Before we parted that night, we sent for paper and pens and set down what we would wish to have done on our behalf by the other should one of us be killed or rendered incapable of performing our duties to our families."

He reached into his pocket and produced a rather crumpled piece of paper which he handed first to Lady Clinton. "Perhaps you can verify that the writing is that of your brother, my lady?'' he requested.

She nodded, read the note, then handed it to Catherine, who also read it while her brother fidgeted impatiently, then she passed it along to him.

"That seems to be perfectly clear, my lord," Lady Clinton said, "and provides completely for the present unfortunate circumstances. But do you not find it a little difficult to add my brother's problems to those you yourself must already have?''

He shrugged. "Certainly no more than he would have encountered had I been the one who was killed or wounded, and I am absolutely sure that he would have done the utmost he possibly could for my family.''

"You have a wife and children, sir?'' It was Catherine who asked the question, and she suddenly needed to know, for he had not seemed at all like the married men she had met.

Coverdale smiled and shook his head. "I have a mother, an older married sister, and a younger brother who is not yet of an age to be of much help, I'm afraid. He's off on a walking tour of Scotland for the summer. But I do also have an estate agent and bailiffs who are most competent.''

Mark was still carefully examining the document and then with a slight nod he returned it to its owner without comment. There was no doubt that he was in a position to know well both his father's hand and his turn of phrase.

"I have been noticing how remarkably alike you two are,'' Coverdale said to Catherine and Mark. "As you do not at all resemble your father, I assume it is your mother you take after.''

"Our mother's side of the family, anyway,'' Catherine said with a smile. "But in a year or two, when Mark has reached his full height, I doubt that it will be more than a slight resemblance.''

She glanced over at Mark while she spoke, and was startled to see a quite guilty expression on his face. It was gone in a moment, but it left her with the strangest of feelings—almost a foreboding.

"Sir John's other concern was that his only daughter be

brought out in London, and a suitable husband found to take care of her," Coverdale said, watching Catherine's face as he spoke.

She felt the warmth mount in her cheeks as they turned a rosy pink, then noted the amusement in his eyes as he observed her embarrassment.

Not one to dissemble, she said sharply, "My papa must have forgotten that I am still in mourning for our mama, and even were I not, where would the funds come from to provide suitable clothes with which to attract this suitable husband, may I ask?"

"That is also something which must be discussed," Lord Coverdale murmured, his eyes twinkling, "for, with all due respect to you, Lady Clinton, this part of town is hardly fashionable enough for a young lady's come-out. I am sure you will agree."

Lady Clinton gave a rare, throaty chuckle. "It most certainly is not, my lord, but my sister-in-law, Lady Stanhope, spends much of the year at her London town house in Grosvenor Street. She would enjoy nothing better than to bring out my niece, for whenever we meet she bemoans the fact that her own children are now all grown, and that I never had any that she could fuss over."

"I am very well acquainted with Lady Stanhope, for she and my mama have been friends since before I was born," Coverdale said, quite obviously delighted at the conicidence, "and if she is willing to present Miss Hayward, then that settles everything. Between her and my mama, Miss Hayward will, without a doubt, have the finest send-off a young lady could ever wish for."

Catherine had been listening to the interchange with growing hostility, for she resented plans for her future being made so arbitrarily, without either of the planners even thinking to consult her as to her wishes. "That settles nothing," she said decisively, "at least, not until I have met both ladies—and, of course, discovered the gold mine that will pay for everything save gowns—for those I can make myself."

"Far be it from me to discourage such enterprise, Miss Hayward," Lord Coverdale said softly, "but it would be much wiser to seek the services of a first-class modiste. The *ton* is quick to notice gowns made by inferior modistes, let alone homemade ones.''

Although Catherine was decidedly embarrassed, her outward reaction was fury that this lord would insult her efforts without having seen any of the garments she had made, for the simple gowns she now wore were old and worn and, of course, the black dye for mourning had not improved their appearance.

She had spent nothing since coming to London, and had just about enough money to buy a dress length at one of the warehouses she had seen on her walks. She would go back there tomorrow, she decided, and purchase something suitable for when she was out of mourning. She would have ample time, while her aunt was training her girls, to cut and stitch a gown in one of the latest styles, and would then tell no one where she had obtained it.

With quite obviously no idea that he had insulted Catherine, Coverdale turned to Mark and suggested, ''Would you like a little fresh air? We could go for a drive in my curricle and see if the problem at Cambridge can be resolved to everyone's satisfaction.''

Of course, this was exactly what Mark wanted to do, and he could not conceal his delighted grin as he hastened upstairs for hat, gloves, and cane while Lord Coverdale took his leave of the ladies, promising that, if possible, he would return in a day or so with his mama, Lady Coverdale, and, if possible, Lady Stanhope also. Mark, livelier than he had appeared all day so far, was close behind Coverdale as the tiger brought around the curricle.

As the door closed behind them, Lady Clinton looked thoughtfully at her niece. ''Though most gels of your age would jump at the chance of a come-out, you're none too pleased about it, are you? Have you taken a dislike to your papa's friend?'' she asked, resuming her seat and signaling for her niece to do the same.

''Not at all, for if he can wean my young brother away from that unacceptable cit, Gordon, he'll have my wholehearted approval,'' Catherine said emphatically. ''But I am afraid that Lord Coverdale's ideas are rather too much for Papa's pockets, if not his wishes.

"I agree completely that Mark must go back to Cambridge and make up his lost time, and I'm quite sure that the prank he played was not of major consequence. To be frank, I wish he could go back tomorrow, before he gets into serious trouble here, but I know he'll have to wait until the new term commences," she said a little sadly.

"He may be able to send him a little early to study with a tutor and catch up somewhat," Lady Clinton suggested. "But I am concerned more about you than Mark. I never wanted a come-out, but I should have thought you would enjoy it."

Catherine sighed. "I have a very good idea how Papa must have overestimated our financial position. There's no money available for me to have a come-out, Aunt Genevieve. Papa was indulging in pipe dreams, that's all. Fortunately, it's too late now this Season, for it will be completely over and forgotten by the time Papa gets back from Belgium. And then he's still going to need a lot of nursing, I'm sure."

"Between his batman, my girls, and myself, we can look after my brother and allow you the opportunity to find a husband," Lady Clinton said firmly. "You cannot possibly wish to remain an old maid, looking after your family for the rest of your days. You've too much life in you for that, Catherine."

There was a rueful expression on her niece's face. "I had hoped for better, I must admit," she agreed, "but only too often things do not turn out quite the way we would like them to. It might be the best thing for everyone if I catch Lord Coverdale alone after he leaves Mark at the door, and tell him not to waste his mama's and Lady Stanhope's time."

Lady Clinton was horrified at the idea. "You'll do no such thing, my girl. It's always best to sleep on it before turning down, out of hand, an offer that might not be made again," she advised. "Or, better still, speak to my sister-in-law yourself, and find out just how much the most simple of come-outs might cost. You know what I mean, no special ball, perhaps not even a presentation, but just some evenings at Almack's and a party or two. And I'll be the judge as to whether a gown of your own making can pass for one by a top modiste."

"But suppose money is spent that could have been put to better use, and then I don't meet anyone who wishes to marry me,"

Catherine bemoaned. "I'd never forgive myself for being so wasteful."

Lady Clinton shrugged. "You're a good deal better looking than I ever was, my dear, and if I could catch a husband, then surely you can. Of course, Lord Clinton was quite a lot older than I would have liked, but we rubbed along very nicely until he died. And then, as you must realize, he left me most comfortably situated."

They both heard the sound of the front door closing, which meant that it was now too late to talk to Lord Coverdale even if Catherine had still wished to.

A moment later Mark came hurrying into the drawing room, an unusually bright smile lighting his face.

"He permitted me to drive them for just a short distance," he said, sounding much like an eager schoolboy. "And they're every bit as fine as they look. Such sweet goers, and beautifully matched."

"Did you have any difficulty in holding them?" his sister asked. "They were most certainly letting the groom know how anxious to be off they were."

"Oh, no, of course not." His voice had taken on an infuriatingly superior note. "It's not the first time I've handled a highly bred pair such as they are, you know."

"I'm sure that Lord Coverdale kept a very careful eye on you, just the same," Catherine retorted. "He appears to be excessively proud of them and most unlikely to risk your damaging their mouths."

Her brother looked as though he was about to explode.

"Never mind all this talk of horses," Lady Clinton said impatiently. "Does Lord Coverdale feel he can persuade them to accept you back at Cambridge?"

Mark flushed. "Yes, he believes so. He is going to take a run up there next week and do whatever is necessary, and while he's there he says he can arrange for me to go up a few weeks early and study privately under one of the masters to make up for the work I have missed."

Catherine was very glad to kow that at least one of them would be taken care of. As far as her own problems were concerned, she meant to take her aunt's advice and speak with Lady

Stanhope. Then, after that she would decide for herself whether or not to take advantage of at least a small taste of the London society life. If nothing should come of it, it would at least be a memory to store away, and no one could say that she had not tried to conform.

Lady Stanhope was, without a doubt, the most sophisticated lady that Catherine had ever met. But then, Catherine had been brought up in the country, and her mama, though the daughter of an earl, had been too ill those last few years to mingle with even the local gentry.

The meeting took place, of course, the following morning at the house in Grosvenor Street, and on this occasion Catherine was accompanied by her aunt, who had already broached the subject of her visit in a note she had sent to her sister-in-law.

An attractive, tall woman with graying blond hair and light gray eyes, Lady Stanhope was about forty years of age. A childless widow, she was quite delighted at the prospect of helping Catherine meet the right people.

As they sat sipping tea and nibbling on dainty pastries and cake, Lady Stanhope explained that Lady Coverdale had hoped to join them, but had succumbed to a slight cold and felt it best to stay in her bed for a day or so. Then she carefully eyed her protégé-to-be.

"You're a little older than the usual crop of chits making their come-out each Season," she said bluntly, "but I'm glad to see you carry yourself well. The worst thing a tall gel can do is slouch. But I'm not sure about that hair, for it's barely a shade away from red. It's such a pity powdered hair went out."

Catherine tried to conceal a grin. She had a feeling that she was going to like this outspoken, middle-aged lady, and a come-out under her auspices might be a vast amount more interesting than she had at first thought.

"Must do something about that walk, though," Lady Stanhope continued. "It just won't do to stride out in that way. We'll get you a dancing master, for I've no doubt you need one, and he can also have the task of teaching you how to walk like a lady. I assume that you really do want to make a come-out and find a husband, and that it's not just one of your papa's ideas."

"I don't really have any choice, my lady," Catherine said frankly. "The alternative is to remain a spinster and live the rest of my life either with my papa, who will no doubt marry again once he's recovered, or help Aunt Genevieve look after her girls." She gave her aunt, a half apologetic smile, but she knew without question that she could not spend the rest of her life doing that kind of good work.

"It's too late, of course, to bring you out this Season, even though the victory celebrations have extended it somewhat," Lady Stanhope said quite decidedly. "It would do no harm, however, to get you a few more stylish black gowns than that one, and take you around town a bit now so you'll not feel so strange when the Little Season begins. I'll come for you in the morning and we'll pay a visit to my modiste."

She saw Catherine's emphatic shake of the head, and a deep frown creased Lady Stanhope's brows.

"If it's having gowns fitted you dislike, you should think yourself fortunate this time for you'll not need more than two or three for now," she said gruffly. "Unless you're wearing lace for evenings, no one really notices the difference between one black gown and another."

"To buy additional gowns in black that I'll never wear again would be a complete waste of funds I don't have," Catherine said firmly. "If I can procure a copy of a current *La Belle Assemblée*," I can add more stylish trim to the gowns I have now and no one will be the wiser."

Lady Stanhope gave her a sharp glance, then nodded. "You have a point there, assuming that no one has yet seen you," she admitted, "save, of course, Coverdale." Then she went over to a small cabinet and took out the magazine Catherine needed. "Here, take this home with you and see what you can do. But don't skimp on trim, mind you. Buy the best you can find, for it will be well worth it in the end."

Lady Clinton replaced her empty cup on the tray. "We must be leaving now, Clara, for I have to meet with a young girl who came all the way from the Isle of Wight to seek work or her fortune here—to no avail, of course. I'll have to take you with me this time, Catherine, for there'll not be time enough to take you home first."

"So you're still looking after half the waifs and strays of London, Genevieve?" Lady Stanhope asked. "If you should ever decide to give it up, you know, you can always come to live with me, for I'd be more than glad of the company."

"I don't look after them long, for there's not one been with me more than a six-month. When I place them in a good position, it's rarely they leave. That's what makes it so worthwhile," Lady Clinton said sharply, then her face softened into a smile. "But I thank you for your generous offer and if ever I grow tired of what I do, I promise I'll consider it very carefully."

The snort Lady Stanhope gave her sister-in-law showed how little she expected such a thing to happen, but she smiled as she took her guests to the door.

"I'll tell the dancing master to call on you tomorrow morning," she said to Catherine. "What time would be best?"

There was to be no possibility of escaping this, Catherine realized, so she murmured that ten o'clock would be a good hour, and went quickly down the steps to help her aunt into the carriage. She did not see Lady Stanhope's smiling shake of her head, for it would never have occurred to her to allow a footman to help either her aunt or herself up the couple of steps. Her aunt saw it, however, and once they were settled inside and on their way, Lady Clinton turned to her.

"Now that you're going to mingle with the *beau monde*, my dear, I believe you should learn a few of their ways. For instance, although I find that I enjoy your assistance far more than that of a footman, you are actually supposed to allow the servant to assist me and then accept his aid yourself—unless a gentleman is present to perform those services, of course," she said with a smile. "How did you like Lady Stanhope?"

Catherine, whose face had shown quite clearly how little she cared for such niceties as accepting aid from servants, now smiled broadly.

"I enjoyed her very much," she said, "particularly her blunt manner of speech. I suppose that she could get away with a great many things that I could not."

"Of course," Lady Clinton assured her, "but she had to put

on a lot of years before she was able to do so. And now I believe we are coming to St. Martin's Church, where the young girl we are to collect is waiting in the charge of the curate.''

''Is this how the girls you are presently training came to you?'' Catherine asked, for she had always been curious as to how her aunt found the girls she cared for.

''One of the ways,'' Lady Clinton said with a slight nod, ''but this young girl would have been admitted to St. Martin's Poorhouse, which is close by, had not the curate intervened.''

Catherine could not help but shudder at the very thought of being sent there.

''Bad though it sounds, my dear, there are a great many worse places in London than the poorhouse, I'm afraid,'' Lady Clinton said just before she stepped out of the carriage.

Catherine stayed in the carriage while her aunt was helped down, and she could not help wondering if Lady Clinton had actually been into the places she spoke of. It seemed that there was a great deal more to her aunt than her appearance would have you believe.

A few minues later Lady Clinton returned, took her seat once more, and they started toward Westminster Bridge.

''Where is she?'' Catherine asked, having expected the girl to travel inside the coach.

''Until she has had a bath, her hair washed, and her own clothes burned, she is in no fit state to ride inside, my dear,'' her aunt said quietly. ''She has been on the streets of London now for a good many days.''

''How old is she?''

Lady Clinton shrugged slightly. ''She says she is sixteen, but I believe her to be no more than thirteen, or perhaps even twelve. She's quite small, and does not look as though she has had a decent meal for some time.''

''Poor girl,'' Catherine said softly, adding, ''I'm afraid I had not thought of this side of your work, Aunt Genevieve. I saw your girls always so neat and clean and thought of it as more of a school for maids than anything else. You must feel extremely proud of what you achieve.''

Lady Clinton made a self-deprecating gesture. ''It was something that needed doing. Once I no longer had a husband to look after, and had the means to help in even this small way, I felt that I must do so.''

The earlier remark Catherine had made about her aunt's work came back to her, and she felt ashamed of her thoughtless comment. If she was soon to mingle with strangers, she must keep a tighter control of her careless tongue.

By design, she was first out of the carriage, this time allowing the footman who put down the steps to assist her, and while he helped her aunt, she glanced up at the forlorn-looking waif who sat on the box next to the coachman.

The girl's hair might be any color, for it was so dirty and matted that it was impossible to tell, and as she scratched herself alternately with one grubby hand and then the other, Catherine instinctively stepped back. She was left in no doubt now as to her aunt's reluctance to allow the girl inside, for the small creature was quite obviously infested with lice.

Then Mrs. Blenkinsop, a large, motherly woman who was the only house servant her aunt employed, came hurrying forward. She worked as Lady Clinton's housekeeper and acted as a second tutor and matron to the young girls who resided here. Catherine had thought her rather a tartar when she heard her giving instructions to the girls, but now she saw the other side of the woman as she called to the girl to come down off the box. Despite the girl's now surreptitious scratching, Mrs. Blenkinsop placed a comforting arm around the frightened creature and, murmuring soothingly the while, steered the young girl toward the back door.

Lady Clinton was watching them also, and heaved a sigh as they slipped out of sight behind the corner of the house. "She's in good hands now," she said quietly, "and I'll warrant you'll not recognize her the next time you see her. And now we both need a little luncheon before going out again to procure the black trim you need for those gowns of yours.''

At this Catherine demurred. "You wore yourself to the nub this morning, Aunt Genevieve. Why don't you take a rest this afternoon and we can go for the trim tomorrow?''

But Lady Clinton shook her head. "My sister-in-law is doing us a favor to agree to take you around informally like this, and

I'd not like to see her all ready to take you out and you with nothing to wear. I'll have a short rest after luncheon while you look at the different designs, then we'll go and find the things you'll need to make the alterations.''

There was nothing Catherine could do but acquiesce, so she studied the book Lady Stanhope had given her and finally drew up a list of trims which could be used to make several of her old gowns more fashionable. Then in the early afternoon they set out to procure the necessary items, which proved a difficult, but, fortunately, not impossible task so close to the end of the Season.

''Well, though we went to considerable trouble, at least we saved more than half of what the same things would have cost several months ago,'' Lady Clinton said as they stepped into the carriage and started for home. ''Are you sure you will be able to make the necessary changes yourself, my dear? Though a little out of fashion now, your gowns were extremely well made for a country modiste.''

''I made them myself, Aunt Genevieve,'' Catherine said with a degree of pride, ''so there will be little difficulty in matching the stitchery.''

Lady Clinton chuckled. ''So that is why you were so angry with Lord Coverdale when he spoke disparagingly of homemade garments. I feared, for a moment, that you were about to say something you would have considerably regretted afterward.''

''I was,'' Catherine admitted, ''but he was doing so much to help Mark, and in the most tactful way possible, that I could not but forgive him for the insult. However, I cannot help wondering where the money is going to come from to purchase the fabric and all the accessories I will need for even a small number of gowns once I am out of mourning.''

''By then it is more than possible that my brother will be back from Brussels and able to produce the necessary funds. I am sure he would not have mentioned your having a come-out unless he had the ready money with which to pay for your clothes,'' Lady Clinton said calmly.

She showed a great deal more confidence than Catherine felt was warranted, but as it was some weeks away, she decided to take it one step at a time. Who could tell? Perhaps she would meet some tall gentleman during this next month who would be enchanted by her, and marry her before it became necessary to spend money she did not have on a come-out she did not truly want. If Lady Clinton wondered why her niece was smiling rather ruefully, she most tactfully did not pose the question.

The following morning, at the appointed hour, a rather strange-looking French gentleman arrived, and informed the maid who answered the door that he had been hired by Lady Stanhope to attend a Miss Hayward.

He was quickly shown into the drawing room and Lady Clinton informed.

As a dancing master, he left much to be desired, for he was a full eight inches shorter than Catherine, and even if the steps had been performed to perfection, the two of them would have appeared singularly odd. With Catherine tripping over either her own or his feet every other step, little progress was made in that direction.

In the matter of changing her unladylike walk, however, he was far more proficient. He carried a baton with which to keep time, and when Catherine took the first long step after a series of smaller ones, she was not completely sure whether she walked into it or he hit her, but she was not about to take any chances.

"If you so much as touch me with that thing just once more, I give you my word that I will wrap it around your head. Is that clear?" she asked him, speaking dangerously quietly.

He looked at her in astonishment for a moment, then he placed it on a nearby table and they proceeded once more.

After two exhausting hours of walking backward and forward across the drawing room, taking increasingly smaller and smaller steps, while a now-seated Monsieur Rievaux either clapped his hands or audibly groaned, Catherine collapsed into a chair.

"Now, mademoiselle," he told her, standing above her and obviously enjoying the novelty, "you practice four hours each day and I come back in two days to check on your progress." With an elaborate bow and a wave of his hand, he hurried from the room, leaving Catherine wondering if he really meant to return.

She had no wish to upset Lady Stanhope, however, so she faithfully practiced, putting her needle aside every two hours to walk daintily back and forth until she was certain she must surely be wearing out her aunt's carpet.

When Lady Stanhope came to call four days later, it was to find such a tremendous improvement that she clapped her hands in appreciation.

"How diligent you have been, my dear," she told Catherine. "I would never have believed that you would apply yourself so seriously to the task, but I am quite delighted."

While her aunt entertained her sister-in-law, Catherine slipped quietly upstairs to don the first of the three black gowns she had finished altering.

Lady Clinton saw her first as she came into the room, and professed amazement at the modish appearance she had achieved.

"I believe you mean to make Coverdale eat his words," she told her niece, then turned to her sister-in-law, who was staring open-mouthed at Catherine.

"If I didn't know better, I would swear that gown had been made by my very own modiste," Lady Stanhope declared. "How talented you are, my dear. But you must not let any of the ladies of the *ton* know that you made it yourself," she cautioned.

But Catherine did not need to be warned, for she was not one to go about bragging of her talents. She was vastly relieved, however, that her workmanship would solve one of the things she had been worrying about.

It did, of course, come a long way behind the problem of her papa's recovery, for she still had a dreadful fear of losing him, and with Lord Coverdale now in Cambridge on her brother's behalf, there was no way for word to be received should he have taken a turn for the worse.

Three

MARK HAD NOT yet left for Cambridge, but he had informed his new friend, Gordon Smith, that he would be doing so very shortly and that young man clearly expressed his displeasure with this turn of events. Having found the perfect twiddlepoop, he had no intention of letting him get away.

Smith, a youth just one year younger than Mark but a vast amount more worldly, had always borne a grudge against the members of the upper classes and took the greatest of pleasure in fleecing them on any and every occasion. The first time he saw Mark, he was standing watching the crowds as they entered Vauxhall Gardens, and Gordon realized at once that he had found a young man ideally suited for implementing a scheme he had devised some time ago.

His dislike of the aristocracy extended, of course, to his so-called friend, but he was careful not to let the young man realize it. He did, however, make sure that if there was any danger of their being caught, he could get away himself and leave Mark to take the blame.

They had already pulled off his scheme quite successfully on two occasions, but this time Mark was somewhat reluctant, making up excuses for not participating again. "I'm not sure that I'll be able to borrow one of Catherine's gowns at the moment," he told Gordon. "You see, she's taken them out of her armoire and is working on some of them right now to make them a little more fashionable. She might miss just the very one I want to borrow."

Gordon gave him a sly grin. "I didn't like to say so, old man, but I thought the two you wore were a little outdated,'' he said, sounding as though teasing. ''If you could find one that she's already altered, you'd look much more the part, you know.''

''You're probably right,'' Mark said. ''And I could use a little more of the ready when I'm up at Cambridge, for there's been no mention of increasing my allowance.''

''You see,'' Gordon said smugly, ''you'll still need me even when you're at your fancy university. You'll have to come back every few months just to make enough to go on with, for it won't be easy holding your own with some of the wealthier students. Not now you've got used to having a little something to jingle in your pockets.''

Reluctantly, Mark agreed to meet him that night in the disguise of a woman and, as before, lie in wait for a likely victim to entice into the darker, winding walks of Vauxhall Gardens. After robbing the man, they would escape over the wall and be back in his aunt's stables within just a few minutes.

On the two previous occasions it had seemed quite a lark, but now, as Mark donned his sister's clothes, he could not help thinking what a good thing it was that Catherine's maid had left on a visit shortly after they reached London, and that she had not the funds to hire someone else but occasionally used one of their aunt's girls. For this reason, she had altered her gowns in such a way that they might be donned, if necessary, without assistance. The new trim was a decided improvement, he noted, and as she had not worn the gown since adding it, he had best be careful not to rip it on anything when he climbed over the wall, or she would know right away that it had been used.

He waited until he heard Catherine and their aunt come up the stairs to retire for the evening, then he put on the chestnut-colored wig that Gordon had procured for him, and covered it with one of his sister's shawls. These were the only items he had borrowed from her, for her shoes and gloves were far too small for him, and Gordon had obtained some for him in larger sizes.

He did not take a reticule with him, for he needed one large enough to hold a gentleman's watch and fob, cravat pin, money purse, and heavy rings. Gordon would bring such a one with him and then take it back after they reached the stables, for he knew a place where everything could be sold quickly with no questions asked.

Surprisingly, Mark required little powder and paint, for his skin was still soft, his beard mere down, quickly removed, and his eyebrows as thin and shapely as a girl's. But these would not show this night, for once away from the house he would put on a black lace mask—the kind worn by many ladies who went to Vauxhall Gardens alone and had no wish to be recognized.

The house was quiet at last, and he slipped out through the back door and hurried to the usual meeting place. Gordon ran a practiced eye over his companion, then gave a nod of approval. Mark said nothing, and would not do so now until they had achieved their objective, for unless he spoke it was virtually impossible to tell that he was not a female. He took the reticule, placed a gloved hand upon the arm that Gordon held out, then they walked into the Gardens, paying the entrance fee which was, indeed, a paltry investment.

Following the crowd at a slow pace, they appeared little different from any of the other couples who were out to enjoy a pleasant evening's entertainment, but soon they left the crowd behind and proceeded along dark secluded walks until they were in the quietest part of the Garden, where just an odd lamp here and there cast a dim light.

A faint murmur of voices could be heard, and an occasional giggle, and Mark turned to his friend, giving him a questioning look. Gordon nodded, then seemed to melt into the darkness while Mark moved toward a patch of lamplight which faintly illuminated a bench.

A couple passed, arms entwined, murmuring soft nothings to each other. Then Mark went over to the bench and sat, the skirt of his gown spread out and his eyes downcast in a meditative pose.

It must have been a full ten minutes before anyone appeared, and then it was only a poorly dressed old man. His eyes lit up when he saw what he thought was a young lady, but as he started to walk toward her, Gordon stepped out from behind a tree.

"She's mine. Be off with you," he snarled, and the old man made a murmured apology and hurried away.

He had barely enough time to slip back behind the tree before a well-dressed gentleman, appearing slightly the worse for drink, came into view. His eyes gleamed at the sight of what looked like a lovely lady sitting on the bench, and his soft chuckle could be clearly heard in the quiet of the night.

"What have we here?" he murmured. "A lady in distress? Were you waiting for me, my dear?"

He took a seat by the side of Mark and began to slip off the mask. "Let me see what you look like? Ah, yes," he said approvingly, then groaned as he received a glancing blow to the back of the head from the weapon in Gordon's hand.

"Quick," Gordon ordered. "I don't know how long he'll be out."

Mark put his mask back in place and started to empty the man's pockets into his reticule, holding it out to Gordon while he pulled a diamond ring off of one finger and a ring with a large ruby from the other.

Once everything was in the bag, they dragged the man behind a tree where he would be out of sight of passersby, and set off as quickly as they dared for the high wall at the back of the Gardens.

Gordon was over in a minute, but it took Mark longer, for he needed to be more careful lest he damage his sister's gown or lose something out of the bag he still carried. Then, as previously agreed, they made their separate ways to Lady Clinton's house and around to the stables in the rear.

"I'll take the bag now," Gordon said, "and I'll meet you at the usual place tomorrow, three o'clock. You go first and make sure the coast is clear."

Peering outside and seeing nothing, Mark made his way to the back door, which he had left slightly ajar, and five minutes later he was in his bedchamber and stripping off his disguise. He put the wig and other items away first, then hung the gown and shawl in his own armoire, ready to return it to Catherine's chamber as soon as she left it in the morning.

Dropping into bed, he had no difficulty whatever in falling

into a sound sleep as though he had nothing whatever on his conscience.

It was a couple of mornings later that Catherine received a note from Lady Stanhpoe enclosing an invitation to an informal outing to Richmond on the following day. Lady Stanhope's note suggested that Catherine write an acceptance directly to her hostess, Lady Coverdale, and then asked if she might take up Catherine in her carriage and drive her there. A footnote asked if she would wear the gown she had shown to her the other day, as it would be quite perfect for the occasion.

"Why did she not invite you, Aunt Genevieve?" Catherine asked. "I would have much preferred your company to that of a group of people I don't know."

"But you know Lady Stanhope by now, my dear," her aunt said gently. "I really do not have either appropriate clothes or the time to attend such occasions. That's why I was glad for Lady Stanhope to take you in hand. There will no doubt be a number of other young people there, and you'll enjoy their company once you get to know them. I have a feeling that you did not mingle with very many young people at home, for you seem much more comfortable around older folk like me."

Catherine gave her a weak smile. "It was not because I don't like people of my own age, Aunt Genevieve," she said, "but because I went out so rarely. Mama needed a great deal of nursing care, and there was no one else to do it."

"Well, all that's behind you now, and you'll gradually make friends among the young ones, and then when the Little Season begins you'll already know everyone and have a wonderful time." Lady Clinton frowned and rose hurriedly. "My goodness, I'd best hurry downstairs, for those girls will be sitting around doing nothing—just waiting for me to set them to work."

Her aunt went down the stairs to the kitchens, while Catherine went up to her bedchamber to check and be sure that the gown Lady Stanhope would like her to wear had not become creased from hanging in the armoire. She had given her maid a few weeks off, once they arrived in London, so that she could visit her family in Sussex. The girl's mother was not feeling at all well, and with so much help available from Aunt Genevieve's girls, Catherine thought it a good time to pay Maggie back for some of the nice things she had done for her.

As she reached inside the armoire she had the strange notion that the gown was not in quite the same place as she had put it several days before, after wearing it to show to Lady Stanhope. Perhaps one of her aunt's girls was training as an abigail, and had been learning how to care for gowns, she thought, but if so she would have liked to have been told.

Pulling the gown out, she noticed some marks around the hemline that she knew had not been there when she altered it, for she had carefully washed and ironed it before starting to work on it.

Frowning, she spread it out upon the bed, and was soon convinced that it had been worn by someone since she had tried it on to show to Lady Stanhope. She disliked making accusations on so little evidence, and decided not to mention it to her aunt just yet, but to wash and press the gown, and restitch a piece of trim that must have caught on something and torn. On closer examination she found that it had obviously caught on a twig which was still sticking to the fabric, and realized that whoever borrowed it had worn it outside.

She would need to take her good shawl with her in case the weather should change before they returned, but when she looked in the drawer where it was always kept, she found that it also appeared to have been misplaced.

Now completely puzzled, she searched all her drawers until she found it at last, pushed into the corner of one of them, and even had it not been used, it was creased so badly that it, too, would need to be washed and ironed.

Frankly annoyed, but relieved that she had thought to look now instead of waiting until she was about to wear them, Catherine put the garments over her arm and went downstairs to wash and press and then repair them where needed. On the way, she passed her aunt, and noticed her puzzled frown, but some instinct told Catherine not to say anything as yet, so she did not stop but hurried along to the laundry room.

The girls were receiving instruction from Mrs. Blenkinsop, and some of them turned around when they saw where she was going, but when she made no request for assistance, none was offered.

These were by no means the first garments she had washed, and she doubted that they would be the last, so she set to work and in no time at all they were clean and hanging to dry over a high rack.

As she walked past the girls once more, she noticed one smaller than the others, and realized that her aunt was right, for the girl did not look at all as she had done the day they brought her from St. Martin's Church. It was not until she reached the top of the stairs that it occurred to her that not one of those girls could possibly have worn her gown, for they were all shrimps in comparison to herself.

While ironing the garments early the next day before getting ready for her outing, she thought of it again but could find no solution. It was a puzzle, she decided, and one that could not be readily solved.

Once in Lady Stanhope's carriage, however, Catherine became far too interested in that lady's descriptions of the Thames at Richmond, and of the other guests who would make up the party, to think about the matter again.

The carriage stopped once more to take up two young ladies who appeared to be a little younger than Catherine, and from then until they reached Richmond the carriage was filled with the liveliest of chatter—something Catherine was not accustomed to hearing save when she went belowstairs at her aunt's house.

At nineteen years, Miss Josephine Waterhouse was just finishing her second Season in London, and this time she had been fortunate enough to find the gentleman of her dreams. He had only the day before journeyed west to speak with her papa, but there was little doubt that his offer would be found acceptable.

"Viscount Broadwith's family has an estate not forty miles from our home," she explained, quite breathless with excitement. "And though he and I had not previously met, I know my papa is acquainted with the earl's brother. There is no doubt that Lionel will be found eminently suitable, for Mama says he is just right for me. And I will be able to have Cynthia come to stay and meet all the eligible gentlemen before she comes out next year."

"And I am to be one of Josie's bridesmaids," Miss Cynthia Waterhouse trilled. "I do hope Papa will agree to have the wedding at St. George's in Hanover Square, for it would be so grand—and just everybody who is anybody would be there."

Catherine tried hard not to smile, but the twinkle in her eyes gave her away to Lady Stanhope, if not to the sisters.

"You don't want to be married from home, Josephine?" Lady Stanhope asked. "I chose to be wed in our own village church, and I never regretted it, for there was something so warm and comforting about being surrounded by people I had known all my life, and who I knew to be most sincere in their good wishes."

The older girl shrugged slightly. "I suppose it will depend upon when it takes place, for it would be useless to be married in London in, say, September, when town would be dreadfully thin of company."

"Oh, Josie, that would never do," Cynthia wailed. "Say you'll wait until May next year, when all the gentlemen will see me and realize how lovely I would look as a bride."

Catherine was relieved when Lady Stanhope changed the subject.

"Have either of you picnicked on the Thames at Richmond before?" she asked, and when they shook their heads, she went on, "It's a quite delightful spot, and Lady Coverdale certainly seems to have chosen a good day for it. You do have wraps with you in case it should turn a little chilly, don't you?"

The Waterhouse sisters shook their heads, and Josephine said, "When we left, Mama was busy looking after our brother, Ned. He must have been dipping rather deep last night and was quite out of sorts this morning, so she forgot to tell us to bring our wraps."

"What a pretty lace shawl, Miss Hayward," the younger girl remarked. "I'll warrant you did not need your mama to tell you to bring it along. You appear to be much more sensible than we are."

The girl was giddy but harmless, and Catherine could not help but smile. "Perhaps I'm a little too sensible sometimes. My younger brother thinks so, I am sure," she told her. "I do hope it won't become chilly. Your gown is so pretty that it would have been a shame to cover it with a wrap."

"How nice of you to say so, Miss Hayward. Our mama said that it was not fair for Josephine to have all the pretty gowns just because she was coming out, so she persuaded Papa that I should have some also."

The girl had charming dimples when she smiled, and Catherine felt sure that this sister would not go more than one Season unwed. She might do very well indeed once her older sister was married and out of the way.

She said as much to Lady Stanhope when they had left the carriage and were walking down to the river, the Waterhouse sisters hurrying ahead.

"Cynthia is sweeter, more like her mama," Lady Stanhope agreed. "But, you know, most young ladies from seventeen onward have only one thought in their heads, and that is not so much to make a suitable marriage but to find a handsome husband. You appear to be an exception to the rule, my dear, if you do not my saying so, and you seem a little quiet today. Is there something wrong?"

Catherine shook her head. There was something wrong, of course, but even if she knew where her young brother was getting his money, she could hardly squeak on him, and she had not the vaguest idea. The mystery of her gown having been used was most perplexing, but it never occurred to her that Mark was the one who had worn it.

They were walking along the grassy bank of the river now and could see Lady Coverdale greeting some of her guests. By her side was her older son, Lord Coverdale, and a tall young lady, much like him in appearance, whom Catherine assumed to be his older sister.

"I'm glad Coverdale was able to get back in time," Lady Stanhope said, "for it's always so much easier to entertain guests when there is a host present also. It was such a relief to his mama, of course, when he came back from Waterloo with only a leg wound, for the rumors going around of the number dead and severely wounded were terrifying." She suddenly realized how thoughtless she was being and, pausing, placed a hand on

Catherine's arm. "My dear, I am so sorry, for your aunt told me, of course, how badly your papa was wounded. I have heard little about it since, however, and was wondering how he is going along?"

Catherine shook her head. "I'm afraid we have not yet heard. I was hoping that when I saw Lord Coverdale today he might have some news for me."

"Perhaps he will," Lady Stanhope said comfortingly. "Let's go over and ask him."

The two older ladies embraced as though they had not seen each other for months, and Coverdale smiled warmly at Catherine.

"If we can get some time alone a little later, I will tell you how I went along at Cambridge. Don't worry," he added, as he saw her frown, "it's all good news."

Lady Stanhope performed the introductions and Lady Coverdale clasped Catherine's hand firmly. "I've head so much about you, both from my son and from Lady Stanhope, my dear. I believe that between us we can make sure that you have a pleasant introduction to society in the way your mama would have wanted. You perhaps do not realize that she came out at the same time as my younger sister, and I have fond memories of when she ran tame in the Grosvenor Square house."

"No, I didn't, my lady," Catherine murmured, touched because she had finally met someone who knew her mama. "Perhaps you could tell me more when you have the time."

"Of course, I will be glad to. Edwin, why don't you take Catherine down to the water's edge where the young people are gathering, and introduce her around?" Lady Coverdale suggested. "Almost everyone is here now and in a little while we will serve a light nuncheon."

Lord Coverdale held out his arm and Catherine took it to walk down the slope toward the group of young men and women gathered below.

"From my conversation with your brother, he seemed to expect that he would not be taken back at Cambridge, but I'm glad to tell you that it was nowhere near as bad as it sounded," he told her, adding, "Provided he makes a determined effort to catch up with his studies, they have no objection to his returning there next term.''

Catherine turned to him, a warm smile on her face. ''I'm so pleased, and I'm sure Papa will be also. Mark is not a bad boy, but I'm afraid he is very easily led, and when he cannot get what he wants he is inclined to become extremely difficult. Perhaps if he had been spanked when he threw tantrums as a little boy it would have cured him, but Mama did not have the heart to punish him,'' she said wryly.

''He should have gone to Eton, as I did. They had quite remarkable cures for childish tantrums,'' Coverdale told her with a grin.

''Mama could not bear to send him away, as you probably guessed,'' Catherine said, having a very good idea what those remarkable cures were. ''You did not, by any chance, hear anything more about Papa, did you?''

''I don't believe so, but I came directly here this morning from Cambridge, so there is a remote possibility that some word may be waiting for me when I get home. Have you met any of the young people gathered below?''

''Two of them. Miss Waterhouse and her sister Miss Cynthia Waterhouse rode here in Lady Stanhope's carriage.''

He seemed so much friendlier than he had been the previous times when they had met that Catherine was completely disarmed and the faint hostility she had felt toward him receded.

As he made the introductions she knew she would never remember all of the names, and the girls, at least, did seem to be much younger than herself, but then it was customary for young ladies to marry men ten to fifteen years older than they were.

The nuncheon Lady Coverdale had selected was light and delicious, and served with clear, bubbling champagne that seemed to prick Catherine's nose and make her want to laugh and enjoy herself.

Afterward, boats were waiting to take anyone who so desired for a trip on the river, and Catherine went with Cynthia Waterhouse and two young men, and though she found it difficult to chatter gaily, and felt as if she was playing the part of a chaperone, she enjoyed the feeling of floating peacefully along without a care in the world.

She had never attended anything like this before. Everyone was so friendly, and she was a little too far away to notice, even if it had occurred to her to do so, when a carriage pulled up and several gentlemen got out and went over to greet Lord Coverdale.

"Coverdale," one of them called, "I had no idea you were back in town."

"Haven't been back yet," he said, "but stopped off here for I knew Mama was giving a party. I'd forgotten how much fun these things can be."

"Speaking of fun," Sir James Blanchard, an acquaintance since college days, said quietly, "a young lady had some fun with me the other night that I did not at all appreciate."

Coverdale raised an eyebrow. "What kind of fun, Blanchard?" he asked.

"I was robbed," he said, "at Vauxhall Gardens, and I still have a lump on the back of my head to prove it." He raised a finger to a spot on his sandy-colored head and winced.

"Were you a trifle foxed?" one of the others asked. "It's not like you to fall for something like that."

"I'd had one or two, of course, but not that much, and just thought I'd take a stroll down some of those dark paths they have. It's usually good for a laugh or two if you see someone you know there," he said with a shrug.

"And did you?" Coverdale asked dryly.

"I didn't get a chance," Sir James said bitterly. "There was this lovely young thing sitting on a bench under a lamp, sobbing as though she was lost or something, so I went over to her to see if there was something I could do to help."

He paused.

"And, of course, there was, wasn't there?" one of the other gentlemen asked with a grin.

"Never found out," Sir James said disgustedly. "I'd just eased off the mask she was wearing, when something hit me hard on the back of the head and I knew nothing at all until several hours later. My head was bleeding, but I got up and made my way to the entrance, then found that my watch and fob, both of my rings I inherited from Papa, my diamond cravat pin, and a purse full of money were all gone. I never stood a chance. Must have been someone waiting behind the bench to knock me out. And what a head I had the next day!''

"You'd better tell us in case we get into the same position. What did this beauty look like?'' one of his cronies asked.

"She was in mourning, or so I thought. Black gown, black lace shawl over her head, black mask. That's as much as I had a chance to see, I'm sorry to say,'' he murmured. "Could have been anyone. Could have been that young lady stepping out of that boat right now, for all I know.''

All heads turned to where Catherine was being assisted out of the boat. She turned to wait for her companions, and Sir James said, "The black gown with the unusual trim around the hem and neckline, the lace shawl, and that chestnut-colored hair . . . I wonder . . ." he growled.

"Now just a minute, James,'' Coverdale said sharply. "I happen to know that young lady quite well. Her father was with me at Waterloo and was so badly wounded that it is still not known if he will recover or not. The last thing she needs at this time is to have someone like you spreading untruths about, to damage her reputation.''

"Is she in mourning for him already before he's gone?'' a wag asked.

"The mourning is for her mother, who died less than a year ago,'' Coverdale snapped, furious at the turn of conversation. "What are you fellows trying to do to the poor girl?''

"I'm not trying to do anything to her,'' Sir James said with a shrug. "I told you the woman I saw could have been anybody, for all I know.''

"But as you realize, I'm sure, insinuations can do more damage than outright accusations. Do you want me to go and ask her directly if she was in Vauxhall Gardens the other night and hit you on the head?'' Coverdale had no intention of doing so, of course, and knew he had already said too much.

"All right, I made a mistake. It wasn't her.'' Sir James turned to the young men who had accompanied him. "I don't know about you, but I think this is the dullest party I ever almost attended. We know when we're not wanted. What do you say

to going over to see what's showing at the Theatre Royal? I
know a place where we can get a halfway decent meal first,
before it begins.''

As the gentlemen walked back to their coach, Coverdale heard
his mother's soft voice behind him. "I'm afraid that was very
badly handled, Edwin. You turned friends into enemies, and
all they have to do now is find out Miss Hayward's name and
her reputation will be ruined beyond repair. Is there nothing
you can do to make amends?'' she asked anxiously.

"You see the gown she is wearing, Mama," he said softly.
"Is it one that a modiste might make several copies of? I mean,
identical copies?''

Lady Stanhope had joined his mother and it was she who
shook her head and answered, "I happen to know that it was
a slightly outdated gown which she altered herself. She is
extremely proficient with a needle. And the ruffled trim is the
very latest thing, so she added it to make the gown look like
new. It could be considered an original. She showed it to me
the other day, to be sure that I did not think it looked homemade. Why do you ask?''

He scowled. "It's better that you don't know, Lady
Stanhope," he said. "I was going to suggest that I take her home
instead of you, my lady, and explain to her on the way what
has happened, but on second thoughts I think it might be better
to do nothing different to what we would normally do. If
Blanchard or any of his cronies are going to make trouble,
there's nothing we can do to prevent them at this point. I'll go
around to see her in the morning. I meant to, in any case, for
surely by now there will be news of her father waiting for me
in town.''

Lady Coverdale nodded. "There is a letter from Brussels
waiting, Edwin. It arrived too late to send it on to you.''

Although the party continued for some time, and the guests
had not the slightest idea that anything strange had taken place,
Lord Coverdale, his mother, and Lady Stanhope shared the wish
that everyone would soon go home.

When they had waved good-bye to the last guest, mother and
son made their way separately back to London, but they met
in the drawing room within minutes of their return.

"What do you mean to do first tomorrow?" Lady Coverdale asked.

Coverdale looked thoughtful. "I believe I'll test the water before I pay Miss Hayward a visit," he said quietly. "If a rumor is started by one of the men present, it will be this evening, and by tomorrow it will be the *on-dit* and I shall hear about it at my club."

"How dreadful if that poor girl is given a bad reputation before she has even begun to be seen around," Lady Coverdale said sadly.

Four

As LORD COVERDALE entered White's and made for the dining room, he became aware of a sudden lull in conversation, then heard it start up again as he took a seat beside his old friend and comrade, Sir Geoffrey Wardle.

"What brings you to White's at this hour?" Sir Geoffrey asked him in a deliberately casual tone. "It wouldn't have anything to do with that rumor flying around about a friend of yours, a Miss Catherine Hayward, and Sir James Blanchard, would it?"

"Why don't you tell me just what is the latest *on-dit*, Geoff, so that I may either confirm or deny it," Coverdale asked quietly.

"It quite obviously grows the more interesting with each telling, but from what I have been able to ascertain, the lady set her cap at Sir James, was rejected, and then arranged for him to be attacked and robbed in Vauxhall Gardens, with herself as the bait to draw him there." Sir Geoffrey smiled wryly and his eyebrows rose expectantly.

Coverdale shook his head sadly. "I cannot believe that he has not denied it, for I know it for a fact that they have never met, Geoff. When he saw her yesterday, at a distance, it was perfectly obvious that he did not know her. He was merely using her to illustrate his point. He said the woman in Vauxhall Gardens could have been anyone—could have been that girl just stepping out of the boat over there for all he knew. And the only similarity at first appeared to be the fact that she was wearing a black gown. When he left us, he did not even know her name, but I suppose it was not at all difficult for him to find out who she was from one of the other guests.

"Mama said I handled it badly, and she was right, of course. If it had been anyone else I'd not have become so indignant but, dash it all, I have a responsibility toward her," he said, glaring fiercely.

Sir Geoffrey looked puzzled but said nothing.

Coverdale sighed. "I was with her father the night before Waterloo, and I promised that I would let his family know if anything happened to him, and more or less keep an eye on them. You know the kind of thing—he was to do the same for mine if I was hit badly."

"He's dead, then?" Sir Geoffrey was startled.

"No, thank God." Coverdale shook his head. "He was in a bad way, though. I managed to get him to some nuns and left him there. Just got word yesterday when we returned from Richmond that he's coming along but still doesn't know who or where he is. It'll be a month or more before it's safe to move him."

"I'm not going to ask how you did all that with a badly wounded leg, Edwin. Seems to me he and his family owe you a great deal." He looked thoughtful and then asked, quietly, "Are you sure that the girl wasn't the one in Vauxhall Gardens that night? How much do you really know about her? Have you actually asked her?"

"I know that she'd never been to London before her father brought her here to stay with his sister. He'd never actually bought out, but had been recovering from an earlier wound, and then on leave, looking after his dying wife when the war ended. His wife passed on and then when it became obvious that there'd have to be another battle to put Napoleon down for good, he just had to be a part of it."

Sir Geoffrey nodded. "There'd have been no victory without him and men like him. So what do you mean to do now?"

"I'll have to go and see her. She probably never even saw Blanchard yesterday, let alone met him before, and doesn't even know there are any rumors going around. She lives with her aunt in a house on Kennington Lane." Coverdale heard his friend's low whistle before he realized the reason. "Oh, no!

That will surely finish her when word gets out, for it's no more than a stone's throw from Vauxhall Gardens.''

"Rather damning, I would say," Sir Geoffrey agreed. "Whereabouts on Kennington Lane?''

"It's a large house on the corner of Devonshire Place. The back of the Gardens, where the dark walks are, must be quite close," Coverdale said, then he rose, as did Sir Geoffrey.

The two gentlemen made their way through the dining room, nodding first to this acquaintance and then that one, as though they had not a care in the world. It was a sign of the high respect in which Coverdale was held that not one single gentleman stopped him to ask about the latest *on-dit*, though it was well known that his name had been linked with it.

Coverdale was wrong in supposing that Catherine had not heard the rumor, for, shortly after an early luncheon, Lady Stanhope had called on her aunt. Lady Clinton had, of course, sent for her niece at once.

"Sit down, my dear," Lady Clinton said, much less disturbed about the problem than was her fashionable sister-in-law. "It would appear that there has been a case of mistaken identity.''

Taking a seat across from the two ladies, Catherine looked questioningly at them, for she had not the slightest idea what her aunt was talking about. She was wearing the second of the three gowns that she was updating, and Lady Stanhope noticed this immediately.

"What a pity that you did not wear that gown to the picnic yesterday," she murmured, "for then I would not be here now bringing you this dreadful news.''

"Dreadful news, my lady?" Catherine asked quickly, fear in her eyes. "Is it about Papa?''

Confused for a moment, Lady Stanhope shook her head. "Oh no, I've heard nothing about your papa," she said, frowning. "I'm afraid it's about you. It seems that a certain gentleman was attacked in Vauxhall Gardens a few evenings ago, and that one of the culprits was a young lady. I did not see him until he was just leaving, but it seems that he saw you at Richmond and decided that the wicked young lady was you.''

"Me?" Catherine asked, frowning, for the idea was ridiculous to say the least. "Is Vauxhall Gardens the kind of place where such things as that occur?"

"No, not at all," Lady Stanhope said emphatically. "I have been there many times and have never had the slightest problem, but then I would not think of entering the ill-lit, dark walks at the back of the gardens where gentlemen go to meet a certain kind of female."

Insulted at being classed as a certain kind of female, Catherine inquired, "What happened to this so-called gentleman?"

"His name is Sir James Blanchard, and he was knocked unconscious and robbed, or so he says. But I am inclined to doubt that he was entirely blameless in whatever happened to him," Lady Stanhope said sharply.

"I'm afraid I still cannot imagine what part I am supposed to have played in all this," Catherine said. "I am quite sure I have never met anyone by that name."

"He was apparently at the picnic yesterday," her aunt interposed.

Catherine frowned and slowly shook her head. "I know that I was introduced to dozens of people, but I do not recall a Blanchard. What does he look like?"

As Lady Clinton did not know the man at all, it was left to her sister-in-law to answer.

"He's in his thirties, I would say. A little plump, though I doubt he would admit to it. He has sandy-blond hair which is usually exquisitely arranged, and he is inclined to look at one through his eyeglass," she said slowly, frowning. The other two ladies were so intent on hearing all, that they did not notice the doorbell sound as Lady Stanhope continued, "I did not care very much for that young man before, and now I must say that I dislike him intensely."

"But I have still not the slightest idea what I am supposed to have done to him," Catherine reminded her, a little impatiently.

Lady Stanhope hesitated, for she did not quite know how to phrase it politely.

All three were startled to hear Coverdale say calmly, and rather more quietly than usual, "I'm afraid that one over-dramatic version is that you set your cap at him, were rejected, then sought revenge by having him attacked and robbed in Vauxhall Gardens. You even took part in the attack yourself."

He was standing in front of the door, which he had closed quietly behind him, and Catherine looked at him in amazement. Part of her wanted to laugh out loud at such a ridiculous idea, but this quickly turned to anger as she realized what dreadful things this unknown person was accusing her of. Keeping herself firmly under control, she forced a faint smile as she said, "You cannot be serious, my lord. As I just explained to Lady Stanhope, though I have been living close by, I have not yet been inside the Gardens. She tells me, however, that things of that sort are not a usual occurrence."

The smile quickly faded as she looked from one face to another, and now her eyes were as troubled as theirs. "You are serious, aren't you?"

Lord Coverdale sighed. He had closely watched her expressive face as it showed first incredulity, then amusement for just a moment, followed at once by quickly controlled anger. He walked over and took a seat where he could continue to watch her.

"I'm afraid so, my dear," he told her. "The whole thing seems to me to center around the gown you wore yesterday. Is it true that you recently retrimmed it to make it more fashionable?"

He leaned forward as he asked the question, and clearly saw the look of fear that came into her eyes, though it was quickly hidden.

She nodded. "Yesterday was the first time I had worn it save for when I put it on to show Lady Stanhope so that she could see if it was suitable for me to wear to the picnic." Her voice was barely a whisper.

"How long ago was that?" he asked gently.

"Just a few days, I think," she said, looking at Lady Stanhope and receiving a nod of confirmation.

He slowly shook his head as he considered the only other possibility. "Could anyone have borrowed the gown without your knowledge, and then returned it afterward?" he asked.

"I suppose it is possible," she said, "but I cannot imagine why they would do so. Can you?"

Lady Clinton spoke up. "Are you thinking about one of my girls, perhaps?" she asked. "Although I don't believe that any one of them is as tall as Catherine, such a thing cannot be ruled out. They all have access to her room when she is not there, for we do not lock doors here, and several of them have been in there at times helping her dress since her maid is away."

"Is the maid ill?" Lord Coverdale asked, grasping at anything a little different from the usual.

"No, but her mama has been for some time," Catherine told him. "She did not beg for time off, but I offered it since my aunt allows me to use her girls when I have the need. There could be no possible connection, for I sent her off long before I started stitching the gown."

Lord Coverdale looked thoughtful for a moment, then appeared to reach a decision. "I have my curricle outside," he said. "With your permission, Lady Clinton, I would like to take your niece for a drive. May I have the pleasure, Miss Hayward?"

"Aren't you afraid that people we meet might start to ask me embarrassing questions?" Catherine asked tartly.

Lord Coverdale shook his head. "No, not at all. It is far more likely that they will simply cut you dead, but as you do not know many people as yet, the chances of more than a half dozen doing so in one afternoon are remote," he said calmly. "What I wish to find out is if they will dare to cut me also for being in your company." He did not add that the chances were most unlikely, for the standards for gentlemen were very different from those for ladies.

"Then the answer is no, my lord, I would not like to go for a drive with you under those circumstances," Catherine said, offended by his callous attitude.

"But you *will* go with me, won't you?" It was more of a statement than a request. "Unless you face up to them they will decide that you are most definitely guilty. Come along, my dear. Show them that you have too much pride to sit at home and feel sorry for yourself."

Her chin rose imperceptibly and for a moment she glared at him furiously, then she rose. "If you do not mind waiting a few moments, my lord, I'll be delighted to accept your invitation," she told him frostily.

A mere ten minutes later, he handed her into his curricle and they set out, taking much the same route as they had on the last occasion, but this time it was afternoon, and Coverdale avoided St. James's Street and made straight for the park.

"Just remember," he said, "they can't actually eat you alive. You have a wonderfully straight back. Keep it that way and hold your head high."

At first she saw no one that she knew, but then in the distance she recognized the Waterhouse sisters being driven by a gentleman she had not seen before.

As they drew nearer she saw the heads go together as if debating what they should do, and then, as they were almost alongside, Miss Josephine Waterhouse looked completely through her and called, "Lord Coverdale, how nice to see you again."

His glance passed over the young lady as though he could neither see nor hear her, then he turned to Catherine with a smile so infectious that she could not help smiling back. "I'm sure you're enjoying the drive more today, my dear, without a pair of chattering magpies beside you," he remarked, driving on.

Catherine had not complained yesterday, so she wondered how he had known what they had been like, then realized that he must have been in their company on many such occasions and found them just as giddy and silly as she had.

"That's two down, and perhaps a half dozen to go," he said once they were out of earshot. "Was it really so bad?"

"Do you think they'll ever speak to you again?" she asked him. "You were even ruder than they."

"You really don't understand yet the double standard that prevails here, do you?" he told her wryly. "An eligible gentleman can do no wrong."

Catherine almost made a sharp retort, then knowing full well that it was not he who had made the rules, she said with a wistful smile, "After that experience, I must say that gentlemen are very lucky indeed, and do not completely appreciate their good fortune.''

He placed his hand on hers for a moment. ''Don't worry, you'll come about, my dear, for I'll not let them ruin you,'' he promised.

There was a slight smile on his face, but as she looked into his eyes she knew that he was making a promise he meant to keep, though she could not imagine how he could be so confident.

There were two more similar encounters, but Catherine did not really know the ladies at all, having met them only at the picnic table the day before. They quite obviously knew who she was, however. After that, Coverdale decided they had done enough for the first afternoon.

''I think we'll go back now,'' he said, ''for I achieved exactly what I wanted to. Perhaps we will do it again tomorrow?''

''I don't know,'' she told him honestly. ''It's really most unpleasant to sit here and be snubbed so dreadfully.''

''Just look forward to the day when they'll find out they were wrong and will fall over each other trying to make excuses for their behavior. Then you'll be able to get your revenge by being cool and ungracious.''

He laughed when she protested and told him, ''I'll do no such thing, my lord.''

''I know you won't,'' he said, ''but I just wanted to hear you say so.''

They drove back in silence, Coverdale going over and over in his mind possible solutions to the problem, while Catherine wondered if her brother could be the culprit. He had certainly been obtaining money from somewhere, and this seemed to her to be just the kind of thing that his friend, Gordon, would thoroughly enjoy. Surely, she thought, if it really was Mark, he would confess when he realized that she was being blamed for it.

When they reached Kennington Lane, Lord Coverdale stepped down and escorted Catherine to the door. Only then did he recall that he had never passed along the news of her father.

He looked quite stricken and, noticing, Catherine asked anxiously, ''Is something wrong, my lord?''

Shaking his head, he told her, "No, nothing at all is wrong, but with all this ridiculous fuss I am afraid I failed to tell you that I had word about your father. He's now out of danger, but unaware as yet of his surroundings. They feel it will be at least a month before he is well enough to travel back to England."

She gave him a tearful smile, grateful to know that the danger was past, but Coverdale was still angry with himself for overlooking something of such importance to her.

"I do beg your pardon, my dear," he said earnestly. "I should have conveyed the message to you at once."

"Please don't blame yourself," she begged, "for it was just the kind of news I needed after that dreadful drive. Now I'll be able to think of Papa this evening instead of those rude people."

He left her then, and she went indoors smiling quite happily.

Once she had removed her hat and gloves, she went in search of her aunt, eager to convey the good news.

She did not have far to look, for Lady Clinton was sitting in the drawing room, a puzzled frown on her face.

"Did Lord Coverdale not come in with you?" she asked, then continued at once, "I was hoping that he might, for I found this afternoon that you omitted to tell us something quite important."

Catherine's eyebrows rose. "Did I, Aunt Genevieve? What was that?"

"I questioned each of my girls individually, and every one of them swore that they had not worn your gown, or even taken it out of your armoire," Lady Clinton said, her expression severe. "But three of them told me, privately, that they had seen you go into the laundry room and wash both the gown and shawl the day before the picnic."

"Yes, I did," Catherine readily admitted. "Fortunately, I took the gown out a day ahead of time and found that the hem was dirty. The shawl was not dirty, but it was creased, and washing it seemed the easiest way to get the creases out."

"Don't you think you should have mentioned it this afternoon?" Lady Clinton suggested sternly.

"To be honest, it worried me a little at the time, for it was perfectly clean when I worked on it, of course. Then I realized

I must have dirtied it myself when I wore it for Lady Stanhope to see, and simply did not notice. As I recall I went into the garden afterward to pick flowers for the table. I'm so accustomed to Maggie checking my clothes that I probably just forgot to do so.'' She looked appealingly at her aunt and asked, ''Do you feel that it's really important?''

Lady Clinton sighed. ''Perhaps I'm making more of it than is warranted, my dear. And you would hardly try to hide the fact that you washed it, would you, when you knew you had been seen performing such an unusual task for a lady?'' She smiled wanly, then asked, ''Where did you go this afternoon, and how was the drive?''

Catherine shuddered. ''We went to the park and it was quite dreadful, as you can probably imagine, but Lord Coverdale was wonderful. Can you believe that he cut the people who wanted to speak to him and ignore me?''

''I believe he feels responsible, in part, for the rumor's getting started in the first place. You see, Lady Coverdale heard his quarrel with Sir James Blanchard and told him that he had handled the matter very badly. My sister-in-law heard her say so,'' Lady Clinton said.

''Perhaps he's not always the most tactful person, but I am sure he didn't mean to make things difficult for me,'' Catherine murmured, ''and before he left he was most upset for he had quite forgotten to tell us that Papa is no longer in danger, but is still unaware of where he is or what happened. They think it will be at least a month before he'll be well enough to travel to England.''

''That's good news, anyway, my dear. And we'll just have to wait patiently until we get him home and can start to build his strength back up again.'' She smiled at her niece. ''The time will pass quickly, but you mustn't expect him to look his old self when he first gets back.''

''I know,'' Catherine said softly, ''for I've seen him come back thin and pale, and with a shakiness he wouldn't admit to, but we'll soon have him fit and strong again, won't we?''

''That's the way, my dear,'' her aunt said firmly, ''we must look at the bright side of things. If Lord Coverdale has been able to make the arrangements, your brother will soon be resuming his studies, with a tutor first and later at the university, and we'll no longer have to worry about him. Which reminds me, I have not seen him today as yet. Did he say he would be in for dinner tonight?''

"I haven't seen him today either. That's strange, for though I know he's away a great deal, he usually seeks me out to let me know when he'll be back. Perhaps he did not wish to disturb us earlier," Catherine suggested.

"If you mean when Lord Coverdale was here, that young man would not have been so considerate, I'm sure, for he is anxious to find out what, if anything, has been arranged for him in Cambridge," Lady Clinton snapped. "Youngsters these days have no consideration for other people."

"He's not bad deep down, Aunt Genevieve," Catherine said, hastening to her brother's defense. "Mama spoiled him, you know, for it was always easier for her to say yes than to get into an argument with him. If Papa had been home more, it would have been a very different matter."

"Of course it would, but my brother always had a hankering after wearing one of those fancy uniforms, even when he was little," Lady Clinton said, smiling as she recalled the two of them in those days. "I thought he'd got over it when he married your mama, but then after you two came along, and the fighting started in Spain, he just had to go. There was no stopping him."

"I'm thankful, at least, that he refused to take Mark back with him this time, for I don't think I could bear it if he had been wounded too. But, you know, that's one of the reasons why my brother has been so difficult to handle these last few weeks. Papa has never been exactly tactful, and he made Mark feel as though he was just a halfling, rather than a grown boy as old as many of the soldiers already fighting over there. But then that's Papa, and once he got his uniform out again I'm sure he already felt like a major, giving orders left and right."

Tears suddenly filled her eyes as she thought of him as he was now, hurting so badly, and miles away from those who loved him.

Her aunt put an arm around her shoulders. "You did everything you could to prevent him going, I know, my dear. And we'll have him back soon, probably lying there giving us all our orders like a sultan in a harem. And won't we just love it!''

"The trouble with you nobs is that you worry too much,''
Gordon sneered. "Getting your share of the spoils doesn't worry
you at all though, does it?''

"But I never thought for a moment that Cathie would be
blamed for what I did,'' Mark said. "What rotten luck it was
that she should have been at that picnic, wearing the very gown
that I had borrowed, when that fellow came along.''

"It's not the way I heard it,'' his friend said slyly. "It seems
that she's been setting her cap at him and he wasn't interested.''

"That's not true and you know it,'' Mark said angrily. "She'll
never be able to show her face in society after this, so how is
she to find a husband?''

"If you're thinking of confessing all like a good little boy,
I'd not advise you to do so, for I'm not taking the rap for it,''
Gordon warned. "You knew the risks involved when we started,
and you're not backing out now.''

"I'm not denying anything I've done with you, and I'll admit
that I went into this with my eyes open as to the risks,'' Mark
averred, "but neither of us could have guessed that this would
happen.''

"Suppose—'' Gordon said, lifting a warning hand and adding,
"now you'd better not do it, for I'm dead against it—but just
suppose you confessed to your sister that it was you that fellow
Blanchard joined on the bench. What good would it do save
start one more story going around? People believe what they
want to believe, you know, and it wouldn't clear her name.
They'd either say you were trying to protect her, or that you
were both in it together.''

Mark thought for a moment, realizing that what Gordon said
was true. Nothing he admitted to now would change things for
Catherine. It might even make them worse.

Gordon put a hand on Mark's shoulder. "Stop worrying about
it, will you? You didn't deliberately set out to hurt your sister
any more than I did. It was pure coincidence. We couldn't have
known this might happen, for the chances of something like this
are one in a thousand. Let's go over to Lenny's place and have

a go at doubling our money. There're sure to be some green-horns around who are willing to part with their dibs.''

When Mark hesitated for a moment, Gordon went on, ''Come along. You'll need all the money you can lay your hands on when you get up to Cambridge. And with your pa still over in Brussels, there'll be no funds coming from him for a long time. Wouldn't it be a treat if you made enough to get that sister of yours a nice bit of jewelry that would take her mind off her problems?''

It wasn't a bad idea, Mark thought, for poor Catherine had little in the way of jewelry save for a pin that their mother had given her—and she did not even have that now, for he had borrowed it without her permission to pawn for much-needed funds. Gordon had handled it for him, but when he tried to redeem it, the pin was gone.

Gordon watched Mark's expressive face and added, ''I know a fellow who would let you have a real nice brooch or, better still, a necklace for next to nothing.''

Mark grinned. ''All right, let's go then. But just one thing. Don't you come up with any more wild ideas like having me dress like a woman. I've finished with that for good.''

They went off arm in arm, for Mark's earlier resentment toward Gordon had gone, and once more he trusted the younger man to teach him how to get along in a city that was so vastly different from anything he had ever dreamed of.

Several hours later he let himself into his aunt's house and crept quietly up the stairs. He would have liked to have awakened Catherine right away and shown her the beautiful necklace he had bought for her with the money he had won that evening.

Gordon had taken him to a place that had looked closed from the outside, but the proprietor had gladly opened up for his young friend and had shown him so many lovely baubles that he'd had a difficult time deciding which to get for her.

She would look like a queen wearing it, but perhaps he should wait until her birthday before giving it to her, he decided, for by then some of the scandalmongers might have found someone else to talk about.

When he lit the candle in his room, he found a note propped against it from Catherine, warning him that their aunt was annoyed at not having seen him at all that day. It also said that she had some news for him, and he was left wondering whether it was about their father, or if perhaps Coverdale had succeeded in securing his return to Cambridge.

Five

CATHERINE NO LONGER had any desire to continue stitching her black gowns, so she took out the length of apple green fabric she had purchased earlier and started working on a gown for some time in the future. She would be officially out of mourning in another two weeks, but had neither sufficient money nor sufficient interest to think of making any change in her attire for the present.

She was in the upstairs sitting room, busily working on the new gown, when her brother came in, stooped down, and dropped a kiss on her forehead, causing her to look up in surprise, for though she knew that he loved her in his own way, a display of affection from him was rare indeed.

"I found your note when I came in last night and was extremely curious," he said with a smile, "but knew better than to wake you from a sound sleep to find out your news."

"I should think so," she told him, her eyes twinkling. "I wanted to tell you that Lord Coverdale heard from the nuns, and Papa is out of danger, but it will be a month yet before he's well enough for the journey home."

Mark sighed with relief. "You've no idea how very much I want to see him again," he said, realizing that if he were here at this moment he would make a clean breast of everything to him.

"It's likely he'll need a much longer recuperation this time, Mark. Aunt Genevieve is talking of keeping him here for the time being, where there are so many more pairs of hands to help in his care, rather than have him go directly to Hayward House.''

"That's a lot of balderdash," Mark snapped, the affection of a moment ago forgotten. "A fine daughter you are if you won't even look after your father in his own home. And you may just as well, for if the rumors I heard yesterday continue, you'll not be able to set a foot outside this house again without shaming yourself and everyone with you.''

Catherine looked at her brother in astonishment, unable to understand the reason for such a vicious attack. Then she became furious.

"I'm sure that if you feel so strongly about Papa's going directly home, you must mean to look after him also. That is, of course, if you even have any idea of how to begin, for you never raised one finger to help me with Mama, if I recall correctly,'' she snapped, her eyes flashing angrily.

The door swung open and Aunt Genevieve came hurrying in.

"Children," she scolded, as if, indeed, they really were. "Have you any idea how easily you can be heard downstairs? And here Lord Coverdale has just arrived to talk to you, Mark, about Cambridge. What must he think?''

Grinning a little sheepishly, Mark made for the door, but Catherine remained seated, her anger having turned to an inconsolable sadness.

"Come along, my dear," Lady Clinton quietly urged. "You know very well that he'll be as sorry as can be later for speaking to you in that way.''

"If I know Mark, he'll persuade Lord Coverdale to take him off in his curricle. You go down, Aunt Genevieve, and I'll join you in a little while, when they've gone.''

"Very well, but just let me say this. No matter what your brother wishes, your papa is not returning north until he's much better. You've had enough nursing to do for your mama without starting all over again. He's staying here where he'll have all of us around him to wait on him hand and foot," Lady Clinton said decidedly.

Catherine sat perfectly still, her sewing forgotten as she once again wondered about that gown with the dirty hem. Had all that shouting and blustering been her brother's guilty conscience at work? But, if so, how could he possibly speak to her as if she had been the wrongdoer?

When a tap sounded on the door of the sittingroom, it startled her, but she called, "Come in," thinking it was one of Aunt Genevieve's girls. When Coverdale entered, she looked at him in complete surprise.

"It's quite all right," he told her. "I have your aunt's permission to come up here, and no one will disturb us—not even that brat of a brother of yours." Her eyes widened, and he grinned. "Yes, I did hear what was going on up here, and I must say that I admire your spirit for standing up to him."

He sat down in the chair facing her. "I've been the rounds again, and things are no better, I'm sorry to say, than they were yesterday. One thing has been added, however." He paused, though he knew it was best that he tell her than have her hear it from someone else, such as her brother. "Word is that Blanchard had put you in the family way."

"My goodness! Without even having met me?" she suggested, laughing at first, and then wanting desperately to be alone and able to cry, for it was all so very dreadful.

"Exactly," Coverdale said softly. There was a pause, then he said, "For some time now I have been aware that I will have to marry in the not too distant future in order to continue the line. Of course, I do have a younger brother, which relieves the pressure somewhat, but one can never quite tell what might happen. The trouble is, however, that I cannot abide the simpering misses who seem to predominate in the Marriage Mart each Season.

"I have very much admired the way you have reacted to being placed in what can only be described as an intolerable situation. You are completely innocent in this matter, that I do know, and you have somehow managed to keep it in its proper perspective."

Catherine was now perfectly still, for she knew quite well where all this was leading, and that she would have to regretfully decline, for she could not allow him to shoulder her burdens in this way.

"I am asking you to marry me, Catherine." He held up a hand when she would have spoken. "No, my dear, permit me to continue. If you are looking to fall madly and passionately in love before you wed, that I cannot promise you, but I myself would much prefer the kind of love that grows through sincere warmth and affection, rather than a fire that quickly burns itself out. What are your feelings about marriage?''

Catherine's cheeks suddenly started to burn, and she thought of how ridiculous she must look, for she did not usually embarrass so easily. But she knew she could not dissimulate but must answer him truthfully.

''I had thought that I might meet some good, kind gentleman, not necessarily of rank, whom I could look after, take care of his home, and with whom, if possible, I could start a family.'' She was discomfited or she would not have added, ''I know that must sound as though I am looking for a position as house-keeper, but I did not mean it to.

''Had I known you for several trouble-free months and you had then asked me to marry you, I would have agreed readily, but I cannot do so now and permit you to shoulder problems that are not of your making, my lord.''

''But they are not of your making either, my dear Catherine,'' he said quietly. ''I am afraid I did play some part in them, however, for had I placated Blanchard when he was speaking of the attack upon his person, he and his companions would not have left the picnic in anger. Better still, I should have introduced him to you and then he would have known at once that he had the wrong party. However, what is done cannot be undone. Will you agree to think about it for a day or two before giving me such a swift answer? I am in earnest and I believe we would rub along very well together.''

''Yes, my lord,'' she began, but Coverdale interrupted.

''Please call me Edwin,'' he asked, smiling gently.

''Yes, Edwin,'' she said softly, liking the sound of it. ''I will think on it and, no matter what, I am indeed honored that you asked me.''

''I do not want you to be honored,'' he told her with a grim smile. ''I want you to marry me and be happy. I'll leave you now to think further on it. I see no reason to put you through the ordeal of yesterday afternoon, but if you happen to have a riding habit with you, I should like very much to bring a mount around and take you riding early tomorrow morning.''

Her eyes brightened in anticipation. ''I'm afraid my riding habit is not very fashionable, but perhaps there will not be too many people out at that early hour?'' she asked hopefully.

''Almost no one at all,'' he told her with some amusement. ''We may, in fact, be the only ones in the park if you can be ready by a half past seven o'clock.''

''Oh, I'll be ready, I promise,'' she assured him.

He took her hand in his, and she felt a very pleasant, warm sensation at his touch.

She went with him to the door, where he turned and said, ''By the way, your brother will be leaving tomorrow for Cambridge, which I think might relieve you of some of your worries. He'll work with a tutor there until classes start.'' He smiled at her, then stroked her pink cheek with his forefinger. ''Until tomorrow, then,'' he said softly, before turning and walking swiftly along the corridor and down the stairs.

Catherine walked back to the sitting room and picked up the piece of fabric she had been stitching, but the needle and thread remained motionless in her hand as she thought back on her first proposal of marriage. It had not been exciting, and he had not knelt on the carpet, but it had nonetheless been a lovely, warm experience. It was such a pity that she could not accept, for she had begun to like him very much.

She heard footsteps outside her door, and hoped desperately that it would not be Mark, for she did not wish for another confrontation with him at the moment.

When her aunt came in, she was at first relieved, but then she realized that Lady Clinton had guessed Edwin's purpose when he asked to see her alone.

''I hope you did not refuse him,'' Lady Clinton said quietly, ''for if you did you might just regret it for the rest of your life.''

''I did, but I don't think he took it as a final answer. He's bringing a mount for me early tomorrow morning so that we can ride in the park.'' Catherine gave her aunt a rather tentative smile.

''That's all right then. He means to be patient with you, I

suppose. You do realize that after all the gossips are through you will be completley unmarriageable, don't you?'' her aunt asked, not unkindly.

Catherine nodded. ''It's not really fair for him to have to shoulder my problems when he did not cause them in the first place. How can I let him do such a thing, Aunt Genevieve?''

''Once you're married, people will forget eventually, but I have a feeling he won't let the matter drop but will fight to clear your name,'' Lady Clinton observed. ''I believe he's that kind of man.''

''I haven't said I will marry him,'' Catherine reminded her aunt.

''You will, if you have any sense, my girl. And you'll do it quickly, I think, for it's pointless to wait when the Season is now over, for all intents and purposes. You would not want to socialize much, in any case, the way people have been talking.'' Lady Clinton touched her niece's cheek. ''Don't let foolish pride prevent you from making an excellent marriage. He's a grown man and knows what he wants by now.''

''Does Mark know that Lord Coverdale meant to propose to me?'' Catherine asked.

''Not as far as I know. You'd better tell him if he's leaving for Cambridge tomorrow,'' her aunt said gruffly. ''Or perhaps you'd better not, if you haven't made up your mind, for he's sure to try to influence you.''

''I wouldn't let him. He's done enough damage already,'' she said a little bitterly.

Lady Clinton's eyes narrowed. ''Just what do you mean by that, young lady?'' she asked sharply.

''Nothing important. I love him, but he makes me as cross as crabs sometimes.'' She smiled a little sadly at her aunt, but was obviously not inclined to say more.

''He seems to listen to Lord Coverdale in a way he never does with anyone else, including your papa, for I thought he might refuse to leave for Cambridge at such short notice, but he appeared to welcome it,'' Lady Clinton said tartly.

''He is probably bored with London already, for how much can he do on the small allowance Papa left him?'' Catherine asked, not wanting their aunt to know of his dubious activities.

Her aunt's eyebrows rose. "I have it on good authority that he always carries a vast amount of money around with him, and even leaves quite a lot in his bedchamber," she said. "My girls would not steal, but some of them know every possible hiding place, and cannot resist taking a look. Are you sure he did not get it from your papa?"

"As Papa gave me so little, I had assumed he had been equally sparing with my brother's allowance, but I could, of course, have been mistaken, Aunt Genevieve," Catherine said hurriedly, though her eyes gave away her anxiety. "Please don't worry about it, for Papa was always more generous with Mark than he was with me."

"If you say so, my dear," Lady Clinton murmured, "but I can't think what my brother was thinking about to give him all that much and only a mere pittance to you. I'm going to see how Bertha is getting along with luncheon. Will you be ready in half a hour?"

"Of course. I'll just finish this sleeve and then join you downstairs," Catherine told her, trying hard not to reveal her misgivings.

No one was surprised when Mark was not home for luncheon, for he seldom was, but when he returned in the late afternoon and announced that he would be spending the evening at home, neither Catherine nor her aunt could believe they had heard correctly.

"You needn't look so surprised," he said a little resentfully. "I'm leaving tomorrow morning on the stage to Cambridge, where the tutor Coverdale has hired will meet me. I had thought you might be pleased to spend my last evening with me, Cathie."

"Of course I am, and if you had but given her more notice, I'm sure Aunt Genevieve would have ordered something a little more special than the simple dinner we usually enjoy," Catherine told him.

"I'd best go and see what we can add to make it more substantial," Lady Clinton said, rising, "for I'd not wish you to be hungry, my boy, before you get to the first stop."

When she had left the drawing room, Mark said, "I'll not be here for your birthday next week, and I had bought something for you. If I give it to you now, will you promise not to open it until the day?''

"Of course, but I hope you didn't spend money on me that you'll need once you get to Cambridge,'' Catherine told him, forgetting about the money her aunt had told her about earlier in the day.

"I told you I had quite a bit of money,'' he said impatiently. "Gordon has put me on to one or two things that paid off, and I thought it was time you had something pretty. Why do you have to spoil everything by asking so many questions? I'm not the greenhorn you seem to think I am. I know how to take care of myself.''

Catherine had no wish to put a damper on what would be their last evening together for some time, so she held back the riposte she would have normally made and simply murmured, ''I know, but just the same, do be careful, for you're the only brother I have.''

He was giving her a warm hug when Lady Clinton came back into the room to inform them that supper would not be long now. "Why don't we have a glass of sherry first? As you know, I don't often indulge, but with you leaving in the morning, Mark, I believe we should wish you a safe journey and success in your studies.''

"I'll certainly drink to that, Aunt Genevieve,'' he said, ''and let's have another toast, too. To Catherine, may her troubles all disappear, and her birthday be filled with nothing but happiness.''

As she watched him toasting her forthcoming birthday, Catherine could not help but wish that they could turn back the clock. Life had not been easy at Hayward House, but her papa had been well and strong, and though spoiled, Mark had not yet met young Gordon Smith and adopted some of his crafty, cunning ways.

But she knew that time could not be turned back, and if she had never met Edwin Coverdale she would have counted it a loss, for she would like nothing better than to marry him, as he asked, and let him take care of her and relieve some of her seemingly endless worries.

Mark led them into the dining room, his aunt on one arm and his sister on the other, and Lady Clinton's girls served a delicious supper, washed down with a bottle of wine—a rare treat in this household, justified by Aunt Genevieve as practice for her girls in the opening, tasting, and serving of it. If Mark, who did the tasting and pronounced it perfect, had little or no experience, it mattered not, for it was practice for him also.

Catherine thoroughly enjoyed the meal, and when she went to bed that night she looked at the package, then put it away in a drawer until her birthday, for, though she was curious, she would not have dreamed of opening it ahead of time.

Before getting into bed, she took out her old riding habit, hoping that Maggie had brushed and ironed out the creases before putting it away, and she found, of course, that though shabby, it was as good as it would ever be. It had been a lovely shade of green once, and had looked perfect against her mare's chestnut coat, before it, too, had been dyed to the somber shade of mourning.

The next morning, as she quickly dressed after washing in water left over from the night before, she found that she was unconsciously humming softly to herself. And as she hurried down the stairs, there was a smile on her face that even heavy gray skies could not mar. She somehow knew that as long as it wasn't actually raining, Coverdale would come.

Her riding boot was on the bottom step when the door bell rang and one of the girls brushed past her, hurrying to answer it.

Catherine stood there, a gloved hand still on the handrail as the door swung wide, and though he was by no means a small man, all she saw was Coverdale's face, a question in his warm eyes and a smile on his lips.

"Are you ready?" he asked.

"I will be in a moment," she said as she crossed the hall and slipped into the empty dining room to pick up a couple of apples from a bowl on the sideboard. She turned and saw him standing in the doorway watching her.

"Catch," she called, tossing first one apple and then the other to him, and laughing as he adroitly fielded them.

She picked up two more and dropped them into her pockets.

"One for them and one for us," she said, then walked toward him, slipping her hand into his as they went through the door that the girl still held open.

He held her hand firmly as he led her down the steps to where his tiger waited for his curricle.

"I thought we would enjoy our ride more if we drove to the park, where a groom will be waiting with our mounts," he told her as he helped her up. Then he got in himself, took the reins, and proceeded toward Vauxhall Row.

"This way, I'll have you back before Mark leaves and can then give him a ride to the stage," he said cheerfully, as though driving the Haywards about was his favorite occupation.

She turned and met his eyes, and saw the understanding smile in them. "Do you always think of everything?" she asked, for she had not realized that Mark would be going so soon.

The smile touched his lips as he murmured, "I usually endeavor to."

He kept the grays to a steady pace, and soon they had crossed the Westminster Bridge and were heading for Piccadilly and Hyde Park.

She saw his groom almost at once, standing waiting with three horses as Coverdale pulled up the curricle a short distance away and helped her down. Then he walked over to the groom and took the reins of a very pretty chestnut mare, bringing her over to Catherine for inspection. He watched as her face broke into a delighted smile.

"She's beautiful," she murmured, and the mare whinnied as if in appreciation. "What is her name?" she asked as she reached into her pocket for one of the apples and held it for the eager mare to take.

"Beauty, of course, and you have now made a friend for life," he told her as he helped her mount.

Catherine leaned forward and spoke softly to the mare, gently stroking her neck until Coverdale came alongside, then she followed slightly behind him.

She had not been on horseback for what seemed an age, and though the sky was still overcast with the threat of rain at any moment, to Catherine it was a glorious morning, for they had come to a spot where it was safe to gallop without being observed, and they raced, Coverdale allowing her a good start, then holding back his powerful stallion until she had reached the finish point.

She turned to him, wagging a finger. "That was not fair, sir, for I saw you were holding back," she scolded.

"I never said I wouldn't." He tried to look innocent but failed, then laughed aloud. "The trouble is that I'd much rather watch you ride, and for that I must be behind you. You ride the way you used to walk until Lady Stanhope took you in hand."

"How do you mean?" Catherine protested, laughing.

"You put your whole heart into it, and I can see you now as an old lady striding around the countryside, visiting all the sick in the cottages and telling them what they should do to get better, for I distinctly notice a streak of your Aunt Genevieve in you."

"Do you think that's a bad thing?" she inquired, serious for a moment.

"Not at all, Catherine. Lady Clinton is a good woman. She's a little outspoken, but her heart is in the right place. But you must not think of copying her, for her life would never do for you," he said softly, quite serious also.

"Why not?" she asked sharply.

"Because you have too much love to give. I have seen how much you love your brother, who has not half of your strength of character. Your father told me that he hit you before he left, for expressing your views on king and country. And though he could not agree with you, he felt ashamed that he struck you, and was proud that you would not take back the words."

They were slowly making their way back, and Catherine was glad that she wasn't facing him, for unbidden tears had sprung to her eyes at the memory of her papa, and how fiercely angry he had been.

"In case you're interested," he said quietly, "I do not believe that a man—father, brother, or husband—should ever strike a woman. You need never fear such treatment at my hands."

They were riding quite close together and he reached out a gloved hand and clasped hers for just a moment.

"I heartily disliked that mincing dancing teacher," Catherine said suddenly, disturbed at her reaction to his simple gesture, and anxious to change the subject. "I had a strong desire to take the baton he carried and break it over his head, but I controlled it for Lady Stanhope's sake."

Coverdale chuckled. "Did you let him know how you felt?" he asked.

"Yes, I did," Catherine confessed, "and he looked quite frightened and placed the baton on a table out of the way."

"He didn't hit you with it, did he?" he asked, suddenly quite serious.

"You need not worry. I could not say whether he placed it where my leg would hit against it, or he tapped my leg, but I left nothing to chance. I made quite sure that he was aware of my feelings in the matter, and what I would do if it should touch me again."

Coverdale started to laugh. "I must say that I'm beginning to feel rather sorry for the fellow now. You must have scared him half to death. Dare we risk another gallop, I wonder? There are still few people around."

"Why not?" she asked dryly. "Could I possibly go any deeper into disgrace then I already am? And, in any case, I'd much rather earn their displeasure than be condemned out of hand."

"Won't you allow me to protect you from that displeasure, Catherine? Once you take my name they will not dare to cut you. In fact, you'll be all the rage, I promise."

"I really don't care what they think, Edwin," she said with a shrug. "But I do have the feeling that Papa will marry again, for he's the kind of man who needs a wife. Should he do so, I would not care to remain at home."

She seemed almost to be talking to herself rather than to him, telling herself what her alternatives were, so Edwin felt it best to keep silent for now and let her think the matter through.

After another short gallop they dismounted and got into the waiting curricle. Catherine's cheeks were a healthy pink from the exercise, which she had thoroughly enjoyed, and she was hoping that he would offer to take her riding again, for to her it had been a very special treat.

When they reached the house, Coverdale helped Catherine

down, then went with her into the house while his tiger waited with the curricle.

Lady Clinton looked up from her escritoire when they came in, and excused herself for a moment. She was just writing a note for one of her girls to take, and she quickly finished it, then folded and sealed it. She rose and followed the girl to the door, then closing it firmly behind her, she turned to face them.

"My nephew left a half hour ago, Lord Coverdale, though it was my understanding that you were returning in time for Catherine to bid him farewell, and that you would then take him to the stage. However, his friend, Gordon, came in a hackney and, despite my protests, Mark went with him. I did overhear that dreadful boy make some disparaging remark about your not trusting Mark to board the stage unless you took him there yourself," she said.

Catherine turned her back to them, trying to stop her disappointment from showing. She did not know when she might see her brother again, but he cared so little that he had not even stayed for her to bid him good-bye.

Coverdale was across the room in an instant, placing his hands on her shoulders and turning her around.

"Don't let him upset you, my dear," he urged. "He is selfish and extremely thoughtless, as you well know. And that young rogue, Gordon Smith, has been exerting far too much influence upon him. It will be good for Mark to strike out on his own for a change, once he gets up to Cambridge."

"*If* he gets to Cambridge," Catherine said, "for it all seems rather strange to me."

Coverdale heartily disliked leaving Catherine in such low spirits after the joy she had derived from her ride. That brother of hers needed taking in hand, and he decided that he was just the man to do it, so when Lady Clinton asked if he was, by chance, free to have lunch with them later, he accepted her invitation. He had a couple of appointments first, he told her, but would be back by twelve o'clock at the latest.

Six

"HOW MUCH do you know about this friend of Mark's?" Coverdale asked the two ladies as they leisurely sipped their sherry. Because of an accident in the kitchen, luncheon was delayed and would not be ready for another fifteen minutes yet. "Is he older or younger than Mark?"

"I only met him once," Lady Clinton said, frowning, "and I really couldn't say. He certainly spoke and behaved as though he was the older of the two."

"I asked Mark, and he told me that Gordon is a year younger than himself," Catherine told them. "But he is not at all the kind of person I like Mark, or any of us, for that matter, to associate with. I'm afraid that sounds terribly arrogant. I gained the impression that Gordon rather despises us, but I knew better than to tell this to my brother or he would have become even closer with the young man."

Coverdale's eyes narrowed. "You don't, by chance, think he has some kind of hold over your brother, do you? From the way Mark spoke to me yesterday, he had every intention of waiting for me to drive him to the stage, though I did give him the ticket in case something unforeseen should occur."

He was watching Catherine's face and saw the look of worry that came into her eyes. "What is it, Catherine? You seem extremely concerned about something. Has it anything to do with this fellow Smith?"

She considered unburdening herself and telling him of her worries, and might even have done so had her aunt not been present, but Mark was her brother, and she felt a strong sense of responsibility toward him. She did not know how her aunt would react if she were to tell her of her suspicions. For that matter, she did not know how Edwin would behave, either, for if she was correct, her brother could be in extremely serious trouble. It was better to hold her tongue.

She shook her head. "I'm probably behaving like a mother hen with her only chick, but this is the first time in ages that we have been apart, and I'm just extremely sorry he did not give me the chance to wish him a safe journey," she said with an apologetic smile.

She was grateful when one of the girls came in to tell them that luncheon was ready. Coverdale rose and, offering an arm to each lady, took them into the small dining room.

While the meal was being served they indulged in light conversation, but once the girls had left the room, Lady Clinton brought up the subject of her nephew once more.

"It is such a pity that my brother is not yet well enough to be home, for he could at least tell us how much of an allowance he had given to Mark. That boy seemed to me to have a great deal more money than a boy of his age should be carrying around. And, as I said to you before, Catherine, one of my girls saw a substantial number of coins in one of his drawers when she did his room." She misinterpreted Coverdale's raised eyebrows, and added, unnecessarily, "I trust the girls completely as far as stealing is concerned, but old habits die hard and some of them cannot resist looking in places where they have no right to be."

"I may be able to explain that," Catherine put in hurriedly. "I thought he had forgotten that it is my birthday next week, but he may have been leaving money here so that he didn't spend it all. You see, yesterday he brought me a gift in a wrapped box and made me promise that I wouldn't open it until the day."

She gave them a wry smile. "I know I must have sounded ungrateful, but I told him he shouldn't have spent money on me that he might need in Cambridge, and he became quite angry. He said that Gordon had put him on to one or two things that had paid off, so I suppose that explains how he had so much more money than I thought, although what things he was talking about I have not the slightest idea."

Coverdale said nothing, but he seemed to be in a deep study, and shortly afterward he excused himself on the grounds of having to take his mother on a visit to a relative that afternoon.

He did not go directly to Grosvenor Square, however, but stopped at the inn from which young Mark's stage had left. It was somewhat of a relief to find, after a coin had changed hands, that a young gentleman had boarded the stage alone, and that his companion had taken himself off in a hackney.

Lady Coverdale was waiting when he returned, and after a glance at his face she forbore mentioning that she had expected him to lunch at home. He had told her only that he was taking Miss Hayward for an early-morning ride in the park.

"Did you meet anyone in the park this morning, or was it too early for most to be about?" she asked brightly as they left Grosvenor Square and turned into Grosvenor Street.

"I'm happy to say that we did not meet anyone," he told her gravely, "for it is really most unpleasant for Catherine to receive the cut direct when she has done nothing whatsoever to deserve it."

"You are quite sure about that, aren't you, Edwin?" Lady Coverdale asked, frowning slightly as she realized the two young people were now on a first-name basis. "It would put you in an extremely awkward position, you know, should the gossip turn out to be true."

He had to wait until a phaeton passed before turning into Park Lane, then he looked at his mother in surprise.

"How can you possibly ask such a thing when you saw for yourself what happened at your picnic? It was the first time that Blanchard had ever set eyes on Miss Hayward, and he admitted as much." Coverdale was astounded that his mother could have the slightest doubt.

She sighed. "I know, but he could have been pretending, couldn't he? Perhaps you are right, though, for it was the gown he recognized, not the girl. She is not at all like the majority of young ladies in town, but that, I am sure, is why you have taken an interest in her."

There was a pause, while Coverdale appeared to be considering something, then he said quietly, "I mean to marry her, you know, if she will have me. She has a quality that is hard to find, and I believe we would rub along extremely well together.''

It was a complete surprise to Lady Coverdale, for though she was aware that he was paying the girl a vast amount of attention, she had thought it was because he was sorry for her, losing her mama less than a year ago and then almost losing her papa.

''Then you have not fallen madly in love, or anything like that, my dear?'' She was smiling pleasantly as she asked, but she knew the answer.

There was a twinkle in his eye as he glanced at her briefly. ''I cannot conceive of ever finding myself in that besotted state, Mama, nor do I think it the best condition on which to base a lasting marriage. I know you loved Papa very much when he died, but I have somehow never imagined that you were madly in love before you wed.''

''Things were different in those days, Edwin,'' Lady Coverdale began, looking a little flustered, for she was not used to discussing such matters with her children. ''I did fall in love, for it was quite the thing in those days to do so before settling down. But he was the curate and only a third son, and he wrote me love poems, as I recall. It was just before I reached my seventeenth birthday. But one married the person one's parents chose, and made the best of it that one could. Your father and I had our disagreements at first, of course, but you're quite right, for I did grow to love him very much, and still miss him dreadfully.'' She gave a little sniff, and Coverdale reached out a hand to squeeze hers.

''Miss Hayward has refused me, you know.'' He tried to sound casual. ''But I have not the slightest doubt that she will accept my proposal within the next few days.''

''That would sound dreadfully arrogant, Edwin, if I did not know the circumstances. It must have been terrible for her when you took her in the park and she was treated so abominably.'' She shuddered, then added, ''I wish you would bring her to tea one day so that I can let it be known that I am standing behind her also. I would, of course, make sure that most of my friends who would not dream of cutting her would be there.''

''Perhaps I should bring her for luncheon first,'' he suggested, ''so that you can really get to know her. She is probably a little nervous of going anywhere to tea in case she is made to feel uncomfortable.''

"You're right, as usual, Edwin. Make it soon, though, before the whole thing gets out of hand,'' she told him.

She was a little more worried than she sounded, for it was very difficult to go against the majority of the *ton* in this way, but she had been hoping for a number of years now that Edwin would marry, and if Catherine was to be the one, then she must give them both all the support she possibly could. She liked what she had seen of the girl, and under any other circumstances would have been delighted with his choice. And he could, of course, always take her into the country until the gossip died down.

It was not the luncheon that made Catherine decide to accept Edwin's proposal of marriage, but the tea the day after.

Lady Coverdale had been very careful in making sure only her best friends would be there, to conceal any awkward moments, but, unfortunately, the haughty Mrs. Drummond-Burrell chose that afternoon to pay a call. She did not at first recognize Catherine, for they had never met, but then another casual visitor dropped a word in her ear. With great deliberation, leaving her tea undrunk and the cake she had selected untouched, she slowly rose to her feet, ignored her hostess, and glared at Lord Coverdale, who had stayed at Catherine's side the whole time, then stalked from the room without a word. Lady Coverdale made no attempt to stop her, but ignored her completely, continuing her conversation as though nothing untoward had occurred.

When the last guest had left, Catherine turned to Edwin. "Is there somewhere private where we may talk?'' she asked him softly, and without a word he steered her into his study.

"After what just happened, I imagine you would like to withdraw your offer of marriage, Edwin,'' she said as soon as they were alone.

"On the contrary,'' he was quick to respond, "I wish to renew it, and hope that this time you will make me the happiest of men.''

"You're quite sure?'' Her eyes were huge with anxiety.

"Absolutely," he told her, smiling.

"Could it be soon?" she asked, "for I'm not sure that I can go through this kind of thing much longer."

"Would you like our marriage to take place on your birthday, which is in three days' time, I believe? I have a special license almost burning a hole in my pocket," he told her, stroking her cheek with a finger.

She nodded. "That would be perfect if it could be arranged so quickly," she said with relief. "I'd like Mark to be there, though. Do you think he could get here in time?"

"I'll send my coach up for him tomorrow," Coverdale promised.

Lady Coverdale expressed her delight and started at once to make arrangements for a small wedding in the house, and when Coverdale took Catherine back to her aunt, Lady Clinton was even happier.

"I've thought the two of you were just right for each other since the first time I saw you together," she told them. "I know that you'll both be extremely happy once you get away from London."

As she went off to order champagne to be put on ice, Coverdale remembered something.

"You know the gift that Mark gave you, that you were not to open beforehand," he said to Catherine. "Would it be breaking your promise if I took a peek at it?"

Catherine looked puzzled. "It wouldn't signify, I suppose, as long as you did not tell me what it is," she said quietly. "Would you like me to go and get it now?"

"Perhaps it would be as well. I'll take it home with me so that I can rewrap it and return it to you tomorrow."

She hurried out of the room and up to her bedchamber, wondering why Edwin wanted to see it, then decided that he probably wished to make sure he did not get her something too much like it. It was usual, she had heard, for the groom to buy a gift for the bride.

After taking out the small package, she sat down on the bed for a moment, feeling that everything was happening the way she had wanted, but wishing it had not been so fast and under such unusual circumstances. It would all have been so perfect, were it not for that awful man seeing her gown and starting the rumors. She liked Edwin very much, and felt he would be the most comfortable of husbands, but she had never liked having to do things in a hurry. However, once they were married, and retired to the country, it would be a much more peaceful existence.

Then suddenly she realized that she had not the slightest idea where Edwin's country home might be, or, in fact, if he really had one. Jumping up, she left her chamber and hurried downstairs, anxious to find out right away where she would be living in a few days' time.

"Here it is," she said, placing the package in Edwin's hand. "But don't forget, under no circumstances do I wish to know what is inside until my birthday."

As he slipped it into a pocket, Lady Clinton came into the room, followed by one of her girls, carrying a tray with glasses and an opened bottle of champagne.

"Someone must have been expecting a celebration," she said brightly, "for there was one already keeping cold in the cellar. Perhaps you would like to pour, my lord?"

Catherine sipped the sparkling wine, only the second time she had tasted it, and found that she liked it very much. By the time she had finished her first glass and had a small refill, she had forgotten her curiosity about where she would live and it was not until she and her aunt were alone, after supper, that she thought of it once more.

"Do the Coverdales have a house in the country?" she asked her aunt as they sat in the drawing room drinking their tea.

"But, of course," Lady Clinton told her, surprised at the question. "I should have thought that you and Lord Coverdale would have already discussed where you will be living, but perhaps everything has happened a little too quickly for you to think about it before."

"I'm afraid it has," Catherine agreed, "and I completely forgot to ask him."

"Well, my dear, I believe they have a couple of large estates in the country, but the one they seem to stay at most often is on the Kentish coast, not far from Dover. I have not been there, of course, but I recall my sister-in-law telling me of visiting there once. It sounded quite a delightful place, near a village called St. Margaret-at-Cliffe. I'm sure you'll like it there,'' Lady Clinton said, smiling benevolently at her niece.

Catherine breathed a sigh of relief. "I'm sure I will also,'' she said, "I've heard that Kent is very beautiful.''

She bade her aunt a good night then, for she was feeling a little sleepy from the champagne, and wanted to be up early to finish the green gown she was making, and which she had decided would be all right for the wedding.

She had reckoned without Lady Coverdale, however, for her future mother-in-law sent a note to the house on Kennington Lane the very first thing the next morning, asking if she might call on Catherine and her aunt at eleven with a view to shopping for a wedding gown.

Catherine looked at her aunt in dismay. "I have a green gown that I was hoping to finish in time for the wedding,'' she said, "and I have no funds with which to buy anything else.''

"Under the circumstances, I see no reason why your husband-to-be cannot buy the gown,'' Lady Clinton said brusquely. "I'm sure that must be his mama's intent.''

Catherine opened her mouth, about to protest strongly, but her aunt just shook her head firmly.

"I'll send her a note that we will be delighted to join her, for one thing you cannot do is get married in green. Don't you know that it is supposed to be very unlucky?''

"But green suits me, and I often wore it before I went into black,'' Catherine told her.

"You've not been married in it, though, have you?'' her aunt retorted sharply. "In any case, it's best to take no chances. Marriage is a risky enough undertaking without that.''

After the last remark there was nothing more Catherine could say, so she went upstairs to get ready for their outing, hoping that a readymade gown, which is what it would have to be, might not be too costly.

Lady Coverdale was gracious and charming, and incredibly patient, according to Aunt Genevieve, but all Catherine wished to do by the end of the afternoon was to bury her head in her pillow, as she was doing now, and never see another gown, bonnet, pelisse, slipper, or glove for the rest of her life.

There was never any mention of money throughout the whole day, but she knew that a quite ridiculous amount had been spent, and she felt deeply in debt to Edwin, for she was sure he would be the one who had to pay for everything.

And then, of course, there had been the snubs, the tittering behind kerchiefs, the ladies who gathered their skirts about them so that they would not come into contact with her own. She had held her head high until her neck positively ached, telling herself proudly that they were the ones who should be ashamed, for she had done no wrong, but it did not stop the hurting.

If Mark had been home she would have asked him directly if he was the culprit, for no one else in the house could have worn her gown. But even were he to admit to it, nothing would change, for she could not see her little brother go to prison.

When a knock sounded on the door and the girl said that Lord Coverdale was here to see her, she wanted to tell him to go away almost as much as she wanted to see him.

"Thank you, Betty. Tell him I'll be down in a moment," she said, before bathing her eyes and brushing her hair. Then she went down the stairs and into the drawing room where Edwin waited for her alone.

He came toward her and reached out to take both of her hands in his. "I know it was a dreadful day," he said gently, "for my mama told me about it. I wanted to come and tell you how sorry I am for putting you through such an experience. I had thought that the shops and modistes would be quiet at what is really past the end of the Season, or I would have escorted you myself. But it's over now, and you need not face those people ever again if you do not wish to."

"The modiste said something about a fitting tomorrow," Catherine began, but stopped when he shook his head.

"I have sent word that she is to come to Grosvenor Square herself tomorrow morning," he said firmly. "I cannot be present, for I have been told that I must not see the gown before the wedding, but I will send a carriage for you, and Mama will take care of everything."

He leaned forward and placed a gentle kiss on her cheek. "Don't worry, you won't ever have to go through that again, for by the time we return to London—in a year or two, if I have my way—those same people will be vying for your attention."

There was something very sweet and tender about that gentle kiss, and afterward it seemed to Catherine that all the tension and worries of the day had suddenly disappeared.

"When do you think Mark will get here?" she asked, a little ashamed of herself for feeling less eager to see her brother after the events of the day.

"Some time tomorrow, I should think," Coverdale said. "And you may not see much of him, because I will probably take him to be outfitted for the wedding. Although it will be very small, he should still be dressed properly."

"Thank you for coming," Catherine said softly. "I feel much better now."

"In that case I'll be going, for you need to get a good night's sleep after this day. I cannot come for you myself, but I'll send the carriage about ten o'clock in the morning," he told her, then, kissing her lightly on the cheek once more, he left the room.

Coverdale had not told Catherine the truth when he indicated that he did not know when her brother would be arriving. He had told his coachman to be back by two o'clock at the latest, and no matter what his young passenger might prefer, he was to come straight to Grosvenor Square. He had a great deal to say to that young man, and he meant to do so without his sister's knowledge.

When he had opened the package that Mark had given Catherine for her birthday, he had found a diamond and emerald necklace—one that was quite familiar to him, for he had seen it on a number of occasions around the neck of one of London's most well-known hostesses. Her husband was a friend of his, and the necklace, along with other jewelry, had been stolen some six months ago in a daring burglary at their country home.

Coverdale wanted to know where Mark had obtained it, although, of course, his friends would be glad to have it back with no questions asked. But, more important, he wanted to ascertain what part young Mark had played in the incident in Vauxhall Gardens, for he now had no doubt that it was Mark who had worn his sister's gown. And he meant to find out whether it was the first or the last of a series of such incidents.

No matter which it might be, it was disgusting that he had allowed his sister to be disgraced in the eyes of society for something she had not done. He was sure that even now she had no knowledge of what had occurred, though the sad expression that sometimes came into her eyes made him wonder if she had her suspicions.

He had kept the box and the paper that the necklace had been wrapped in, and intended to see that Mark bought her another gift tomorrow, of a size to fit into the same box. That way she need never know that her brother had first given her a necklace that was stolen property.

He was sitting at his desk in the library, going over what needed to be done about the matter, and was surprised when the door opened and Lady Coverdale came in.

"I just returned from the card party, and was wondering how Catherine was when you saw her," she said with an understanding smile.

"She was all right, I believe, when I left her," Coverdale said, "but it must have been a terrible day, and she has had too many of those of late."

"I know." There was nothing but sympathy in his mother's eyes. "I felt so awful for her, but dared not say anything that might change the proud way she held up her head and looked straight through those dreadful women. She behaved for all the world like a duchess, and will make you an excellent countess within a day or so now."

"She's gone through an awful lot for her age, first nursing and losing her mother, then trying to look after that rascal of a brother, and her father lying there in Brussels for so long at death's door. I mean to take some of those worries off her shoulders, if I can," he said with determination.

"Are you sure you're not just a little in love with her, my dear?" Lady Coverdale asked.

"Perhaps," he said, smiling gently. "I really don't know, but she does rather grow on you, you know."

"I agree. I wanted so much to put my arms around her today and protect her from those wretches. The gown is lovely and she'll make you a beautiful bride," she told him, "and now I must get a little sleep or I'll look terrible in the morning."

He smiled. "You'll never look terrible, Mama. I often think you're ageless, for you seem to have a remarkable amount of energy."

"For one so ancient?" she asked, laughing. "Perhaps, but I hope you'll give me some grandchildren to play with before I'm too old to enjoy them."

"You can count upon it," Coverdale said with a grin. "And if Catherine and I decide to take a trip to Europe in a year or two, to make up for the honeymoon we missed, we'll let you look after our little ones."

She left the room with a happy smile on her face, quite sure that all was going to turn out well for her son and his marriage of convenience.

Seven

COVERDALE DID NOT see Catherine when she came to the house for the fitting of her gown. He had felt it best that she think he was out, for though he would have much enjoyed her company, the last thing he wished was to have her still in Grosvenor Square when her brother arrived. In the event, she missed Mark by less than a half hour.

Seated at his desk in the library, Coverdale heard his coach pull in, and then Winters, the butler, directing the young man into the drawing room to await his master's pleasure. Then, when Winters came into the library to intone in somber tones that Mr. Mark Hayward was here, he instructed him to wait five minutes, and then bring the young gentleman in to join him.

His head was down as though working on some complicated problem when Mark came in, but he looked up, smiling, and asked him to take a seat. "I'll be through here in just a moment, Mark," he told him.

"Look here, Coverdale," Mark said impatiently, "I know you have gone to a lot of trouble to bring me to town for your wedding, but I am anxious to get over to Kennington Lane to make sure that this is what Catherine really wants, and that there's nothing havey-cavey about it. You must admit that it is rather a hurried arrangement."

Coverdale appended his signature to a document, then carefully placed the pen in its holder before looking directly at the young man and saying, sternly, "You're quite right, Mark. It is hurried, and I believe you had a great deal to do with making such haste necessary."

"What do you mean, sir? If she's in a family way, I certainly had nothing to do with it," Mark said angrily.

Coverdale jumped to his feet and came around the desk, towering over the young man. "How dare you cast aspersions upon your sister's character?" he growled, looking so fierce that Mark instinctively shrank away from him. "You know quite well that it was not she who sat on that bench enticing tipsy gentlemen to come nearer. It was you, who had crept into her bedchamber and borrowed her gown and shawl. You were just the right height, weren't you?" Coverdale thundered.

"I swear I was not pretending to be her, you must believe me," Mark begged. "I wouldn't have deliberately got Catherine into trouble."

"You wouldn't?" Coverdale said sarcastically. "Then it was pure concidence that made you select a chestnut-colored wig?"

"Gordon brought the wig. He said it was one he'd used once before I knew him," Mark said, horrified now. "I never thought anything about its being the color of Cathie's hair."

"Perhaps you didn't, and perhaps you never realized that your friend didn't like her and meant to make her a scapegoat," Coverdale said, his voice dangerously quiet now. "But once she was accused you did nothing to help her, did you? You even made disparaging remarks to her—like the one you made to me earlier—when you knew it to be a fact that she was completely innocent."

This time Mark looked down at his feet, unable to meet Coverdale's accusing eyes.

"I happen to know that your father gave you very little money when he left for Antwerp, thinking, of course, that you would be staying with his sister and not need much pocket money. Just how many times have you and your young friend tried this little caper? And how much did you make in money and jewels?" Coverdale asked sternly.

"That was only the third time," Mark mumbled, gazing at the toe of his boot.

"Dammit, look at me when you're speaking to me," Coverdale snapped. "What was your total reckoning from the three nights?"

"We got sixty-five guineas in cash, sir, which we divided

evenly, and Gordon took the jewelry and sold it to a man he knows. As I didn't take the risk of getting caught with it, he kept whatever he made on that," Mark told him quietly, now looking directly at Lord Coverdale.

"But you have a lot more than that now, don't you? Where did the rest come from?" Coverdale was determined to find out everything so that he could decide how to deal with the matter.

Mark, biting nervously on his lower lip, hesitated before answering, then said, "Gordon has some friends who run a gaming hall, and we went there and doubled our money each time."

"By cheating, I suppose," Coverdale suggested.

Mark nodded. "Gordon showed me how to do it. It was easy money," he said unhappily.

Coverdale was not finished with him yet by a long way. "Have you any idea what would have happened, Mark, if you had been caught in Vauxhall Gardens?" he asked quietly, and when Mark shook his head, he said, "You would have been arrested, held in prison with all kinds of ruffians until your hearing came up, which might have taken months, and then when found guilty you would most likely have been transported to Australia to work as a bondsman there, if you were fortunate enough to survive the voyage."

Mark's fresh complexion had turned deathly white. "What are you going to do, sir?" he asked quietly.

"At the moment I honestly don't know," Coverdale said, then added, "but there is also another matter that I do know what to do about. Your sister told me that you had given her a package and specified she must not open it until her birthday. I persuaded her to let me see it, and she agreed, on condition that I must not tell her what it was."

"I didn't steal that, sir," Mark protested rather weakly. "I bought it for her."

"Had you no idea that you were buying stolen goods?" Coverdale asked. "Come now, Mark. If Gordon took you to buy the necklace, you must have realized that the place was probably the same one where he sold the things the two of you were stealing."

Mark nodded, then said, "I wanted to get her something nice to make up for the trouble she was having."

Coverdale sighed in disgust. "If she had worn it she would have been in far deeper trouble, I can assure you," he said with a cold smile. "You see, Mark, I immediately recognized the necklace as one stolen from the home of some friends of mine about six months ago."

The young man looked up, an expression of horror on his face. "Oh, no," he said, dropping his head into his hands.

"Have you any idea what has been happening to you?" Coverdale asked.

Mark looked puzzled. "I don't know what you mean, sir," he said.

"I would surmise that your young friend was using you," Coverdale said quietly. "I would like to make a guess that the money and jewels you took were always carried by you until you were clear of Vauxhall Gardens, for one thing. Am I correct?"

Mark flushed, slowly nodding, for he was beginning to understand. "They were dropped into the reticule I carried, which was one that Gordon brought with him. Then when we were clear of the Gardens he gave me half of the money and left with the reticule under his coat," he said slowly.

"Exactly, and was it Gordon's suggestion that you borrow your sister's gown and wrap?"

"Yes, sir. He said he had observed that we were almost the same height, and black would not be noticed as much as a colored gown." Mark looked down and shook his head as he began to realize what a fool he had been. "And it was he who said he could get me a nice piece of jewelry to give to Cathie for her birthday."

"I thought as much," Coverdale said. "I have already returned the necklace to my friend, who has agreed not to ask any questions about it. I did, however, keep the box and wrapping, and I would suggest that you go out with me this afternoon and buy some small gift that will fit into the box, then rewrap it and I will return it to her this evening."

"Thank you, sir," Mark said gratefully, his voice barely a whisper and his mouth trembling as he tried not to lose control.

"I assume that your young friend does not know that you are back in London for a few days?" Coverdale said.

"I probably would have been in touch with him, sir, although we did quarrel when he took me to the stage. Now, of course, I would not think of seeing him." Mark said bitterly.

"Before you go back to Cambridge I would like you to tell me what means you used to contact him, for I intend to make sure he does not try these little games on anyone else," Coverdale said firmly. "If you have some compunctions about doing so, I would remind you that he could have irreparably damaged your sister's reputation with the combination of the incident with Blanchard and the necklace."

Mark nodded. "I'll give it to you, sir, for I'm sure you are better able to deal with him than I am."

Coverdale rose. "Do you have suitable morning dress in which to give Catherine away tomorrow?" he asked, and when the boy nodded, he suggested, "Why don't we take care of the matter of the gift, then go to Kennington Lane and see how your sister is feeling today. Although I know she was here this morning, I have not yet seen her."

Mark got quickly to his feet. "You will take good care of her, sir, won't you? As I am responsible for your having to marry her, I would not want to think that she might be unhappy."

"You're not entirely responsible for this, Mark, for I am sure I would eventually have come around to seeing her as someone I would like to spend the rest of my life with. I might not have seen her courage in adversity, however, were it not for you."

They went into the hall and Coverdale ordered his carriage brought around, then said to Mark, "Come along and we'll see if my Mama is at home. I'm sure she would like to meet you."

"Her ladyship is in the conservatory, my lord," Winters said quietly.

"I just thought about something," Mark said, smiling a little sheepishly. "Cathie will be a lady by this time tomorrow."

"Your sister has always been a lady," Coverdale said with mock severity. "Tomorrow she will become a countess."

Coverdale had not given a thought as to where the wedding would take place, and was surprised to find that furniture was being moved into the conservatory. He saw his mother giving instructions as to the placement of the pieces, and led Mark over to her.

"It was Catherine's idea to have the wedding in here," she told him, "and now I see that she was quite right. It will look beautiful with the fruit trees and masses of flowers."

"How many people will be here?" Coverdale asked, as he watched more chairs being brought in.

"Not many, I'm afraid, for it is such short notice. Perhaps thirty guests, I would say, at the most," she said, sounding disappointed. "And this is Catherine's brother, I know, for I would have recognized him anywhere. You're not so much losing a sister, young man, as gaining a family, for I'm sure Catherine will want you to stay here when you're in town. Lady Clinton's home is a little too far from the activities of the Season, and you'll find Grosvenor Square much more convenient, I know."

"I'm afraid that we're going to leave you to do all the work, Mama," Coverdale said, "for we're going over to Kennington Lane to see Catherine now. What time will she be here tomorrow?"

"I'm sending the carriage for her and Lady Clinton at nine o'clock, and she'll get dressed here, so you had better stay out of the way, Edwin. It's most unlucky for the groom to see the bride beforehand, you know," she told him, quite seriously.

He smiled, and Lady Coverdale could not recall when she had seen her son looking so happy.

"Off you go, then," she told them, shooing them out of the room, "for I've much to do if I'm to have everything ready by eleven o'clock in the morning. I'll see you tomorrow, Mark. Make sure your sister gets a good night's sleep, and don't let her worry about anything."

They had a couple of stops to make before going to see Catherine. The first was at a shop which sold elegant scarves for evening wear, and Mark picked out a lovely one in fine gold and green silk that would make a good birthday present for his sister. Fortunately, it could be folded small enough to fit into the box that had held the necklace.

The other stop was at a famous jewelers on Bond Street, where the proprietor hastened toward Coverdale and handed him an already wrapped box which he slipped into his pocket with a nod of thanks.

Then they started for Kennington Lane. After they had crossed the bridge at Westminster, Mark said with a grin, "I see now what Lady Coverdale meant about Grosvenor Square being more convenient. Having never been to any of the really fashionable places, I didn't realize just how much out of the way we were. You need not worry, though, for I will not take advantage."

"Catherine and I may not be in town very much at all this year, and it is too far away to make plans for next Season. But if my mother is in town and asks you to stay, then by all means take advantage of it," Coverdale told him, knowing full well that she would keep a very close eye on the young man.

A few minutes later they stopped in front of Lady Clinton's house and alighted. Coverdale gave instructions to his man as to the time he should return, then followed Mark into the house.

Catherine was hugging her brother, then she turned, saw Edwin, and came slowly toward him. Now that the time was drawing nearer she was feeling increasingly nervous in his presence, for it would not be long before he was legally responsible for her—owned her, in fact.

He held out his hands, and she placed her own in his, then impulsively leaned forward and brushed his cheek with her lips.

"Mm," he murmured, "that was nicely done. No second thoughts?"

She shook her head, still smiling. "How about you?"

"None whatever. I'm looking forward to arriving in Kent and having the place to ourselves—except, of course, for about forty or fifty servants."

There was no more time for private conversation, for Lady Clinton had ordered tea, and good manners demanded they join her in the drawing room.

Although Catherine answered the questions asked of her, the brief conversation with Edwin had taken her mind away from the more imminent problems of the wedding and started her thinking of what would happen after the wedding, both during the journey and once they reached his home.

She wondered if the servants in Kent would be surly and

difficult to handle, but then she thought of Lady Coverdale, and knew that she would not have let such people remain in her employ for long.

It would be lonely in the carriage if Edwin decided to ride alongside all the way to Kent, for Maggie was still away, and everything had happened so quickly that she had not thought to send for her to come back. Perhaps Lady Coverdale would lend her a maid, for she would need one when they stopped at an inn overnight.

"You seem to be deep in thought, Catherine. Did you suddenly discover you had forgotten something important?" Edwin asked, a warm gleam in his eyes.

"As a matter of fact, I did." She saw that her aunt had heard and looked startled. "I just realized that I sent my maid off to see her family for a week or two, and now it's too late to call her back."

"That's not a serious problem," he said, smiling. "You can either borrow one of Mama's, and we'll take her with us, or choose a girl when we get to Kent."

"I should not like Maggie to think that I had brought her down here and abandoned her, though," Catherine said seriously. "My aunt can tell you what happens to abandoned girls in London."

"Then perhaps Lady Clinton would not mind putting the girl on the stagecoach when she returns, and sending her down to us," he said equably.

"Of course. How silly of me not to think of that at once. I seem to be getting myself confused because there is so much happening." Catherine gave him an apologetic smile.

"It would be strange if you didn't, my dear," he said kindly. "Here you are endeavoring to cram weeks of wedding preparations into just three days."

Catherine nodded. "I didn't realize it was going to become so complicated when I agreed. I had in mind that you, me, Mark, my aunt, and your mother, that's all. And your sister, of course, whom I met at the picnic, though at the time I did not know we would become related."

"We can always elope tonight, if you want to," he suggested, grinnning. You could climb down the ivy beneath your bedroom window, and I would have a coach waiting below to catch you.''

"And have a mother-in-law who would not speak to me ever again?'' she returned glibly.

He shrugged. "Some daughters-in-law would count that a blessing.''

"Not me,'' Catherine said emphatically. "I think she's quite wonderful. Do you know that she has never asked me a single question about Blanchard and Vauxhall Gardens?''

"Nor will she, for she knows you had nothing to do with it and would not think of upsetting you by bringing up the matter,'' he said. "When we were youngsters and Papa had thrashed us for some terrible prank we'd been up to, Mama behaved perfectly normally with us afterward, not scolding, but not sympathizing either.''

"I can just imagine her being that way,'' Catherine murmured, but her cheeks went a deep pink as she thought of the children they would have, and wondered if she could behave nearly as well. She looked up at Edwin and realized that he knew what she was thinking, and she suddenly felt hot all over.

To cover her confusion, Catherine rose to refill their teacups, then passed some of the wafer-thin sandwiches which one of the girls, aspiring to be a chef, had made.

"This morning Lady Coverdale appeared to be holding up remarkably well under the strain of the wedding, Edwin,'' Lady Clinton said. "I simply cannot imagine how she managed to arrange everything at such short notice.''

He grinned and said, "I made the offer to elope to her also, but when she looked as if she might die of shock, I thought better of it.''

"I just had a thought,'' Catherine said. "What are you wearing tomorrow, Mark? You are supposed to be standing in for Papa, I believe, and you will need a number of other things besides morning dress.''

"That's already taken care of, my dear. When Mark brings you in the morning, he will be shown into a guest room where my man will have everything waiting for him.''

"After all that dreadful scurrying around for gowns and things, I'm now beginning to feel completely useless as everything is being done for me,'' Catherine said with amusement.

"Don't worry, Cathie," Mark put in. "Once you're married you'll have plenty to do looking after your husband's every need. That's the only reason a man takes a wife, you know."

"My, you do have a lot to learn, Mark," Lady Clinton said with amusement. "But then, so had we all when we were your age, though we didn't think so at the time."

Lord Coverdale rose. "I'd best be on my way, for Mama needs someone to see that she does not overdo. Will you walk with me to the door, Catherine?"

She stood up and he took her arm, steering her out of the drawing room and into the hall. One of the girls was waiting to open the door, but she took one look at them and tactfully disappeared.

"I won't see you until the service tomorrow, my dear, and so I wanted to give you this now and ask you to wear it with your gown. It's a birthday present, of course, and I hope very much that you will like it," he said softly.

"Whatever it is, I know I will, if only because you gave it to me," she told him, looking into his eyes.

Then she felt his arm around her, drawing her closer, and this time his lips sought hers. She made no attempt to pull away, for she felt excitement stirring inside her and had no wish to stop the delicious sweetness of her first kiss.

He moved away at last, then, as an afterthought, he remembered to give her back Mark's gift. She went with him to the door, waiting until he was in the carriage, then waving until he was out of sight.

As she walked back into the drawing room, Lady Clinton made a tactful excuse in order to leave brother and sister together, and closed the door quietly behind her.

"This is what you want, isn't it, Cathie?" Mark asked, anxiously.

"Yes, but I didn't want it quite so soon. Everything has had to be done in such a hurry that there's been no time for me to— well, Mark, to be courted properly. He's a good man, and a very kind one, also," she told him.

"He's also an army colonel and he knows exactly how to give one a dressing down," Mark said ruefully. "Not that I didn't throughly deserve it. I can't tell you how sorry I am that I got you into this mess, Cathie, but it wasn't intentional—not on my part, anyway.''

"Are you going to continue seeing Gordon?" Catherine asked, realizing that this was probably as much of an admission of guilt as she would ever get from him.

Mark shook his head. "No, I'm not, for I see now what he was trying to do. I had an idea before, and when he took me to get the stagecoach I told him as much, and he was furious. He seemed to think that it was Coverdale's doing, and he swore to get even with him, but I set him straight about that. I told him that I made my own decisions and that Coverdale had not been involved.''

"Did he believe you?" Catherine asked, "for it's a wonder he did not throw you out of the hackney.''

"He had no option, for I made myself very clear," Mark said firmly. "I know that I have come out of it a lot wiser, and I mean to go back to Cambridge this semester and really work hard so that I can give Papa all the help he needs at Hayward House when he's on his feet again.''

Catherine knew that he meant it at this moment, but she also knew that her brother was weak and easily led, and it was a good thing that he was going back to Cambridge right after the wedding tomorrow, for it was quite possible that if he saw Gordon Smith again he might easily slip back into trouble.

They had a quiet, pleasant supper with their aunt, then Catherine excused herself, for she still had to finish packing some of her personal things before going to bed.

When she had finished, she got under the covers, but she was too excited to go to sleep immediately, and when she heard the hall clock chime twelve she got up again, relit her candle, and reached for her gifts.

The silk scarf which was Mark's gift was the loveliest she had ever owned, and she stroked it against her cheek to feel its softness. Then she reached for the box Edwin had given her, tearing the wrapping in her haste to find out what it was, and uncovered a dark blue velvet box. She stroked the smooth velvet, enjoying the anticipation, then lifted the lid at last. A string of lustrous, creamy pearls lay on a bed of deep blue silk, glistening in the candlelight, but they were outshone by the large clasp, in the form of a gold rose with diamond-edged petals and a large diamond in the center.

Carefully, she unfastened the clap and put the necklace on, then, candle in hand, she went over to the mirror on her dressing table and tried it first with the clasp on one side, then with it in the center. Lady Coverdale would know how it should be worn, she was sure, and it would be quite perfect with her wedding gown.

But she couldn't believe that such a beautiful piece of jewelry was really hers.

She woke early the next morning, her twenty-first birthday, and moved through the first few hours as if in a dream. Her aunt insisted that she have a substantial breakfast before they left for Grosvenor Square, and though she was not hungry, she complied.

When the carriage arrived, the piece of baggage she would need for the wedding was placed inside, and her other things were piled on the back.

She was not at all nervous, which surprised her, but she supposed that at some point she would be, and hoped that it might not happen when she was making her responses.

Lady Coverdale was waiting eagerly, her own gown in place, and her abigail all ready to make Catherine the most beautiful bride of the Season.

First, Catherine put on white silk hose that tied at the knees, then dainty white brocade slippers, with delicate bead and bugle work. She had never even seen anything like the fine white lawn drawers trimmed with wide lace that went on next, and could not resist pirouetting in front of the mirror to see the full effect, before putting on her petticoat.

At this stage she called for the abigail to come from the dressing room to help her with the next piece of underwear. Though she had never worn a corset in her life, the modiste had insisted on a short one that had a padded attachment high in the back to make her gown and train fall smoothly. Once this was in place, she slipped into a robe and the other ladies entered to help decide how her hair was to be arranged, for Catherine would not allow it to be cut.

After much discussion and trying on the veil, her abundant chestnut curls were tamed and arranged becomingly around her face with the back hair brought up to form a coronet upon which the veil would rest.

Although cream had recently become fashionable for brides, it had been the consensus of the ladies that pure white would be preferable, for it would serve to make a most definite statement. The gown of heavy white lace over white satin was a perfect choice for one as tall and slender as Catherine. Its low-cut neckline emphasized but did not reveal her small breasts, and the large puff sleeves were almost joined above the elbow by delicate white lace gloves. The skirt barely touched the floor in front and had a train in the back. She immediately began to practice walking back and forth to make sure she did not trip.

Just before the veil was pinned upon her hair, the pearl necklace that Edwin had given her was placed around her neck, with the jeweled fastener in the center.

"I have a birthday present for you, also," Lady Coverdale said softly, and produced a pair of earrings that exactly matched the gold and diamond rose fastening the pearls. Tears came to Catherine's eyes and she swallowed hard.

"Now, now, you must not get upset, my dear," Lady Coverdale said. "They'll seem like nothing once you set eyes on the family jewelry."

Catherine shook her head and put up her hand to touch the necklace. "They'll never seem like nothing to me; I'll treasure them all my life," she swore.

Lady Coverdale bent to kiss her cheek. "I believe you will. I wonder if my son knows just how fortunate he is today," she murmured.

It had all taken a great deal longer than Catherine could have believed, for her aunt suddenly exclaimed, "My goodness, we only have half an hour before the ceremony begins. I'd best run off and slip into my own gown, or I'll miss the whole thing."

It broke the tension that had suddenly set in, for Catherine had to laugh out loud, though she knew that her aunt would be ready on time, for in her own home she took no more than ten minutes to dress for dinner.

"Did my flowers arrive?" she said, knowing it was a foolish question, for Lady Coverdale had left nothing to chance.

"Can you not smell them?" she asked Catherine as the abigail went into the dressing room and came out with a bouquet of white roses, lilies of the valley, and forget-me-nots.

"Oh, yes," she said as she buried her face in them, "and they're so beautiful."

There was a knock on the door and Catherine heard Mark's voice asking if she was ready. Taking a last look at herself in the mirror, she went out to join him.

Eight

CATHERINE FEARED that her brother's eyes might fall right out of his head if he continued to stare at her in such a fashion.

"Whatever is the matter with you?" she asked sharply.

"I simply can't believe it's you," he told her, "you look so beautiful—as though you'd been transformed."

"You don't look quite such a scapegrace as usual either," Catherine said dryly, which served to make Mark laugh and bring him back to his normal self. He did, in fact, look extremely handsome, for Coverdale's man had turned him out in the finest style.

"You'd best let me hang on to your arm going down these steps," she said anxiously as they reached the top of the stairs, "for I'd hate to tread on my gown."

"Just a moment, Catherine," Lady Coverdale called softly from behind. "Let me catch hold of your train and then neither of you will tread on it. Just go carefully, that's all."

Once they reached the foot of the stairs, Lady Coverdale spread the train out behind Catherine and instructed her, "Now, just walk slowly along the red carpet until you come to the conservatory, but don't go in. Wait there until you get the signal to go inside and proceed toward the dais."

To Catherine's surprise, Mark seemed inordinately nervous. She could feel the stiffness in the arm that she was holding, and she asked him quietly, "Are you sure you're all right? I've never seen you quite this tense."

"That's because I've never done this before," he told her curtly.

"Well, neither have I, but I'm enjoying myself. I've just discovered that I like getting dressed up," she said, quite sincerely, attempting to help him over his discomfort.

"There's a vast amount more to this than putting on an expensive gown," he muttered. "What if I say the wrong thing? This is Papa's job, not mine. He should have been here to do this. Can you believe that they're actually writing bets into White's betting book as to when your first child will be born and what color its hair will be? There's a lot of money on it already."

If her papa had been here she would not have needed to get married, she thought, for he would have kept Mark in hand and sent Gordon packing the moment he saw him. Then there would have been no lies told about her, no wagers placed in an exclusive men's club, and no so-called ladies avoiding her as though the slightest contact might actually contaminate them.

With Mark's words the bubble of happiness she had clung to all morning had burst, and now she felt alone and afraid of the uncertain future to which she was committing herself.

Lady Coverdale was quite furious. She had been close enough to hear the exchange of words between brother and sister, and she would very much have liked to slap that young man hard for his complete disregard of his sister's feelings. She had wanted so much for this to be a happy occasion for all of them, for she had now no doubt in her mind that Catherine was the perfect wife for her son.

A signal was given, the music started, and Catherine walked slowly along the red carpet, with her head held high and looking to neither left nor right until she reached Edwin's side. She was aware that there were about a couple of dozen people in the seats behind her, but they were all strangers to her save for her Aunt Genevieve.

Someone took away her bouquet, which she had been holding onto as if to a lifeline, then she felt a comforting warm hand clasp hers and she looked up into Edwin's face. The slight smile and the warmth in his eyes that seemed just for her alone, made everything all right again—or almost. She wondered if he could see her face through the veil, and know how nervous she felt.

The actual ceremony was surprisingly short, and she must

have murmured her responses at the proper times, for no one nudged her and there were no awkward pauses. There was now a plain gold ring on her finger, and she had signed a book where someone pointed and watched while Edwin did the same.

Then he lifted her veil and she felt his strong arms around her. His lips were warm on hers, and comforting, and then she walked, with her hand on his arm, to a different room where tables were set together and covered in white damask cloths.

She wished with all her heart that she did not have to sit at the head of the table, next to Edwin, pretending to eat, when all she wanted to do was fly away with him to some secluded place where there were no *tonnish* ladies or sap-skulled brothers.

"It won't be long now, my dear," he murmured softly into her ear, "and then we'll be able to get away from here and you can relax and be yourself."

With an effort she forced herself back to the present. Incredibly, it seemed he had read her mind and was in agreement, but first there were things that had to be done, and decisions to be made.

"How is Mark getting back to Cambridge?" she asked him.

He smiled. "That's better," he said, smiling, "but you need not worry, for my second coach is taking him back as soon as we leave."

The cake was cut and toasts were made, and though Catherine raised her glass and smiled each time, her lips barely touched the pale liquid.

Lady Coverdale bent over her son and whispered in his ear, and he turned to Catherine.

"Go with Mama, my dear," he told her softly. "You need to change into a carriage dress or something now, and then we should be out of here and on our way to Kent in less than a half hour."

This time she did not have to walk down the narrow carpet, for Lady Coverdale took her to a side door and held her train once more so that she did not trip as they went up the narrow flight of stairs.

When they were in the bedchamber they had used before, Lady Coverdale took Catherine to a couch in front of which was a tray with a teapot, cups and saucers. She poured two cups, then went to a cabinet and added something to one of them before handing it to Catherine.

"Drink this, my love," she said gently. "It will make you feel much better."

They sat for a few minutes, sipping the hot brew, then Lady Coverdale said quietly, "I want to tell you something, my dear, about how I feel at this moment."

Catherine looked at her questioningly.

"Don't worry about the time, for no matter what Edwin said, he will not mind waiting, I know. I heard what that young idiot said to you just before you went into the conservatory, and at that moment I longed to wring his neck. You see, no matter what people say, and no matter how many bets are placed in White's betting book, I know my son, and I have worried these last few years about the kind of girl he would bring home to replace me. But I am not worried any more, for I know you are just the right wife for him, and you must not let young Mark, or anyone else, spoil this day for you.

"I know that you are not 'in love,' as they say, and I was not, either, when I was wed, for it wasn't at all fashionable in those days to love one's husband. But it only takes a little piece of it to start something wonderful. For love grows, you know, year by year, just as do the plants in that conservatory where you were married. But, like them, it will die if it is neglected. It has to be given a little attention every now and then to keep it blooming and growing. If both of you will just tend it with care, Catherine, it will grow and flourish for the rest of your lives."

While she was speaking, she was removing the veil from Catherine's head, and drawing the gloves from first one hand and then the other.

"Why don't you stand up now," she suggested, "and let me unfasten your gown. Then it will take just a few minutes to put you into that blue carriage dress we got for you the other day."

In no time at all, it seemed, the wedding gown was back in its box and Catherine was standing in front of the pier glass placing pins in her new pale blue hat, which was trimmed with deeper blue plumes that curved flirtatiously from the crown to beneath her chin.

Dora, the abigail she was borrowing, came in and curtsied first to Catherine and then to her mistress, causing the former to raise her eyebrows in surprise.

Before removing the box of wedding attire, the girl handed the cases containing the pearls and earrings to Catherine. "You'll want to take these with you, I'm sure, milady," she said.

"Thank you," Catherine said quietly, then when they were alone once more she turned to Lady Coverdale, who was now smiling broadly.

"She was quite correct, Catherine," she said. "As Countess of Coverdale, you now outrank me, for I am only the dowager."

"Not in my estimation, my lady," Catherine said sincerely, "but I never thought that I should like being a countess—and I find that I do," she admitted, smiling.

"You must be quite exhausted, my love," Edwin said gently once they had settled back against the soft squabs of the wonderfully comfortable traveling coach and were on their way out of London. "It must have been exceedingly difficult for you to look and behave as calmly as you did. You see, my mama told me what that idiotic brother of yours said just minutes before the wedding, and I must admit that I was just as angry as she was."

What he deliberately omitted was that while she was changing gowns he had let Mark know, in no uncertain terms, how his careless tongue had ruined his sister's wedding day for her. Mark, of course, said that he had just not thought it would bother her, when he told her, and promised he would be more careful in the future, but Coverdale had little hope of such consideration. He feared that the boy just did not possess a modicum of common sense.

"He is eighteen," Catherine was saying, smiling and shaking her head sadly, "not a boy anymore, but still a very long way from being a man, and it has seemed to me these past twelve months that he is endeavoring to make all his mistakes at once. I am aware that he was the one in Vauxhall Gardens, you know."

"I thought you were," he said, "but I hated to mention it in case I was mistaken. He could have found himself in dire straits had Blanchard seen his seducer more clearly. But I believe he has now learned his lesson and means to settle down at Cambridge and really study this time." He watched her face as he spoke and saw the tiny worry lines crease her brow. "What is it that you fear?"

"That although he may mean to do so, what will happen if Gordon Smith goes up to Cambridge and starts to make trouble for him?" she said.

"I considered that possibility, also, but when I tried to find Smith in his usual haunts, I discovered that he had not been seen for several days. There is a possibility that he may have gone underground, so I have left a very reliable man to keep a lookout for him and, if he surfaces, to do whatever is necessary to prevent him from plaguing Mark."

"Do you always think of everything?" she asked, grateful for his efforts.

He shook his head. "No, I don't, I'm afraid, no matter how hard I try. One of the things I didn't think about was White's betting book—and I should have, for it's exactly the sort of idiotic thing they wager on there."

But what was actually worrying him at the moment was how he was going to avoid making love with her for the next few weeks. Abstinence was the only solution he could think of, for otherwise he might easily get her with child right away, and then all the talk would begin once more.

"Are we going all the way to Westcliffe House tonight?" Catherine asked. "Although I have heard of it, I am not really sure that I know how far it is."

"We could get there if we wished, but it would be a long journey and I know that you are feeling tired after the events of the day," he said softly. "I believe we will stay the night at Maidstone. There is a comfortable inn there, and when we get nearer I'll send an outrider ahead to secure rooms for us. Then, in the morning, we can have a leisurely breakfast, have them pack a picnic luncheon, and reach Westcliffe House in the early afternoon."

"Were I not with you, however, you would ride right through, I'm sure," Catherine said, smiling.

"Perhaps," he agreed, "but you are with me, which is surely a good enough reason to make the journey in comfort."

They rode in silence for some distance, and Catherine's eyes gradually closed.

Coverdale was more than pleased to be back in Kent again, for though his ancestors had originally come from the north, he had been born at Westcliffe House, and so Kent would always be home to him.

He gazed out of his window at the hedgerows filled with briar and honeysuckle, and beyond them white sheep grazed on pastures that looked much like green velvet. Distant farmhouses seemed to have snuggled into folds of lighter green, and here and there fields of golden grain rippled in the wind.

White-nippled oasthouses, silhouetted against the sky, seemed to be waiting for the time, not a month away, when the hops would be ripe and the fields would be a hive of activity, for it took every able-bodied man or woman in the area, hordes of casual laborers from London, and every gypsy in the south of England to pick what was their largest crop.

It was hard work, as he well remembered, for he and a friend had gone picking hops one year—unbeknown to his mama and papa, of course. The hops grew on tall vines, in clusters, and to harvest them the vines had to be hacked down and then stripped of the crop. Even though they had worn leather gloves, and took turns at hacking and stripping, their hands had been sore and blistered for a sennight.

He glanced at Catherine, who looked so peaceful as she slept, her dark lashes contrasting with her creamy skin and the faint touch of pink in her cheeks.

She had never seemed at all missish to him, and so he wondered whether it might not be wisest to tell her his thoughts on a possible early conception. But the best thing was, of course, to see how their first evening together went along for, in any event, he would much rather wait until he was home and in his own bed before he subjected her to what might possibly be considerably uncomfortable the first time.

As things turned out, he need not have worried, for the inn had only two small rooms available, with a parlor between them, and neither bedroom had a bed big enough for the two of them to sleep in, though one had a cot for the maid.

Before they sat down to a light supper, Coverdale took Catherine for a stroll around the county town, as much to stretch their legs as see the sights. Maidstone had been there since medieval times, but most of the buildings now standing were quite new, and housed shops of all descriptions, including a bank and a large town hall which dominated both Bank Street and High Street.

Supper was plain but well-cooked country fare and afterward they found a pack of cards and had a game of piquet, at which Catherine was quite good for a female, but could not be persuaded to play for money even when Edwin offered to furnish it.

It was a time to get to know each other without servants always around, as there would undoubtedly be once they reached West-cliffe House, and he found himself enjoying her ready smile, and the way they could share a joke when others were around by just a glance or a special gleam in their eyes.

The maid his mama had lent her, Dora, was quiet and efficient, and very happy to be going to Kent because her young man worked there, and they had not seen each other since the start of the Season.

The next morning Catherine looked rested and extremely well in a deep green carriage gown with a matching bonnet, and they lingered so long over breakfast that they made a later start than they had meant to. But once in the carriage, they made up for lost time.

Coverdale knew the exact moment when Westcliffe House would come into view, and he made a point of watching his wife's face as she caught her first glimpse of the magnificent house. Her eyes opened wide, and her soft lips formed a distinct but soundless "Oh."

"Will it do?" he asked with amusement.

"I believe it will," Catherine said, laughing, then asked, "Why didn't you tell me how beautiful it was? I had an idea that it was larger than most country homes, but this house is unbelievably lovely as well.''

"Wait until you see the gardens. You'll never want to come indoors unless it rains,'' he said softly. "It was a wonderful place to grow up.''

"Yes, I think it must have been. I don't know how you could bear to be away from it for so long in the wars,'' she told him.

"Don't you see?'' he asked. "There was never any question in my mind. I had to fight Napoleon because of all this, for had he achieved his goal and defeated all of Europe, England would have been next. And what could be closer to France than this lovely corner of our country?''

She nodded, understanding in her eyes. "You did indeed have much more at stake than most.''

He grinned. "And now I'm afraid you're in for an inspection parade to rival many military ones, for there's no doubt that at this very moment old Jarvey will be lining up the whole staff in order of rank.''

Catherine made a wry face. "Is there a back way I could use to sneak in?'' she asked, teasing, then tried to smooth her unruly hair. "How do I look?''

"Charming, if a little disheveled,'' he said, grinning. "Here, let me give you a hand.''

He moved to sit on the seat beside her, then smoothed her hair back and reached for the bonnet she had discarded a couple of hours ago. As he positioned it, and tucked some unruly strands of hair beneath, his fingers brushed her cheek and he heard her quick intake of breath.

Quite deliberately, then, he placed a hand on each side of her face and, his eyes unwavering, he lowered his head until his lips met hers and stayed there, alternately teasing and demanding until, as the carriage came to a halt, he eased away.

As he handed her gloves to her, he smiled slightly and murmured, "I think we'd best continue this later in some other place.''

There was the sound of steps being let down, and then the door opened. Coverdale jumped down first, then reached up to help Catherine.

He took her hand as they walked toward the flight of stone steps leading to the portico and the massive, studded doors beyond, and his fingers seemed to impart some of his strength into hers. Then, as they came to the door and he released her hand to let her go ahead of him, she stepped forward with renewed energy.

It was just as formal, and more, then Edwin had told her it would be, for she had not quite expected such a formidable tartar as the elderly butler who stepped toward her and bowed low.

"Jarvey, my lady," he said stiffly, leading Catherine toward the men and women of all ages standing as straight as soldiers in formation.

"This is the indoor staff, my lady," Jarvey intoned, and started toward the first in line. "Mrs. Lambert, housekeeper," he intoned, as a plump lady in a black dress curtsied.

There were four rows of them arranged in order of rank, with the cook next in line, and it was clear that Jarvey meant Catherine to go with him down each row, asking a question here, making a comment there. She did not let him down, but lived completely up to his expectations, behaving very much as the dowager Lady Coverdale had done when she was here.

Coverdale had urgent mail awaiting his attention, and went directly to the library, while Catherine allowed Jarvey to conduct her on a tour of the ground floor rooms, ending with the great kitchen, laundry room, and still room, but she decided to leave the cellars and upper floors for another day.

"Aren't you tired, my dear?" Coverdale asked when they finally met for a glass of sherry before dinner.

"Exhausted," she told him with a weary smile, "but it need be gone through only once, and though Hayward House is minuscule by comparison, I have run it single-handed since I was seventeen."

"It shows, for you handled Jarvey superbly. I believe, however, that you should have an early night tonight, my dear," he said, then noticed her slight flush of embarrassment.

"Don't worry, Catherine, I'll not disturb you, for I've enough work on my desk to keep me busy until tomorrow morning," he told her, then wondered if he had said the right thing, for she looked not a little surprised.

Jarvey came in then to announce that dinner was served, and Coverdale offered Catherine his arm, but once they were in the dining room he took one look at the long table with a place set at each end, and told the old butler that this simply would not do.

"I do not intend to spend the evenings shouting at my bride, so you'd best put Lady Coverdale's place setting immediately to my right whenever we do not have guests," he told the old man, and was sure he caught a glimmer of approval before Jarvey signaled to a footman to make the necessary changes.

The food was well cooked and well prepared, but Catherine was too tired to eat very much of it and, in any case, she was quieter than usual, for she found it most uncomfortable to carry on a conversation with servants constantly hovering over her.

"You look as though you might fall asleep at the table, my dear," Coverdale said gently. "It has been a very long day for you, and though I'll miss you, I'll willingly excuse you if you feel you cannot stay up any longer."

He was being kind, but suddenly she felt stubborn. "Really, Edwin, I'm quite all right, but I'd rather not go to the drawing room and drink tea alone. Would you mind very much if I had my tea brought in here?" she asked. "I shall not at all care if you smoke, for I grew accustomed to Papa's cigar, and have even missed the smell of late."

"Of course I don't mind. I just hadn't thought of it because you looked so weary," he said at once, giving the necessary instructions. "This is your home now, and I always enjoy your company. Should you fall asleep at the table, I promise that I will carry you up to your bedchamber myself," he teased.

He did not miss the sigh that escaped her lips when at last the servants left them alone, and suggested quietly, "If you would rather the servants disappear between courses, it can be arranged, you know. I am so accustomed to them that I disregard them completely, but I can fully understand your feeling uncomfortable."

"You really wouldn't mind?" she asked, taken aback a little at his astuteness.

"Of course not." He grinned. "Jarvey will probably be delighted. Didn't you see the expression of approval on his face when I told him I wanted you by my side when we dine alone?"

He reached out his hand and placed it over her smaller one, lying on the table. "I want you to be happy here, Catherine, for it's the place where I prefer to spend most of my time, and I hope you will eventually feel the same way."

"There's little doubt that I will, Edwin, for, as I told you, it's the most beautiful house I have ever seen." She sighed. "And I suppose that, in time, I will become as accustomed as you to the constant presence of servants."

"I'm sure you will, and when we have young children running around you'll be glad that there are so many people to watch over them," he said lightly.

She had the distinct feeling that he had made the remark about children deliberately, just to see the pink flush that came to her cheeks. But he at least meant to consummate the marriage eventually then, she decided, for she would have been bitterly disappointed had he not wished for a family.

She did not know whether she felt rejected or relieved that Edwin did not mean to join her tonight, for she could remember all too clearly her mama's hinting that the marriage bed was far from pleasant.

"If it is a fine day tomorrow, I thought you might like to take a ride over part of our property," Coverdale suggested. "I must be out most of the day, for I believe in seeing for myself how things are rather than relying on the word of a bailiff. Even the best of them tend to slacken off when an owner is away for a while. But I hate to leave you alone for such a long time on your first day here."

"I'm not a silly little girl, Edwin," Catherine protested. "I'm sure I could find plenty of things to do here if you were to go off for the day. I must admit, however, that the prospect of a morning ride with you is most appealing. Do you have a suitable mount for me?"

He grinned. "Of course, for I sent your little mare down here a few days ago, and by now she will be eager for an outing also. Would breakfast at eight o'clock be all right, and then we could set out immediately afterward? If we go as far as our northern boundary, and then come back through the village of Westcliffe, you'll meet quite a few tenant farmers and villagers in your first morning here."

"It sounds more like a treat for me than an inspection of your bailiff's performance in your absence, but I am certainly not going to complain, and I will keep out of your way during the times you are conducting business, I promise," she said eagerly, her weariness forgotten for the moment.

But she was much more tired than she realized, and it was not long afterward that she wished Edwin a good night, received a chaste kiss on the cheek from him, and then graciously accepted the escort of a young footman to her bedchamber, where Dora was waiting for her.

"I'll need my green riding habit in the morning, Dora, and am having breakfast with Lord Coverdale at eight, so please be sure to wake me, with a cup of tea, in plenty of time," she told the girl.

In what seemed like no more than a few minutes, she was being tucked in to the large canopied bed, and immediately fell fast asleep, to dream of children with chestnut-colored hair running and playing on those immaculate lawns.

Nine

ONCE CATHERINE had left the dining room, Coverdale went also, but his destination was the library. He had time to do a little more work this evening before retiring to his chamber, he told himself, for his state of mind was far removed from sleep, and he was, if the truth were known, a little on edge.

Setting himself comfortably behind his desk, with several large ledgers before him, he worked for almost an hour before his mind drifted back to his bride, and he wondered if she was abed as yet—and what she looked like with her glorious hair tumbling around her shoulders and her blue eyes heavy with sleep.

Over the years he had kept a number of mistresses, but none for very long, as he had little desire to continue the relationships once they grew familiar and began to expect more from him than he was prepared to give. He had never been ungenerous to them on parting, for he had no wish to leave them without means of support until they could find another patron.

But for him that was now a thing of the past. His relationship with Catherine was very different from anything he had ever imagined, for he found that he wanted her for a friend and companion as much as for a lover. Of course, that might change somewhat, depending upon her measure of affection, but it was something he did not wish to dwell upon too much at the moment. He was quite determined to postpone her initiation into the art of lovemaking until no one, whether holding a bet at White's or not, could even hint that a child she might bear was other than his own.

The thing to do, of course, was to take her for rides around the countryside each day. She had admitted to knowing nothing of the area, and if they were both tired of an evening, it would seem more natural to retire to their own chambers alone at night.

He sighed heavily. It was much easier said than done, however, for if he had needs tonight, what would he be like a week from now? He reached for the brandy decanter and poured himself a goodly portion.

The breakfast room was, to Catherine's surprise, much more cheerful than that large, gloomy dining room, and someone had filled vases with fragrant yellow and white roses, and set them on the sideboard and the dining table.

"Good morning, Jarvey," she said brightly. "Is Lord Coverdale still abed?"

"No, I am not still abed." The deep voice came from behind her and it startled her so that she swung around and almost fell into her husband's arms. He caught her and held her close for a moment, his face so near to hers that she could smell the lotion he had used after shaving.

"Impertinent minx," he murmured softly, before releasing her and standing beside her chair. "If you'll take a seat, my dear, I'm sure Jarvey would enjoy bringing you your first breakfast at Westcliffe House."

The old butler had moved to the sideboard and was awaiting her instructions.

"I believe I'll have a little of the scrambled eggs, one piece of ham, and a spoonful of kidneys," Catherine said. "Oh, and do let me try a little of that finnan haddie on a separate plate. A spoonful will suffice for now, thank you, Jarvey."

"You mean to sample everything before deciding what you really want?" Edwin asked, quite amused.

"But, of course I do," she replied primly, though her eyes sparkled with laughter. "For how can I know if any of them are quite to my taste if I do not first try them?"

The butler put the plates in front of her, then asked, "And for you, my lord?"

"I'll have finnan haddie first, for they never make it this way in London. And I'll help myself to the rest later, thank you, Jarvey.''

After complying with his master's request, Jarvey bowed, then left the room, closing the door quietly behind him.

''Oh dear, does he mind very much not being in the room all the time?'' Catherine asked, feeling sorry now that she had protested last night.

''Not at all. He thinks it quite appropriate, for, after all, we are newlyweds, my love,'' Coverdale said, his blue eyes twinkling. ''And may I say how delightful you look in that green riding habit?''

''At least I no longer shame you with my shabby black clothes, but your mama spent a fortune on things for me, and she would not even let me keep a reckoning of it because, she said, it was her gift to me. Did you repay her for them?'' she asked.

''No, for she would not have permitted me to, my love. It was something she very much wanted to do, and it would have been unkind not to have allowed it, don't you think?'' he asked gently.

Catherine could not reply at once, for she had just taken a mouthful of the finnan haddie and, a moment later, the first thing she said was, ''You were right, Edwin, this is the most delicious I have ever tasted. I must ask Cook for the recipe.''

If Edwin had hoped she had forgotten his previous question, he was disappointed, for she continued, ''And as for your mama spending her money on me, I think that's worse than if you were repaying her. She is a widow, Edwin, and might need the money.''

When he laughed aloud, Catherine looked at him in astonishment, but he merely softened it to a chuckle before saying, ''My dear girl, it has been a practice for generations in the Coverdale family to provide extremely well for their womenfolk. Mind you, they have always chosen them well,'' he said, adding, ''as I did.''

Catherine's cheeks turned a deep pink and she became most interested in cutting up her piece of ham.

''My mother will never want for anything, I can assure you, and if it pleases her to furnish you with a complete wardrobe, surely you would not wish to deny her that pleasure?'' he asked.

''I suppose that when you have the money, you don't think as much of it as when you have not,'' she observed. ''To me it was a small fortune, but then I have never had enough to quite go around.''

''You do now,'' Coverdale told her.

She glanced up at him sharply. ''What do you mean?'' she asked.

''I mean that you have a quarterly allowance to spend on clothes and fripperies, and if there is anything else you would like and cannot pay for from your allowance, you must come to me. But, to be honest, I cannot imagine refusing you anything that you really wanted,'' he said cheerfully, then paused. ''No, I take that back. The one thing you may not do is give money to your brother, for I am giving him an allowance until your father is in a position to do so, and I do not think that it should be exceeded.''

''Couldn't it come out of what you give me?'' she asked, ''for I know that I'll not need any more clothes for ages and ages.''

He did not mean to laugh at her, but he simply could not help himself, though he softened it by placing his hand on her arm.

''I want you to buy things for yourself, my love,'' he said warmly. ''And I have opened an account for you into which I have put a thousand pounds. I shall put the same amount into that account every quarter so that you may pay your own bills, but if we should find that it is not sufficient, then I will make other arrangements.''

''A thousand pounds a quarter?'' she gasped, now quite shocked. ''Why, that is a small fortune, Edwin. I don't believe I have spent a total of a thousand pounds on myself in my whole life, never mind in just a quarter.''

He wagged a finger at her. ''And you are not to pay for any household goods from that. It is for your personal expenses only. And now,'' he said, getting to his feet, ''if you are quite ready, I will have the horses brought around.''

''Just a moment,'' she said softly, walking toward him slowly. ''I don't believe I got my morning kiss.''

He stood watching her and waiting, a small smile playing around the corners of his mouth, his eyes twinkling.

She stood on her tiptoes, for though she was tall for a woman, he was much taller than she, and his arms came swiftly around her, pressing her close. She reached out a hand to touch his cheek, feeling the smooth, clean-shaven skin, and he caught the hand in his and placed a kiss in the very center of the palm. A moment later his lips were on hers, tender and teasing, then hungrily demanding, and finally leaving her gasping for breath.

"I think we'd best be on our way," he murmured, releasing her with some reluctance, "or we'll find ourselves back in your bedchamber."

Catherine said nothing, for she was confused, her feelings in a turmoil and her heart beating more rapidly than she had ever known. Did husbands and wives really make love during the day, she wondered? For surely that was what Edwin had meant.

She was in such a state that she turned to leave, quite forgetting her hat, gloves, and riding crop, and he picked them up and insisted on properly positioning her hat before allowing her to precede him into the hall.

It was one of those lovely days in late summer when there is a crispness in the air, as if anticipating autumn, and Catherine was sure she could catch the smell of apples. She said as much to Edwin.

"I hadn't noticed," he told her, "but then I may be used to it, for they're ripening on the trees now, getting ready for the cider presses.

"We'll go north this morning, I think, for there are some cottages in need of repair that I want to take a look at. My bailiff is inclined to wait until the rain actually pours in before doing anything about it, which means we then have a great deal more work to do to make them habitable," he complained.

"That has been the problem at Hayward House also," Catherine noted. "Our bailiff has been there so many years that my papa feels he cannot replace him with a younger man, for he'd feel bound to pension him off. Unfortunately, that is something we cannot afford to do."

The cottages were the small, half-timbered kind built in late Tudor times, with two small rooms downstairs, two above, and a staircase up the center. The doorways were so low that even

Catherine bumped her head on the solid oak lintels as she went in the back door, and into the parlor also.

"They're well-constructed as a whole, and mostly in need of nothing more than rethatching," Coverdale said. "I would guarantee that it's not been done in the last thirty years."

"How often do they need to be rethatched?" Catherine asked.

"If it's done properly it will last about twenty years, so I'm afraid these are considerably overdue. But if I don't get someone to them soon before the winter sets in, they'll be completely uninhabitable.

"You know, Catherine, I was thinking last night that once I've gone over things here, I should probably take a trip up to Hayward House and see if there's anything I can do to help there for now. Your father'll not be leaving London for some time when he does return from Belgium," he said. "Would you like to come with me and show me around?"

"Of course I would. You must know that I'd like nothing better. But can you afford to take the time to do so?" Catherine asked.

"Someone needs to do it, and who is better fitted to the task than the major's son-in-law?" he countered.

She might have said, "The major's son," but then Mark was a little young for the task, so she held her tongue.

"You're much happier in the country than in London, aren't you, Edwin?" It was a question that needed no answer, for Catherine could sense how much he loved the house and land and the feeling of continuity. He would want a son, she was sure, to take over when he was gone.

"Of course I am," he said quietly, "but times are changing. Nothing is the same as it used to be, as more workers head for the cities. Of course, the landowners have brought it upon themselves by paying wages their workers couldn't possibly live on. It's nowhere near as bad here as in the midlands and north, but when the changes come, they will affect every corner of the country."

Catherine looked worried. "Surely you don't think that there will be a revolution here, as they had in France?" she asked.

He shook his head. "Not a bloody one, for the temperament

of the people is different here. But we're in the middle of a revolution now; the riots these last few years are all a part of it, and the Prince Regent is not popular, you know, with the common people.''

''They would rather have the Duke of Wellington, I suppose,'' Catherine said.

Coverdale laughed. ''Of course they would. He's their hero right now, and there's no question but that he is a brilliant soldier, and very down to earth, which Prinny could never be. In a battle he doesn't just stand back and give orders. He's right there, fighting with his men and encouraging them much of the time.''

''I really don't know how Papa will settle down this time,'' Catherine said thoughtfully. ''He never really did the last time he came home, you know, which is probably why everything is in such bad straits up there.''

His smile held understanding as he said gently, ''I wouldn't worry too much about that. Things are very different this time around, for there's no fighting going on for him to miss, and, I'm afraid, he's not going to feel the way he did before. That's something you'll have to accept, my dear, for it's more than likely he'll feel some of those injuries—particularly in cold, wet weather—for the rest of his life.

''And, speaking of aches and pains, you might have a few yourself tonight, for how long has it been since you spent half a day on horseback?'' he asked, grinning.

''I'll suffer them gladly,'' she said, smiling happily, ''for I don't remember when I enjoyed myself so much. Just stop and listen!''

They had reached the edge of an apple orchard, the fruit rosy red on the trees, and near them was a row of beehives. Then, above the sound of buzzing, larks could clearly be heard as they soared and sang in a blue, cloudless sky.

After listening for a moment, she sighed, then asked, ''Do you make your own cider here on the estate?''

Coverdale nodded. ''I'll have to take you to watch the way the juice is extracted when they reach that stage. They'll be picking soon, by the look of it, and probably are already doing so a little further south.''

"May I watch them making the cider itself?" she asked, eagerly.

"Of course you may, if you wish, as long as you don't get too close, for I would not like to see any part of you made into apple cider. That was always one of our mama's worries when we went there as children," he said with a grin.

"Then, if you children could manage to keep your little fingers out of the press, I am sure that I will succeed also," she told him primly, "for I have always prided myself on my cautiousness. But I want to see more than just the pressing. I'd like to watch the whole process."

"Did that cautiousness include striding around the less salubrious parts of London, completely without escort?" he suggested, his eyebrows raised.

"Let me tell you that I was never once accosted in those parts, but I distinctly felt someone pinch me in an area supposed to be one of the finest, when I was in the company of your mama," she told him.

He chuckled and said, "All your areas are the finest, my love. Just which one did he pinch?"

"Oh!" she said, threatening him with her riding crop, but his horse was already dancing away, out of range.

"As if you yet know any of my areas," she muttered to herself, frowning, "or have any wish to, it seems."

But he caught the words and was at her side in an instant, concern reflected in his eyes.

"I believe we must have a serious talk, Catherine," he said quietly. "Let's ride over to the edge of the woods. I'll tether the horses and then it's but a short walk to a stream where we may talk without fear of being disturbed."

He realized that she had not meant him to hear, but if she was upset enough to remark upon it, she must be feeling hurt and he knew he must bring the matter out into the open. After all, it was her problem just as much as it was his, and neither of them was to blame.

He reached the woods ahead of her, dismounted, and waited to lift her down. After the horses were tethered, he took her hand and led her down a slight slope to where nature had carved a seat from which to view the rapidly flowing stream.

Once he had helped her sit, she turned her head away and kept it averted, following the swift current of the stream with her eyes.

"We must clear the air on this, before it grows into something larger than it is," Coverdale said, "and I suppose it is my fault for not telling you of my intentions right away."

She clearly did not mean to help him out, for she made no comment but just waited for him to continue.

"Until I heard of the wager made at White's, I had every intention of consummating our marriage as gently as possible, on our wedding night," he began. "Then when I heard of the ridiculous bet, I decided it would be in both our interests if we could wait a month before doing so."

"Then you didn't believe that I had nothing to do with it, did you?" she asked, quite shocked. "In that case, why did you marry me?"

"Have you finished jumping to conclusions?" he asked her quietly, waiting for her answer before continuing.

Finally, she nodded, still pouting a little.

"Had I disbelieved you, I would not have married you under any circumstances, which you will realize if you think about it," he went on. "What worries me is that should I put you in a family way the first night, and our child be born prematurely, it would cause debates as to hair color, size of the child, and so on, in order for the fools to endeavor to settle their wagers."

She turned to look at him, realizing now that he had been merely tyring to protect her, and he cupped her face in his hands, leaned over, and placed a gentle kiss on her lips. "I want to make love to you very much, my dear, and because of it, last night was one of the most uncomfortable nights I can ever remember spending. What I am trying to do is to make sure we never again have to be the subject of gossip and ridiculous wagers. Can you understand what I'm saying?"

Catherine nodded. "But why was it so uncomfortable for you last night? Were you worried that I would feel rejected, for I wouldn't have if I'd but known your reason," she told him quite seriously.

"I know, my love," Coverdale said quietly, "but it was my

own feelings that were keeping me from sleep. It is difficult to explain, but I promise you will understand eventually. And now I believe we should go back to the house and see what Cook has prepared for luncheon. Are you hungry?''

"Yes, as a matter of fact I am," Catherine said, relieved now that they had brought the problem out into the open. "Can we race there?''

"Why not? We're not in Hyde Park now," he told her. "Once you're mounted I'll give you a ten-count start.''

Of course he won, for his was the stronger horse by far, and they dismounted and walked into the house arm in arm, laughing together at some silly joke, the earlier tension completely gone.

With Edwin off with his bailiff for the afternoon, Catherine decided it was a good time to see the upstairs rooms and bed-chambers, so she sent for Mrs. Lambert, and soon the two of them were going from room to room, noting things that needed some attention, a rare event for the place was in excellent order, and enabling Catherine to familiarize herself with the layout of the great house.

They were about halfway through when Jarvey came into tell her that Lady Witherspoon had come to call.

"Please tell her that I am not yet receiving guests, Jarvey,'' Catherine said, for she was amazed that anyone would visit a bride on her second day there.

"Nonsense, my dear," a loud voice came from the top of the staircase. "I'm not a guest—I've spent half of my life in and out of this house.''

When Catherine stepped into the hall, it became apparent why the caller had taken so long to get up the stairs, for she was quite heavy, carried a stick, and walked with a decided limp.

"Nonetheless, my lady, I am neither ready to receive visitors nor dressed to do so," Catherine said quietly, and was about to suggest she call at some later date when she felt a decided nudge from the housekeeper. "However, if you are a friend of my mama-in-law, Jarvey will, I am sure, bring tea in the drawing room in a few minutes and I will join you when I have changed.''

"Oh, you don't need to change for me," the caller began, but Catherine had slipped quietly away and Lady Witherspoon had no option but to follow Jarvey down the stairs again and to await her hostess in the drawing room.

"Would you like me to help you, my lady?" Mrs. Lambert asked. "It will be quicker than sending for Dora, and I can tell you, at the same time, who this person is."

"Thank you," Catherine said gratefully, already starting to unbutton her riding habit. "I'll wear the green gown, I think, for I know it is already ironed. But now you have piqued my curiosity. Who is she?"

"Lady Witherspoon was an old flame of the late earl. Before he married, of course. I do not believe she has ever been a favorite of the earl's mama, however, for she is the biggest gossip in these parts, and you'll have to watch your words or they'll be misconstrued and repeated a hundred times."

"Then why didn't you let me just send her packing?" Catherine asked, realizing that the woman probably knew all the gossip that had circulated in London about her.

"Because what she can't find out, she'll make up," the motherly housekeeper said, "and you don't need that. She'd have followed you here into your bedchamber if you'd given her half a chance."

"I'm grateful to you, Mrs. Lambert," Catherine said as the housekeeper did up the buttons on her gown. "I'm not going to be very friendly toward her, but at least I now know how to deal with her. I would suppose that the earl did not expect her to call quite so soon, or he would have told me about her, I'm sure."

It was a good twenty minutes before Catherine entered the drawing room, by which time her visitor had drunk at least one cup of tea and eaten several of the small cakes Cook had provided.

"Please don't get up, Lady Witherspoon," she said coolly, allowing a footman to seat her across from her visitor. "I understand you were familiar with the late earl's family."

"That I was," the other woman replied, "and used to running tame in this house, I can tell you."

"Do you have a home nearby?" Catherine asked, signaling to the footman to refill Lady Witherspoon's cup.

"A couple of miles south of here, toward Dover. My papa had been a sailor and he didn't want to live too far from the sea," she said. "I understand that you come from Norfolk way. Can't say as I've heard of any Haywards in that area, though."

Catherine smiled. She came from a perfectly respectable, old family, and was not going to allow this creature to belittle them. "Then your informant must have been mistaken," she said, "for my father's family has lived in that area for more than five generations, my lady. At present there is no one in residence, however, for my father, Sir John Hayward, is still in Brussels recovering from his wounds, and my brother is studying at Cambridge."

"You got married in . . ." Lady Witherspoon had just started to say, when Coverdale walked casually into the room.

"Ah, just in time for tea," he said, "and I didn't know we had a visitor so soon. How are you, Eliza?"

"Fair," she said, "and I hear I must congratulate you. Your mama must have thought you were never going to wed, and then you up and marry in the blink of an eye."

"When I finally saw the perfect wife for me, there was no point in wasting time," he told the old lady. "And she seems to have fallen in love with Kent, haven't you, my dear?"

"It's like a beautiful garden, but on a large scale," she told him, passing him a cup of tea and offering the plate of cakes.

"I think I will have one," he said, "for I've got to keep my strength up, you know. After a Season in London there's a little too much catching up to do for my liking. But it's probably the last one I'll attend for some time."

He turned back to Lady Witherspoon. "What's the latest gossip around here, Eliza?" he asked.

"You know me, Edwin," Lady Witherspoon said, "not one for gossiping, and nothing much ever happens around these parts anyway. The last time there was anything exciting was when they built the Royal Military Canal and the Martello towers to keep out Napoleon."

"Well, they'll not be needed anymore, for this time they're

going to make sure he stays where he's put,'' Coverdale said firmly.

"I hope so, for the country's spent too much already on wars against him. Next thing, they'll be taxing us even more to help pay for it all,'' Lady Witherspoon grumbled. "Give my best wishes to your mama when you write, which probably isn't often if I know young men these days.''

"I'll give you a hand, Eliza,'' Coverdale said, helping the old lady out of her chair and placing her stick in her hand. "Take my arm and I'll see you into your carriage.''

Catherine rose also. "It was so nice of you to call, Lady Witherspoon. When I start paying calls I'll make a point of stopping to see you,'' she said, smiling coldly.

A moment later, when Edwin came back, she told him, "Your timing could not have been better, Edwin. She was just about to say that we got married in a hurry when you walked in the door.''

"I know. Jarvey sent word to me and I hurried back, for I knew what she would be up to. I must say, however, my dear, that you seemed to be coping with her extremely well,'' he said. "One thing I promise you, though. She's the only one I know of who would have the unmitigated nerve to come nosing around at this time. There are no more like her in these parts.''

Ten

COVERDALE'S PROMISE, though sincerely meant at the time, was one that he could not fulfill, however, for they had a second unexpected caller the next morning.

They were just finishing an early breakfast, for Coverdale meant to show his bride the villages of Westcliffe and St. Margaret at Cliffe, and St. Margaret's Bay beyond, when Mr. Jowitt, the bailiff, asked to see him at once.

"Send him in, Jarvey," Coverdale said sharply, then turned to Catherine and murmured, "I am sorry, my dear, but it may be something urgent."

A heavy-set man, probably in his mid-forties, entered behind the butler.

"Beggin' your pardon, milord, for disturbin' you," the bailiff began, "but somethin' very strange must 'ave 'appened overnight. Cleopatra's foal was missing this morning, and we just found it at bottom of t'quarry, dead by the looks of it. I thought you might want to take a look yourself before you do aught else."

"Oh, no," Coverdale said. He took a quick drink of his coffee, patted his mouth with his napkin, then stood up. "I'm very sorry, my dear, but I'm afraid we'll have to postpone our ride until later. I'll be back as soon as I can."

"Don't rush," Catherine told him, a worried look on her face. "If we can't go today, then perhaps we can go tomorrow. I think I'll inspect the kitchens and herb gardens instead, so you'll probably find me there if you're back sooner than you expect."

It sounded strange to her that a foal would have wandered away from its mother, but Edwin hadn't remarked upon it.

With time on her hands it felt pleasant to go out of the house alone and around to the back where she soon found what she was seeking.

There was not, of course, any comparison between her garden at home and the well-laid-out rows of peas, kidney beans, and broad beans, their pods fat and ready for the table. She recognized the new leaves of cabbages, Brussels sprouts, and broccoli that had just been planted, as had carrots, turnips, and beetroot, and knew that they would be well supplied for the winter months ahead.

She picked leaves of fresh mint and sage, rubbing them between her fingers and enjoying the fragrances.

There was a bench around an old oak tree, and she sat down for a moment, quite concealed from the house, looking toward the apple orchard she and Edwin had passed the day before.

She had no idea that anyone was near until she heard a voice close to her ear, saying in a sad, sing-song tone, " 'E's gone after the foal, 'asn't 'e? But it's too late now. 'E can't bring this'n back no matter what, for it were dead afore it went over.''

Catherine swung quickly around, and saw a young woman of about her own age, who smiled at her strangely. She was not poorly dressed, in that her clothes were of reasonably good quality material, if not well fitted, but her hair looked as though it had not seen a comb for days.

It was her eyes that were the strangest thing about her, though, for they were not vacant, as were those of so many afflicted people, but they were bright and held a look of cunning.

"What do you know about it?" Catherine asked the girl.

She looked startled at first, then her face seemed to close up. "Pa tol' me this mornin'," she said, almost sounding normal for a moment. "But I knew before 'e said it. You're the new lady, an' I'm Nell, Crazy Nell they call me, 'cos I 'ave visions. They dursen't put me away as long as I 'ave visions.''

Mrs. Lambert came bustling around the other side of the tree. "Off with you, Nell," she said, "and don't you come around bothering her ladyship.''

"I'm sorry, my lady," Mrs. Lambert went on. "She's a bit addlepated, if you know what I mean, but she's harmless enough."

Catherine was just about to say that it was all right, the girl was not bothering her, when she realized that Nell had left as silently as she had arrived.

"She's such a trial to Mr. Jowitt, the bailiff. It's not easy to lock her in and go do his work, for she is cunning enough to pick the lock and get out every time," Mrs. Lambert said. "Was there anything else you wanted us to plant for the winter, my lady? We've got onions and leeks over there, and a whole lot of potatoes a little further along." She pointed to a corner where large patches were devoted to the vegetables she named.

When Catherine smiled and shook her head, Mrs. Lambert said, "Jack, the gardener, is around most days, so if you think of anything, just let me know. There's a pretty rose garden just down that path, if you'd like to take a look at it, you know."

"I thought there must be, for I've been smelling them constantly," Catherine told her, smiling. "Please don't let me keep you from your work, for I know you're very busy, Mrs. Lambert. I'll just wander around, and as long as I can see the house I can find my way back."

With a smile and a little curtsy, the housekeeper turned and walked back to the house. Catherine watched the direction she took, and saw where the back door was, then walked slowly toward the rose garden.

It was there that Coverdale found her a half hour later, enjoying the morning sun and the fragrance of the flowers.

"I'm sorry I had to leave like that," he said, bending to kiss her cheek, then sitting down beside her, "but it was a most unfortunate and costly accident."

"Are you sure that it was an accident?" Catherine asked, thinking of Crazy Nell's words. "Surely, foals don't get out of the meadow and wander around loose during the night?"

"It would seem that this one did," he said, a little grimly.

"Was the foal very valuable?" she asked.

He smiled wryly. "I'm afraid so, my dear. Didn't you know that accidents only happen to the valuable ones? I believe it's a little late now to start out. Shall we wait until after luncheon and then have our ride?''

''Of course,'' she said, feeling that she might have agreed to anything at that moment, for he had placed his arm along the back of the seat, and his fingers were stroking her neck and shoulder, causing the most delightful sensations.

''Have there been other accidents?'' she asked, wondering if he was speaking from previous experience.

''Not for a long time,'' he said, ''for when I came back from France the first time, I took great care in selecting the best staff I could, and then paying them what they were worth. That is why I am even more concerned about this, as one of my best stable hands swears that he found the gate still closed this morning.''

''And you don't believe that the foal found it open, then nudged it shut with its nose,'' Catherine said dryly.

''Hardly.'' He reached out a hand. ''Come along, my dear, and let's see if luncheon is ready.''

He led her back the way she had come, to the front door of the house. In the distance she saw a figure just entering the woods, and for some reason it looked familiar, but she realized she must be mistaken, for as yet she knew no one in the area.

Catherine was wondering whether or not she should tell her husband what Nell had muttered. He might say that she was foolish to listen to anything the girl said, but, on the other hand, it might start him thinking further about how the foal could possibly have got out of the field. She did, however, decide it was best to wait until after luncheon before bringing up such an unpleasant subject again.

''I think I'm getting to know you a little better,'' Edwin said as he finished the last mouthful of apple pie. ''You've been quiet throughout the meal and now you have decided to tell me what is troubling you—or at least I hope you have.''

She smiled. ''You're very observant, my lord,'' she said, feeling inexplicably pleased. ''I have been sitting worrying a little about the young woman who came up to me this morning in the garden. Her name was Nell, and she said people call her Crazy Nell.''

''She's my bailiff's daughter, a little deranged at times, but completely harmless," he told her. "You mustn't let her worry you, for she bears none of us any ill will. What else did she say to you?"

"That the foal was dead before it went over the cliff." She had tried to make her voice sound quite matter of fact, for she believed the girl was right, but she was anxious to find out what Edwin's reaction might be.

"Was she very sure about it?"

Catherine nodded. "It almost seemed, for a moment, as though she had been there at the time and seen it," she told him.

"She may be right. A couple of my men went down to get it, so we'll soon know, for we may be able to tell that much, though not what actually happened, unfortunately," he said thoughtfully. "I'll have a word with Jowitt and see if he can find out anything more from the girl."

She knew that her own papa, the only man she had ever really known, would have rejected the ramblings of a crazy female quite out of hand. In fact, he would not have listened to one who was not crazy, for it was his expressed opinion that their duties were in the house, and matters outside were none of their concern.

Though she could not bring herself to feel badly about her papa, Edwin was rising in her estimation every day.

"If you're quite finished with luncheon, my love, we can start out now," he told her, "for I must be back by five to meet with Jowitt once more. And I do believe that the horses will by now be getting a little restless."

"And we mustn't let that happen, must we, my lord, or that fierce stallion of yours may try to take his revenge," she said, laughing as she reached for an apple.

"He'll most certainly do so if you give that apple to your mare and I have nothing for him. It's surprising how quickly they come to expect such treats . . ." His next words were cut short as he stepped aside and put out a hand to catch the apple that Catherine tossed dangerously close to his head.

"Just you wait, young lady," he warned, laughing. "I'll catch you unawares next time."

He put an arm around her shoulders to take her to the door, but as he looked down at her smiling face he knew that he could not wait even a moment to taste those inviting lips. She gasped when he pulled her close, for it was unexpected, then her whole body seemed to accept the inevitable and she relaxed in his arms and gave in to the delightful temptation of his kisses.

The sound of voices in the hall disturbed them, and Coverdale lifted his head and gazed at her face. It was no longer that of a laughing girl but, rather, that of a woman with eyes glazed and unfulfilled passions aroused.

"I'm sorry, my love, I should not have done that, for this is not the place," he murmured, gently releasing her.

Then he opened the door and placed her hand on his arm to lead her into the hall and out to where the horses did, indeed, wait most impatiently, perhaps wondering why it took several nudges with their great heads before they were given their apples.

Once mounted, Catherine and Edwin rode in silence for a while, each deep in thought.

Coverdale was soundlessly cursing Blanchard for his part in the contretemps that had placed him in such a position that he could not even kiss his bride without this tremendous urge to complete what he had started. But he knew that the fault really lay with Mark and his friend, Gordon. He had been attracted to Catherine since the first time he had seen her, striding along Kennington Lane, though then the absence of a maid had led him to envision a quite different relationship with her.

As they rode along in silence, Catherine felt mostly confused, for this was, indeed, only the second time that she had been really kissed, and her body responded in the strangest way imaginable. One thing of which she was certain was that she had not wanted Edwin to stop, and had felt quite let down when he had released her. She had actually needed his strong arm to hold as they had left the dining room.

It took but a short time to reach Westcliffe, which was little more than a few houses clustered together along the road that led to the ancient parish of St. Margaret at Cliffe.

As they rode slowly down the silent main street, Coverdale explained, "It's quiet here because this is the time of year when even the womenfolk and little children go off to help with the crops, and only a few older ones remain behind to look after the babies. They need the extra money, of course, to tide them over the winter months when there is less work available. This year there are a great many of the returning soldiers helping with the harvest, so they will be finished more quickly than usual.''

Edwin's remarks brought to mind the figure that Catherine had seen disappear into the woods, and she recalled that it had seemed strangely familiar.

''Are you using any of the soldiers at Westcliffe House?'' she asked.

Coverdale shook his head. ''Not at the moment, but we'll probably do so when the hops are fully ripe.''

He noticed her puzzled frown, and said, ''Did you have a special reason for asking?''

Catherine shook her head. Now she was not really sure of what she had seen, for it had been no more than an impression, but she had the feeling that the figure had been wearing a red jacket and gray trousers.

It was becoming windy, and the sea could not be far away, for she could smell it as they rode the short distance to the chalk cliffs at St. Margaret's Bay. Noisy seagulls soared overhead and the tide was coming in, so that Coverdale had to almost shout to make himself heard.

''It's hard to believe that we are less than twenty miles from the French coast, isn't it?'' he said, adding, ''On clear days you can see it from here.''

She had not realized they were so close, and with the battle of Waterloo still so much on her mind, it gave her a rather uncomfortable feeling.

''Now I can really understand,'' she said, ''why beating Napoleon was a personal as well as a patriotic endeavor for you. It would have been dreadful if the French had landed and taken over Westcliffe House.''

''Prinny must have thought so, too, for the Royal Military Canal was built just south of here for the express purpose of keeping out Napoleon, and soldiers were encamped near the little fishing village of Folkestone,'' he told her, adding, ''Quite a number of them are still there, for they found jobs nearby and either brought their families here or married local girls. Folkestone will be a small town before you know it."

She turned the little mare away from the cliff's edge. "Let's not go into Dover today," she suggested, "for we would probably have little time there, and I would like to pick up some thread form the small shop I saw in St. Margaret at Cliffe. Would you mind very much?"

He smiled. "Your wish is my command, my lady," he said. "By all means let us go to Dover another day and spend more time, for there's much that will interest you in the town. But after all those clothes my mama ordered for you, you're surely not still stitching your own, are you?"

She shook her head and said earnestly, "There is no need, though I still believe that she spent too much money on them, for it would have kept us in food for a year. But repairs are often necessary, and I've always had a penchant for browsing in country shops."

They were almost there, and Coverdale groaned dramatically. "Is that a warning that I shall have to wait outside with the horses for a half hour while you examine all the merchandise they have?"

Catherine laughed. "Well, not quite all of it, but I warn you that I am inclined to forget the time when I become interested in something."

He raised an eyebrow, and she relented.

"I promise not to be more than ten minutes, for I can always come back some other day, can't I?"

"Just as long as you bring a groom with you," he told her, remembering those long walks she used to take in London completely on her own. "And don't forget that you will probably find much more to choose from when we do go into Dover."

"I mean to look there also, my lord," she said, chuckling and dropping him a curtsy—not an easy feat with the cumbersome skirt of her riding habit. Then, before he could make a rejoinder, she hurried into the small shop.

If it had been in their village in Norfolk she would have expected to be recognized at once, but it came as somewhat of a surprise to her when the rosy-cheeked woman came from behind the counter and dropped her a deep curtsy.

"My lady, " she said almost reverently, "I never expected to see you in my little place so soon. Won't you sit down? I've a pot of tea just brewed, and I'll bring you whatever you'd like to see, if I've got it. I'm Mrs. Mumford."

Catherine was embarrassed, and gently refused the chair, saying, "I only came in to look for some thread, and I see it's over there. Please don't go to any trouble, for Lord Coverdale is waiting outside with the horses, and I promised I would not be more than ten minutes."

Mrs. Mumford looked so disappointed that Catherine added, "I'm sure I'll be in your shop quite often and the very next time I come, I will have tea with you."

She had scarcely finished her sentence, however, when the shopkeeper curtsied once more, and Catherine turned to find that Edwin had entered also.

"How are you, Mrs. Mumford?" he asked. "It's been a long time since I was in here, but it would seem that it has not changed at all." He turned to Catherine, explaining, "Jim Mumford and I go back a long way, my love, and he wouldn't hear of me holding my own horses."

A man of about forty came in then from the back room. "They're well taken care of, my lord," he said, then he glared at his wife. "What are you doing, woman, letting her ladyship stand?"

He reached for the chair that his wife had offered earlier and this time Catherine agreed to sit down, but not before explaining that it had been offered before, and that she had refused.

"Jim is a true Man of Kent, my dear," Coverdale said to Catherine, "for he was born in Smarden, which is east of the River Medway, and his family moved here about twenty years ago, I would say. Am I right, Jim?"

"Aye, that you are, my lord. You've got a good memory," Mumford said, grinning.

"They were good days. I was ten years old," Coverdale went on. "Jim was about eighteen, and he came to work at the house then, and his mother opened the shop. I was just getting over the measles, and he'd already had it, so Mama gave him permission to take me fishing, for I was driving her to Bedlam, or so she said.''

''Aye, and once you got the hang of it, you could catch more than I could,'' Jim said proudly.

Catherine looked closely at Edwin and could almost see him as a small boy of ten, particularly as he was now, relaxed and talking to an old friend. She was sitting beside the counter where Mrs. Mumford had quietly set out the trays of threads for her selection.

She chose several while the two men reminisced, then she asked, curiously, ''What is a man who is born west of the River Medway?''

''He's a Kentish Man,'' Coverdale said, grinning. ''I'm afraid it goes back a long way, my love, to the time when the Saxons came here to help the early Britons defend themselves against the Picts and Scots. The Saxons that stayed on settled east of the river, while the early Britons went over to the west and are still called Kentish Men.''

Catherine was reaching into her purse for the necessary coins, but Mrs. Mumford quickly said, ''No, my lady, I'll put it on the account.''

''I'd rather pay now for something as small as this,'' Catherine told her, to Coverdale's amusement, ''for I could quite easily forget such a small item, and would not wish to do so.''

She carefully counted out the coins, then rose and said her good-byes, promising to come back soon when she had more time to browse.

Two young lads, the image of Jim Mumford, were waiting with the horses, and Coverdale helped Catherine mount before taking his own horse from one of the lads and giving each of them a small coin. They ran off whooping loudly, as though it was not very often that they saw a coin.

''I'm glad that I married a country girl,'' Coverdale said softly as they set off for Westcliffe House, ''for you have just the right attitude. They're proud people and I warrant that one visit has made you the most popular lady in the entire neighborhood.''

''I get along with country people, for I had to do all the visiting in Norfolk during the last few years of Mama's life,'' Catherine tried to explain. ''You see, from what she told me, she never really recovered from having Mark. And then he was an irritable baby and little boy, and Papa was never very good with children, so she wore herself out endeavoring to keep him quiet and out of Papa's way. That may have been the reason that he bought colors and went off to fight with Wellington, for he was with him in North Germany, then home for a while, and then he was to go to Venezuela but they were diverted to Portugal to liberate Lisbon from the French,'' she explained.

"I'd no idea that he was, more or less, a professional soldier,'' Coverdale exclaimed. "And in that case I'm surprised that he didn't rise to a higher rank than major. Was he in again at the start of the Peninsular Wars, then?''

"Yes, he was, and as for his rank,'' Catherine paused, smiling ruefully, "he was made acting lieutenant colonel on several occasions, but it was never made permanent, mostly, I believe, because Papa has quite a temper, and he would say or do something he shouldn't—then he was back to a major.''

"And through those years Lady Hayward tried to bring you two up and look after the estates? I don't wonder she was not well,'' Coverdale remarked, "or that Mark became extremely spoiled. You must have seen very little of your father from when you were fourteen years old, and Mark about twelve.''

She grinned. "Oh, we saw him from time to time,'' she said, "for he was always getting wounded, though never terribly seriously until this time, and he would come home to recover. Then when he'd driven Mama to her bed and undone all my attempts to make the bailiff do a decent job, he'd put on his uniform and go back to war.''

Coverdale smiled a little grimly. "No wonder you seemed so different from the simpering misses I was accustomed to seeing in London. Believe me, my love, you missed nothing by not having a come-out.''

She looked at him a little sadly. "Yes, I did,'' she said quietly. "I missed falling in love, and being courted properly before getting married.''

"And you missed that because of your brother,'' he said, nodding grimly. "Had he been able to see through Gordon Smith, and not followed him into trouble, I would now be courting you, and we would have married at St. George's in

Hanover Square, if you would have had me.'' He saw the expression of surprise on her face. ''I knew what I wanted the first day I met you—though I must admit that one of my earliest desires was to give you a sound thrashing before starting the courting. First, you all but accused me of cowardice, and then you deliberately arranged for your brother to be out when I called specifically to see him. It was hardly an auspicious beginning.''

Catherine's cheeks had turned to a deep pink, and she had a strange, warm feeling inside.

''Then you didn't ask me to marry you because you felt you had handled things badly?'' she asked him.

''I asked you earlier than I had meant to because of Blanchard. I wanted to give you the protection of my name,'' he said quietly.

They had arrived at the main gate some time ago, and were so immersed in conversation that they had reined in and let the horses graze. Now they were quite obviously getting restless.

Catherine no longer felt she had missed something, for she was much closer to Edwin now than they would have been in a courtship. And though she was not yet sure of his actual feelings, she would have been in the same position if all their problems had never arisen.

Coverdale was watching her, with a slight smile on his face. ''We'd best get these horses back to the stables before they become any more restless,'' he told her quietly. ''If you want to dismount at the house, I'll take them around for I need a word with my head groom.''

She shook her head. ''I'll come with you, if you don't mind,'' she said, ''for I've not seen the stables as yet, and I should at least know where they are.''

He nodded, and they headed toward the back of the house, a little distance from the kitchen gardens.

Once their mounts had been taken by grooms, Coverdale took Catherine's hand and said, ''Come with me and meet Barrows. He's been here since I was a boy, and knows more about horses than anyone I've ever met.''

Though some of the stable boys would probably have liked to grin at seeing their master holding hands with his lady, they would not have dared. Barrows, however, was a different matter and he raised his eyebrows as they approached.

"So that's the way it is?" he remarked. "Must say, I'm right glad to see it."

"Barrows, meet your new mistress," Coverdale said with a smile. "If I'm away at any time, her word is law."

"That's all right with me, milord. Now if you'd picked a gal that didn't know one end of a horse from the other, that would have been a different matter," Barrows said gruffly, before turning to Catherine. "You've got a good seat, milady, and gentle hands, for I watched you ride out."

He was a short man with skin like wrinkled leather, but Catherine liked him at once, for he had eyes that she instantly trusted. She put out her hand. "Pleased to meet you, Barrows," she said. And she knew as she felt his firm handclasp that here she had a trustworthy friend.

Eleven

"WE'VE SO FAR been unable to find anyone who admits to having seen a stranger or strangers around here," Coverdale told his head groom. "You've checked with all your people, I am sure."

"That I have," Barrows said, no longer smiling, "and I'd like to get my 'ands on whoever took that foal out of the field. You must have made an enemy, milord, for no one else would have done a thing like that. I 'ad the veterinarian in to take a look at what's left of the little fellow, and 'e said it was either dead or unconscious when it went over the top of the quarry."

"That is apparently what Crazy Nell said, also." Coverdale shook his head somewhat wearily. "I think it would be best if you keep a man on duty in the stables all night for a while. I wouldn't like the next accident to be a fire in here."

"I've already set everything up, milord. And grooms and 'ands alike know that if I catch any of 'em sleeping they'll be let go the next morning," Barrows declared.

Coverdale nodded approvingly. "That's good, and keep them watching during the day also, for anyone at all they may see wandering around who has no business to be here."

"That I will, milord. Nice to meet you, milady," Barrows said to Catherine, touching his cap in salute.

She smiled, then took Coverdale's arm to walk the short distance to the back door of the house.

When they were out of hearing, Catherine said, "There was something about Barrows's face that I liked very much. I felt I could trust him completely."

"You can, my dear. He's a good man, as long as you love horses, and he seems to be able to tell the ones who do and the ones who don't without them saying a word," Coverdale told her. "I'm sure you must be feeling tired by now, for it's been a long day. Would you like me to postpone supper for an hour so that you can rest first?"

"Oh no, I'm made of much stronger stuff than that, Edwin," Catherine said firmly. "If I looked straight-faced it was probably because I was thinking about that foal. How could anyone want to hurt a little creature like that?"

Coverdale shook his head. "We'll not know until we get to the bottom of it, and I only hope that while we're trying to find out, we don't have any more 'accidents'. ''

"In a place like this, where people have known each other for years and years, I cannot believe that a stranger would not be noticed," Catherine said with a puzzled frown. "At home we always knew when strangers were around, for it was talked about at once."

"It's the same here most of the year," Coverdale said thoughtfully, "but at a time like this when the hops are being harvested, followed by the apples, there's a lot of work available, and we've always had gypsies around looking for it. And then, of course, there are the poor devils who came back from the war to find no jobs to be had. You'd best be sure not to go off alone here, for before long they'll be all over the place looking for any work they can find to bring them a little money or food."

Catherine nodded. "I will be careful, I promise, Edwin, for you know the dangers better than I do. Isn't the harvest a little early?"

"It's always earlier here than further north," he told her, "but this year it's even more so, for we had a particularly good summer for the crops."

They had entered the house and, disdaining the back stairs which Catherine would have used had she been alone, Coverdale led her through to the main hall.

Jarvey cleared his throat loudly to get attention. "Something came for you by post, my lord," he murmured.

Coverdale nodded his acknowledgement and said to

Catherine, "I'll just go and see if anything of importance came in, my dear, and will join you before dinner for a glass of sherry."

He went in the direction of the library, while Catherine went slowly up the great staircase. She would have liked to have gone with him to see if the post held any news of her papa, but did not yet feel familiar enough with Edwin to ask if she might. Her papa, when home, would have been furious with her had she dared to ask about any missive that had come by mail before he was ready to tell her. But then, if Edwin had seemed anything like her papa, she would not have married him, no matter how many people talked about her.

Dora was waiting for her in her bedchamber, with the gown she had chosen for this evening all ready to put on, but first she must get rid of the smell of horse.

After she had bathed, she looked at the lovely canopied bed and regretted not having agreed to postpone dinner a little, for the hot water had not quite succeeded in soaking out all her stiffness. But she had been without her maid for long enough to enjoy the luxury of sitting back and letting Dora dress her hair, then help her into her gown, a rather low-necked, elegantly styled creation in a particularly attractive shade of light amber.

"I must say that Lady Coverdale has excellent taste in clothes, Dora. I never would have thought this particular color would suit me half so well," she murmured, looking at herself critically in the pier mirror.

"It's just right for you, milady," the maid agreed, "for it brings out the color of your hair. There are some ribbons in the same shade that I could twist among your curls, if you like."

Catherine did like, and when she went down to the drawing room to meet Edwin, it appeared that he did also, for he cast her an admiring glance, and insisted that she turn around so that he could see the entire effect.

"Charming, my dear. You have the knack of knowing just what suits you," he murmured, lifting her hand and placing a kiss in the palm.

She smiled ruefully. 'I wish that I could accept the compliment gracefully," she told him, "but I must confess that it was your mother who realized how well it would suit me. She felt that with my height and coloring I could wear the more sophisticated shades.''

"Then I must thank Mama when next I see her, for there is no doubt that she is right. The whites and pastels are not really meant for you, but rather the more exotic colors and elegant styles." The corners of his mouth twitched as he added, "And the fact that you wouldn't accept credit where it's not due is just another sign of that refreshing frankness which I've found so vastly appealing since the first time we met."

Catherine took a seat by the fireplace while he went over to the sideboard where Jarvey had set a tray with a decanter and two filled glasses.

"Even the wine matches your gown," he said as he placed a glass of sherry on the table beside her, then took a seat across. She picked up the glass and twisted the stem between her fingers, watching the colors change as the amber wine caught the glow from the fire.

They sat in a comfortable silence for a while, then Edwin said, "After breakfast tomorrow, before we leave for Dover, remind me to show you the outside of the house and tell you a little of its history. I believe you have already seen the vegetable garden, but there are interesting plants, arbors, statuary, and such which my ancestors acquired over the years that I think you might find quite intriguing."

"I saw the vegetable garden this morning, which will provide us with a quite varied supply throughout the winter," she told him, "and then I followed the dictates of my nose until I reached the lovely rose gardens where you found me. Your head gardener must be extremely knowledgeable."

"I'm sure he is, for he's been here many years, as have the majority of the staff. I loved Westcliffe as a child, but then I left for Eton and Oxford, and after that went into the Army. It was not until I returned, last year, that I realized how much I had missed it." His voice softened as he recalled just how he had felt, coming home at last. "I missed Papa a lot at first, and I tried hard to restore the old place to the way it was when he was in his prime."

Catherine was glad of his arm when they went in to dinner,

for she was feeling quite sleepy. The warmth of the fire and the sherry, after so much fresh air, was having its effect upon her. When she retired, her only regret was that she had to go to her bedchamber alone for, despite his explanation, and even despite his kisses, she still felt rejected, as though he did not desire a closer connection. She could not help wondering if he had a mistress in town—or even out here in Kent—and though she had heard it was accepted in many circles, to her it was abhorrent.

Coverdale had mentioned during the dinner that they would take the curricle into Dover instead of going on horseback, so Catherine wore a sunny yellow carriage dress to breakfast, and as soon as they had finished, he took her on a tour of the outside of the house, starting with a series of paved terraces that faced toward the sea.

She now knew where she meant to pass her time when Edwin was busy with estate duties, for there were attractive benches in sheltered corners just asking for someone to spend a peaceful afternoon on them with needlework, a sketching pad, or an interesting book.

The stone wall of the house had several large niches, about six feet from the ground, some with bowls of trailing plants hanging inside them and others with statues. The one in the center held a quite beautiful and most unusual statue. Edwin said that it was one of his mother's favorite pieces, and went on to tell Catherine how, as a youth, his father had taken the grand tour of Europe, and had come across a sculptor in Greece who claimed he was the creator of some quite remarkable statues. The late earl had purchased the extremely beautiful, life-size statue of a woman with a small child clutching at her skirts, and had it carefully shipped to his home.

Later, when examined by one who claimed to be an authority on the subject, he was informed that it was much older than the previous earl had thought, naming a famous sculptor as the probable artist. He would not even begin to give him an idea of its worth, but said it was irreplaceable.

At this point the late earl had decided to build the niches as an unusual setting for a piece of such value. He had preferred not to fill the others with statuary that would take away from the work of art, but instead had the urns made to hold trailing ivy and other vines.

"There's something very lovely about the expression on her face," Catherine said, "and placed out here, it almost gives you the feeling that she is waiting for her sailor husband to come home from the sea."

"I believe my father felt very much the same as you when he had it placed there," Coverdale told her, "and though it has been suggested that something of such value would be safer if kept inside the house, I've never felt happy about moving it from the spot my father chose."

They had no sooner turned to leave the terraces than Mr. Jowitt came hurrying over.

"I'm sorry to disturb you, my lord, Lady Coverdale," he began, "but I need a decision from you on the reroofing of the cottages. I need to order the thatch today if we're to get it while the good weather holds."

"Would you excuse me, my dear?" he asked Catherine. "I must take care of this now, and will then join you either here, or in the conservatory, whichever you wish."

"Here by all means, my lord," Catherine said, "for I don't at all mind spending some time on this terrace, drinking in what may be the last rays of warm summer sunshine."

It was more than an hour before Coverdale returned, however, for one decision had led to another, but Catherine was comfortable and not at all concerned.

"I do beg your pardon for leaving you so long," he said as he came hurrying toward her. "Perhaps, once we've been to the conservatory, we should have luncheon here instead of in Dover, and then take tea there."

It was of no consequence to Catherine, and an easy matter to catch one of the servants and send word to Cook of the change of plans.

"Be sure to tell her just a light luncheon," Catherine added, "for we'll be having tea not long afterward."

It was in the orchid house that they caught up with the head gardener, an elderly man by the name of Tombs, who Coverdale vaguely recalled as looking much the same when he himself was but a youngster.

Once Tombs found that Catherine was most interested in all aspects of the gardens, he showed her every one of the different kinds of orchids he was cultivating, and was about to begin taking her through the succession houses. She was aware by now, however, that Edwin had not quite the interest she had in each and every plant, and was eager to have luncheon and then start out for Dover, so she regretfully cut short this visit. She begged the elderly Kentish Man to take her on a more extensive tour at a later date.

An hour or more later, after a light luncheon, the curricle was brought around, Coverdale helped her up, and they were tooling merrily along the road that led to the old town of Dover.

"I believe we must arrange some sort of a sign to let me know when you wish to depart, my lord," Catherine said, her lips quivering with amusement. "I am afraid that I am somewhat inclined to forget myself when I become engrossed in one of my favorite occupations, such as gardening."

"How refreshingly frank you are, my love," he murmured, carefully watching the road ahead, for it was quite narrow in parts. "Most wives would not dare to admit that they found Tombs and his orchids more interesting than their husband."

She quickly placed a hand on his arm and said contritely, "Of course I do not, Edwin, and you cannot think it, for after all, it was you who suggested taking me there in the first place."

He laughed aloud. "I'm only funning, my dear, and you mustn't take me seriously. Of course it was I who took you there, and I'm delighted that you're taking such an interest in the old house and gardens. I wouldn't have it any other way."

She heaved a sigh of relief, for she was more than aware of her shortcomings in this respect.

"I would not expect you to have to remain and listen to me discourse on the subject of boxing, fencing, or gaming of any sort, my love," Edwin said gently. "The trouble is, I believe, that we have had very little opportunity to get to know each other before plunging into marriage. If we want to rub along comfortably, then we'll just have to give ourselves more time together.''

The road they were traveling was little more than a country lane, but there was nothing in sight so he turned to look at her for a moment.

''It would seem to me, though, that we have already found a great many more things in common than most couples have when they start out. So long as we can talk about problems I have a feeling they will take care of themselves,'' he murmured, enjoying the vision she made in her cream bonnet with yellow ribbons streaming behind.

Suddenly a look of horror came into her eyes and he turned his attention swiftly back to the road to find a high-perch phaeton racing toward them down the middle of the road. The vehicle was swaying dangerously and the matched pair of chestnuts appeared to be completely out of control.

He pulled the curricle over as far as he dared without putting them into the ditch, then heard the sound of splintering wood as the hub of the phaeton's large wheel ripped spokes out of his own. Instinctively, he reached for Catherine, pulling her against him so that his body would take the impact if they went over, as he feared they might.

Carlos, who had filled the positions of tiger, batman, and valet for a number of years, had managed to jump clear of the vehicle and run for the horses' heads. Calming them in the mixture of English and Spanish to which they had grown accustomed, he checked them as far as he could for injuries they might have sustained.

Coverdale's first worry was that Catherine was all right. ''Try not to move at all, my love, and tell me if you hurt anywhere,'' he said softly.

''I don't think so.'' Catherine's voice was shaky, as well it might be, but she obeyed him implicitly, asking, ''What about you? Are you injured? How is your bad leg?''

''It took a bump, but it'll be all right. The biggest problem now is getting out of here without tipping the carriage completely over,'' he told her.

He had seen Carlos at the horses' heads, and called, ''What shape are they in, amigo?''

"No serious problems, I think, milor'," the little man said, leaving the horses and coming toward his master. "But this wheel," he threw up his hands in horror, "it might go poof at any moment."

"Is anyone injured in the phaeton?" Coverdale asked. "I suppose you'd better find out, though I'm not exactly pleased with the driver."

The little man looked at him and shook his head slowly. "That wheel also must be bad, but the carriage did not stop here, milor'. Perhaps 'round the next bend?" He shrugged meaningfully.

"Is there room to get her ladyship down on the other side?" Coverdale asked.

Carlos nodded. "I think so, if she permits me to assist."

"She will, won't you, my dear?" he asked Catherine gently, grateful that she was not having hysterics, as many young ladies would have been doing long before now.

"Of course," she said quietly. "Just tell me what to do."

He did not release her until Carlos was in place, then he said softly, "Now, try to slide very slowly away from me, my love. I must stay on this side so that the carriage does not tip further."

She did exactly as he instructed and, watching her until she was safely in the tiger's arms and being lowered to the ground, Coverdale once again could not believe his good fortune in his choice of a bride.

Once safely on the ground, she walked carefully over to the horses and stood there, talking softly to them, waiting to see how Edwin was going to get out without tipping the carriage, for he was, of course, considerably heavier than she was.

Carlos asked a question in Spanish, then went to the small seat behind and brought back a walking stick. Slowly and very carefully, Coverdale eased himself along the seat and allowed his man to assist him to the ground, then, leaning heavily on the stick, he made his way to where Catherine stood.

"Don't look so concerned, my dear," he said. "I sustained no more than a bump, and I do believe we came off quite lightly, considering everything." He turned to Carlos. "I think you should go to the bend and look for the phaeton. I would not like someone to be lying there badly injured."

As soon as the little man was some distance away, Coverdale touched Catherine's cheek and said softly, "You are most remarkable, my love. No megrims, no hysterics, just worrying as to how I am and looking to the horses." He shook his head. "Even my mama would have been shaking by now, and asking what on earth we are going to do to get back."

She felt too embarrassed by his compliments to respond to them. "I wish there were somewhere where I could take a look at that leg," she said, frowning. "It is the one that was wounded, isn't it?"

There was amusement in his eyes. "Yes, it is," he told her. "And if it will make you feel any better, when we are back at the house and Carlos is attending me, he will allow you take a look just to reassure yourself."

"Edwin," Catherine said crossly, "I know that I am not your wife in every sense of the word, but I am married to you and must surely be the best person to take care of you. I have experience, you know, for I looked after my papa when he came home wounded."

"But I am not your papa," he said firmly. "The only way I will permit you to look after me is if I can do the same for you. You must have sustained some bruises or strains, despite my efforts to save you from being thrown out of the carriage."

She turned away, her cheeks a rosy red, then, to his surprise and dismay, she looked directly into his eyes and said, on a note of challenge, "You have a bargain, my lord, and I will keep my end of it."

Muttering quietly to himself, he looked along the road they had traveled and saw that Carlos was already returning. Without responding to Catherine, for he was, for once, not sure what to say, he waited until the little man was within hearing distance, then called, "What did you find?"

"Just the carriage, milor'," Carlos called back, "much worse than ours, and the chestnuts almost done for. No sign of driver or passenger."

He was panting slightly as he reached them and shook his head in disgust. "I think I'd have killed him if he was there, for nettles were under the harnesses to drive horses mad. I removed them, but damage was already done."

"Did you recognize the phaeton? Did it belong to anyone we know?" Coverdale asked. "I was too busy attempting to get out of its way to see whose it might be."

"I took these out of the pockets," Carlos said, handing a sheaf of papers to Coverdale.

Without compunction, Coverdale leafed through them, then exclaimed, "But these belong to Lady Summerskill. She's our neighbor to the north and a very good friend of Mama's. I'll warrant the carriage was stolen and the driver is lying unconscious somewhere." He stopped, realizing that Catherine was looking at him with horror.

He grinned. "Just my lurid imagination, my lady," he said by way of apology.

"Is it really, my lord?" she asked sarcastically. "I was told by my mama that men were the most unimaginative creatures alive, but I now believe that she must have been mistaken."

"Yes, well . . ," he muttered, then glanced up. "Look, there's someone coming. Perhaps we can at least get you home, Catherine."

"If you think that you can put me in some stranger's carriage Edwin, and send me home, you're very much mistaken. I ride with you or not at all," she said boldly.

It took only a flick of Coverdale's eyebrows in the direction of the oncoming carriage to make his tiger hurry along the road to intercept the vehicle.

"You go too far, Catherine," Coverdale said in a dangerously soft voice she had not heard before. "You will go in whatever transportation I decide. Is that clear?"

"I am sorry for the way I spoke. It is one of my failings, I know, my lord," she said contritely, "but I beg you, please don't send me off alone with some stranger while you put yourself in jeopardy."

Leaning heavily on his cane, he lifted his other hand, meaning to stroke her cheek, and was shocked when she put up a hand to protect her face.

"One thing you'll learn I don't do, my love, is hit women," he said gently. "If going back alone worries you so much, then I'll not send you off."

This time when he raised his hand she did not flinch from

it, but let his fingers gently caress her face before turning her head and placing a kiss in the palm of his hand.

Coverdale felt a surge of pleasure at the unexpected gesture, and cursed Blanchard silently for having put him in such an impossible position. Then he turned to look at the carriage, which had stopped for Carlos to jump up beside the driver and was now coming slowly toward them. A moment later he recognized the carriage as that of his good friend, Viscount Lionel Lazenby.

"Well met, Lionel," he called as his friend stepped down from the carriage. "I'll vow you couldn't have chosen a better time to pass this way had you tried."

"So I hear, and it sounds rather questionable behavior to me. Have you no idea who the phaeton belongs to?" Lazenby asked, walking toward them.

"Papers inside show it as having been purchased by Lady Summerskill, but I would doubt very much that she bought it for herself. I don't know if you have met her, for she's sixty if she's a day," Coverdale said with a grin. "She probably bought it for that young rapscallion of a grandson of hers, but I cannot see him driving his cattle like that, or departing the scene.

"I don't believe you've met my wife," Coverdale added as his friend came closer. "Catherine, this is an old friend and warrior of mine, Viscount Lionel Lazenby. Lionel, my bride, Catherine."

Lazenby bowed low. "My pleasure, my lady. I trust you found Westcliffe House to your liking."

"Of course," Catherine said happily. "Who could not like such a beautiful house? Do you live nearby?"

"Close enough for Edwin and me to have known each other all our lives." He frowned. "You were not using a stick last time I saw you, Edwin. Has the leg become worse?"

Coverdale gave him a wry grin. "Only since someone tried to run us off the road," he said. "Are you alone? Can you take us up?"

"Of course, and we'll fasten the horses behind, as long as they're not injured," Lazenby said at once.

"I'll keep an eye on them, milor'd," Carlos said, coming to his master's side.

"Allow me to put Lady Coverdale in the carriage first and make her comfortable," Lazenby suggested, aware that his friend would not want anyone watching if he should need assisting into the carriage.

Five minutes later they started back to Westcliffe House, but when they reached the phaeton that had done them so much damage, Lazenby insisted on stepping down. Coverdale appeared content to watch from the window.

"I'll send someone back for them as soon as we get home," he said to his friend.

"Frankly, I wouldn't mind getting my hands on whoever treated them so roughly," Lazenby said disgustedly when he got back into the coach. "Their mouths are torn, and they're going to need very careful handling before they're fit to pull a carriage again."

When they reached Westcliffe House, Coverdale asked his friend to come in, but Lazenby refused. "Far be it from me to disturb a couple who should by rights be on their wedding trip," he said. "Delighted to meet you, Lady Coverdale, and only wish it had been under more pleasant circumstances. Look after Edwin, here, for I know that if he can he'll ignore that leg and do nothing about it until he's flat on his back again."

"She's enough of a termagant already, without you aiding and abetting her," Coverdale growled, slipping an arm around Catherine's waist.

When the carriage had gone, he went with her into the hall and said, "If you'll excuse me for a few minutes, I'll drop a line to Lady Summerskill explaining what happened. Carlos can take it so that he can then show her man where it is to be found."

"And then will you keep your promise and come upstairs to let me have a look at that leg?" Catherine asked.

He sighed, then said, "All right, if you insist, but you'd best not think to get your way every time. It's just that I don't make a habit of breaking promises."

Catherine's smile was mischievous. "I'll see you in your bed-chamber in ten minutes, shall we say?"

"Fifteen," he growled.

Hurrying up the stairs, she went first to her own bedchamber and took out the small case she kept filled with necessary medicines and ointments, then went along to Coverdale's chamber and took a seat near the fireplace to wait for him.

Twelve

IT WAS A full twenty minutes before Coverdale came up to his bedchamber, but the time went very quickly to Catherine, for she found it of the utmost interest to wander around a room that was so personal to a husband of whom she knew so little. To see what he read before going to sleep of a night quite fascinated her, as did the neat manner in which everything was arranged on his dressing table, which she felt sure was his doing more than that of Carlos.

She wondered where his nightshirt and cap were, for her own lay neatly across her bed at this moment. She could see his slippers beside his bed, waiting, so was it possible that he slept naked as she had heard some men did?

The thought gave her a quite odd feeling almost of anticipation, and she then wondered if he shaved both at morning and at night. This there was not, of course, any way of telling from examining the bedchamber, but then she recalled that he always smelled newly shaved at the dinner hour, so it probably lasted until he actually went to sleep.

How awful, she thought, to have to do that twice each day. She had, on a few occasions when her papa had been recovering from wounds and his man had been away, shaved him, and the bristles had been quite rough and prickly to the touch.

As she thought about this, the door suddenly swung open and Edwin came in, pausing just beyond the threshold, a rather grim smile on his face.

"I see you're determined to make me keep my word," he said. "What is that?"

He pointed to the case she had placed on his desk.

"It's healing lotions and balms that I keep made up all the time in case of need," she told him. "At home there was always something happening, and even in London I had to look after a couple of Aunt Genevieve's girls."

He grunted, sounding none too pleased, but a promise was a promise and he was not about to go back on his word.

"If you'll excuse me, I'll change into a dressing gown," he said, watching with interest as a flush started under her chin and went right up to her forehead. He grinned. "Are you quite sure you want to go through with this?" he asked.

"Of course," she told him primly. "I've tended my papa and several other men in the past."

His eyebrows rose, but all he said was, "Indeed."

When he came out of the dressing room, Catherine was pleased to see that he still wore his shirt under his dressing gown, but his legs were quite bare—and covered in dark hairs.

"Where would you like me to sit?" he asked, a small smile playing at the corners of his mouth, but this time she was all prepared.

"If you'll sit on this chair," she said, "and extend your right leg over this stool, I think we can manage very nicely. I know it is the right leg, but whereabouts is the wound?"

He grinned and pointed to the right thigh.

Trying to pretend that it was someone else, preferably a complete stranger, she propped his leg upon the stool, placed a towel over his entire lower body, then turned it back to reveal only the injury.

She forgot all about her embarrassment when she saw that it had, indeed, been banged with the jarring of the two carriages and looked red and painful, though it seemed that nothing had been opened up again. Kneeling on the carpet and working quickly, she applied cooling lotions, then placed a pad over the entire wound and carefully wrapped it.

Coverdale watched her every movement, and when she was finished he said, a surprised note in his voice, "You weren't just fussing. You really are good at this kind of thing, aren't you? I must admit that it feels a great deal more comfortable already."

"Will you take my advice and endeavor to keep it raised like this for the rest of the day?" she asked earnestly.

"Compared to your father's injuries, it is nothing at all, but to me it has been a painful nuisance for some time. If doing as you say will help, then of course I will rest it," he agreed amiably. "Are you prepared to be my handmaiden and wait on me?"

Catherine might or might not be in love, but she knew that at the moment she liked him more than any man she had ever met in her life.

"If you wish," she agreed, her eyes twinkling mischievously. "We could have dinner served up here, as you very well know, and then by tomorrow morning your leg would be almost back to normal."

His leg might be, he thought, but what about the rest of him? Could he bear her closeness and still leave her alone? Then he realized that he was in no condition to touch her, in any case, so an intimate dinner in his bedchamber might not be at all a bad idea.

"I'll just go down and make arrangements," she said, moving swiftly across the chamber.

"You surely do not mean to leave me here alone until the dinner hour, do you?" he asked in mock alarm. "And you cannot think to don an evening gown when I am *en deshabille*, can you?"

This was an Edwin she had not yet seen, for he was playfully teasing her in the most delightful way. "But I cannot wear a dressing gown also. It would just not be the right thing to do," she protested.

He smiled broadly. "On the contrary, that's exactly what an intimate dinner really is, my love, so go now and make all the arrangements. Tell Jarvey to bring the sherry here a half hour before we are to eat, and then come back, through your dressing room, appropriately attired."

"In case it takes longer than you think, would you like your book?" she asked, picking it up from the night table and bringing it over to him.

"Thank you, my dear, but please don't be longer than necessary, for I would much rather have your company than that of the most exciting book yet written,'' he said softly.

He caught hold of her wrist when she would have hurried away, and said, ''I'd like to know just who those several other men you looked after were.''

She did not quite know whether he was funning or not, for he looked serious. ''Oh dear! I should have known you'd ask that,'' she said with chagrin.

''Well, I'm waiting,'' he told her, without even the glimmer of a smile.

''If you really must know,'' Catherine finally said, feeling quite embarrassed, ''they were men who worked for Papa, and all I did was give one something for an upset stomach, dressed a gashed hand, and strapped up a broken arm.''

Edwin was chuckling at her embarrassment long before she finished her list of patients, and the moment he released her wrist she stepped out of his reach.

Feeling quite flustered, she hurried from the chamber and down to the kitchens to see how dinner was progressing and to inform Jarvey of the change of plans.

Then, once all had been accomplished, she put on her prettiest dressing gown, and arranged her own hair in a much softer style, for she had given Dora the afternoon off, and, as Edwin had suggested, went through the door at the back of her dressing room, which she had never realized led directly into his. It was a most interesting and useful arrangement, she decided.

Edwin appeared to be dozing when she came quietly into his chamber, but almost immediately he opened his eyes and smiled when he saw who it was.

''Do you realize that we have now been married for almost a week and I have never before seen you dressed so informally?'' he asked. ''You look delightful, my love, if, perhaps, a little discomfited.''

''What could you expect when I had the task of informing the staff that we were to dine alone in here? Even the inscrutable Jarvey looked pleased with himself, but I don't think for a moment that he believed me when I said you had hurt your leg,'' she said crossly.

''Shall I send for him and give him his marching orders?'' Edwin asked, grinning.

"No, of course not, but you might have sent for him and instructed him yourself," she told him, trying to stay cross with him but not succeeding very well.

"I promise to do so next time," he said soothingly. "Why don't you draw that chair a little closer and sit down, my dear, for I think we should have a serious talk about what happened today. In your absence I gave it considerable thought."

He reached out and gave the chair she had moved another pull closer to him, then when she was seated, he took her hand in his and clasped it firmly.

"At first I thought it was just a case of runaway cattle in possibly inexperienced hands," he said quietly, "and that the driver simply could not pull them over to his side of the narrow road. On further consideration, however, I believe that it was planned and that the driver meant to harm us."

Catherine's blue eyes had grown large with surprise. "But why?" she asked. "Who would want to do such a thing? Does someone here bear you a grudge?"

He shook his head. "Not to my knowledge, but it does not necessarily have to be someone local. You see, from here to Dover we take a smaller road which is fairly straight until it swings to the right just a little before entering the Dover to Walmer Road. It would have been a simple matter for a carriage to wait on the Dover-Walmer Road watching through the trees for our approach.

"If he was far enough back, he would have had time to get up a good speed before swinging onto the narrower road and careening toward us. Once past us, he only needed to swing left so that we could no longer see him—if we were in a position to do so—and he could then abandon the vehicle, as he did, and make his escape across the fields."

"But why would anyone wish to do that?" Catherine asked.

Edwin shrugged. "Why would anyone want to push a foal over the side of a quarry?" he countered.

"Do you really think there is a connection between the two?" Catherine found it difficult to believe. "For it to have been planned, the driver of the carriage would have had to know what time we were leaving and, if you recall, we had originally meant to set out for Dover in the morning."

"Precisely. Someone would have had to tell him we meant to make the trip, and what time it had been changed to, which means someone from Westcliffe House," he said grimly.

There was a knock on the door, followed rapidly by a second one, and Edwin murmured, "It's Carlos." He let go of Catherine's hand as he called for his man to enter.

"The Lady Sumemrskill sends her thanks for letting her know, and her regrets for what happened," Carlos told him. "Her son was there and knew the phaeton was stolen, for it was taken while his tiger slept."

"His late tiger, I assume?" Coverdale asked.

"Exactly, milor'," Carlos said with a grin. "I went with him to see for himself, and when he saw the chestnuts I think he wanted to cry. He talked to them as if they were his children, then he and groom walked them slowly home with just rope around their necks."

"It wasn't him, then," Coverdale said grimly.

"When he left, I went slowly back over the road until I found the place where the horses stood for a time," Carlos said.

"On the Dover-Walmer Road?"

Carlos nodded. "I found this," he said, holding out the end of a cheroot.

Catherine gave a little start, and Coverdale took it and sniffed it, then set it on the table by the side of the chair.

"Were there any more?" he asked, and when Carlos shook his head, added, "Then he probably did not have to wait too long."

"You think we'll find him, milor'?" his man asked, a hopeful gleam in his eyes.

"Eventually we will," Coverdale said grimly. "But for now I believe we have done, or rather you have done on my behalf, just as much as we can."

"Your leg, milor'?" Carlos could not see the bandages for the dressing gown covered them.

"It feels extremely comfortable now." Coverdale grinned. "My wife has hidden talents."

With a smile and a bow to Catherine, Carlos left the chamber.

"You looked as though the cheroot was familiar to you," Coverdale said to Catherine. "I know quite a few people who smoke them, including myself sometimes, but none who would have reason to harm either one of us.''

Catherine shook her head, for she knew her brother had tried at least one of Gordon Smith's, and might frequently do so for all she knew. "Men rarely smoke in front of ladies,'' she said.

Jarvey must have been waiting downstairs for Carlos to leave, for he came in carrying a tray with a sherry decanter and glasses. After he had poured he placed it on the table by Coverdale's hand, then went to the door to let in two footmen with a table, chairs, cloth, and china, and within a few minutes the table had been laid and room found on one of the side tables for the various dishes when ready.

"To your health, my dear,'' Edwin said, raising his glass. "May you be safe from all dangers,''

"And to yours, also,'' Catherine added quickly, before taking a sip, "for surely it's you they intend to hurt.''

"When I know who is behind it, then I will have the answer.'' He sighed. "At least I'm pleased to know that young Summerskill could have had no part in it, and feels so badly about the chestnuts that he is walking with them a distance of some five miles to make sure they suffer no further damage.''

He refilled both glasses, and Catherine sat in silence, wondering who it could be of the fifty or more servants who had known and given out the change of time they were to leave Westcliffe House—and probably the original time, too. It had to be someone fairly close to them to have known about their change from a morning to an afternoon outing.

"You seem to be in a quandary,'' Edwin said. "Is there any way I can help solve your problem?''

She shook her head, smiling a little sadly. "I'm afraid not, for I was trying to think who would have been aware of our change of plan, and there are at least two dozen people who could have known, from gardeners to the kitchen and serving help.''

"Don't worry your pretty head about it any more, my love,'' he told her gently. "These things usually have a way of surfacing eventually, and then later we wonder why we could not have seen something so obvious.''

Though it took a little maneuvering to get Edwin into a comfortable position at the table, once it was achieved the supper was a huge success, for Catherine enjoyed serving the various dishes herself, and afterward, when challenged to a game of piquet by Edwin, she was able to give a reasonably good accounting. So much so that he vowed to give her more practice, for he dearly enjoyed a close game.

"Am I to be allowed on this leg tomorrow?" he asked just before she was about to retire for the night.

"I believe so," she told him seriously, "for after a night's rest it should be able to bear some weight, but you must use a walking stick for a couple of days at least."

"Then, tomorrow morning, allow me to show you the family picture gallery—or rogue's gallery, as we used to call it when we were small. After breakfast would be a good time, for the best light is in the morning, and there are a number of chairs strategically placed in case either one of us should tire." He grinned. "You'd best not make too many rude comments about my ancestors, for you will soon have to sit for a portrait and become one of them."

"Oh, dear, must I?" Catherine was dismayed already, but realized that it might be a good thing to see which were the more attractive poses. "Are you already in the gallery?"

"Of course, standing there in my scarlet uniform, with one hand on my sword. I cut quite a figure, I can tell you," he joked.

Catherine had no doubt that he did, for he was an extra-ordinarily handsome man, and she was quite sure that his would be the finest portrait of them all.

The next morning, as they strolled slowly down one side of the gallery, she knew she had been correct, for he was the best-looking, and she had no doubt whatever that he would outshine her. She told him as much, and he laughed.

"Never, my love," he said, "for we'll have a full-length one painted to match mine, and in one of those unusual evening gowns of yours, you'll make all the other women seem insipid."

"Your mama looks lovely as a young lady," Catherine said, "but then she is still an extremely handsome woman."

"She is, isn't she? And so full of sound common sense. When

I told her we were to be married, she threw herself whole-heartedly into it, you know,'' he said. ''It wasn't at my request that she suggested taking you shopping for clothes. She just felt that your aunt was too far removed from society right now to have the least idea what was stylish and what was not.''

Catherine was looking at a beautiful stained glass window that dominated the south wall.

''It's in the most perfect place,'' she told him, gazing at the window as the light streamed through it, turning the glass to jewels, and softening the face of the madonna as she looked gently down at the child in her arms.

''I found it in Spain where we had been fighting for days to capture a small town that was in a particularly strategic position,'' Edwin told her. ''It was one of the few windows left whole in a long-abandoned mission, and I paid the priest double what he asked for it, but still a small price for such a thing of beauty. It cost me almost as much again to have it crated so that it could not possibly be broken when I shipped it back here.''

''It was worth it, no matter what you paid, for it looks so right, and would be impossible to replace,'' Catherine said softly, marveling at the gentle soldier who could be terribly stern and fierce, and yet fall completely in love with something as beautiful as this window. She remembered also how shocked he had been when she had thought, for just a moment, that he was going to hit her. It was foolish of her, of course, to have let the thought even enter her head, for he was nothing like her father.

Perhaps something of what she was thinking had showed in her face, for quite slowly, giving her plenty of time to rebuff him if she chose, he drew her into his arms and cradled her there, looking down at her trusting face.

''You are becoming impossible to replace also, my love,'' he said softly, then slowly lowered his head until his lips barely touched hers, but even so she felt a warmth begin to seep through her and with it a longing, but for what she did not exactly know. Slowly, almost leisurely, he traced the outline of her lips with his tongue, then gradually deepened the kiss until her heart pounded and her entire body felt aflame with something she could not define. She felt an urgent need to cling to him as closely as she could, and she did not fight it.

Then he lifted his head and looked down at her flushed face. "I must stop now, my love, or we may both regret it," he murmured, relaxing his hold but leaving one arm still about her, for which she was truly grateful, for her legs were threatening to give way beneath her.

He smiled. "At least it would seem that I have not been saddled with a cold wife," he teased.

"I'm so warm all over that I feel I'll never be cold again," she said, confusedly. "I'm only just finding out what kisses really feel like."

Keeping one arm firmly about her waist, he led her back down the stairs and into the drawing room. She was glad that no one was there, for she felt that she must look completely disheveled, but when she looked in the mirror above the sideboard, she was surprised to see how well she looked—and how happy.

"I must meet with Mr. Jowett in fifteen minutes, so I'd best go into the library and make sure I have everything ready for discussion," Edwin told her, not realizing there was a tenderness in his smile that had not been there before. "What are your plans for the day, my love?"

"I believe I'll go back to see the succession houses I missed yesterday," she began, but stopped as she saw one of the servants race past the window. "Edwin, I think there must be something amiss . . ."

Before she could say any more, Jarvey came hurrying in.

"There's been another accident, milord," he said with unusual urgency. "Your father's statue is lying in pieces on the terrace."

"Was anyone hurt?" Coverdale asked sharply.

"Apparently not, milord, for there was no one there when one of the gardeners found it."

Coverdale started for the door, with Catherine close behind carrying the walking stick he had forgotten all about.

"Slow down, Edwin, please," she begged, "for it is not proper for me to be seen running around the house."

He said nothing, but slowed his step, and Catherine was able to slip the stick into his hand, and she noticed that he made use of it at once. She was hoping against hope that some pieces were complete enough for repair to be made, but when she rounded the corner and saw a hundred or more of them, she felt sure that there was not the remotest possibility.

As Coverdale stood there gazing at the remains, and regretting not having moved it to a safer place, Catherine dropped into a crouch and picked up the piece of skirt that had the child's small hand clutching it. Then, paying little heed to the light slippers she wore, she searched for more pieces that might also be kept.

Meantime, Covedale had found a piece of frayed rope, and started to look around him at the terrace beyond this one. Suddenly he found what he was looking for and he called to the servants to keep back, permitting only Carlos to come closer.

He held up the rope. "This was still attached to one of the chunks," he told his man, "and if you look carefully you'll see the deep imprints of a horse's hoofs as it strained, trying to topple the statue. Take a careful look around and see if you can find any more imprints, such as the boot prints of the man who led the horse."

They soon found what they were looking for, and Carlos went inside to find something by which to measure the size of the boot prints. It might be useful if they should find someone who had been in the vicinity of the terrace in the last twelve hours.

Meanwhile, Catherine had found enough pieces of the mother's head and that of the child to effect a repair. That was, of course, if she could persuade Edwin to keep at least some part of the statue for future generations to see. At her direction, Mrs. Lambert, the housekeeper, had brought out a number of large laundry baskets and set the maids to picking up the smaller pieces while she helped her mistress gather together the larger ones.

"There's little point in looking more than a dozen feet from the deep imprint of horse's hoofs," Coverdale called to his man. "We wouldn't have these if the horse had not been straining to pull the statue down, for the ground is not very moist."

He walked back to examine the niche itself and the terrace beneath, and saw Catherine and the female staff busily picking up pieces.

"There's no point in doing that, my dear," Edwin told her despairingly. "It can never be put together again."

"The pieces have to be picked up anyway," Catherine said, understanding completely how he felt at the moment and not wishing to start an argument. "What have you and Carlos found?"

"A piece of rope and hoof prints," he said quietly so that the others could not hear, "and also boot prints, which prove that it did not fall but was pulled down deliberately."

Tears sprang to her eyes. "Oh, Edwin, how dreadful! When is it going to end?"

In front of servants he could not do more than take her hand in his and squeeze it, but it was still a comfort to her. "It's going to end very soon now, my dear. Trust me, and don't forget, you are never to be out of doors alone."

"I won't forget," Catherine promised.

On her orders, the filled baskets were carried back into the house and up to one of the storage rooms until such time as she felt she could discuss with Edwin the restoration of at least parts of the statue. In the meantime, she meant to make a sketch of it from memory before she forgot exactly what it had looked like.

She felt as though she was walking on pins as she went into the house and up to her chamber, for she had been wearing soft slippers quite unsuited for stepping on fragments of the statue. She found, of course, that the slippers would have to be thrown away, and Dora came in just as she was bathing small cuts on her feet, for some pieces had gone completely through.

"Oh, milady, why did you have to step on the bits of that silly old statue," the girl scolded. "It was so moldy that you could easily get an infection."

"Nonsense," Catherine said sharply, "I'll just dry my feet and put some lotion on, and they'll be as fine as fivepence in no time at all. Just hand me the blue case from the bottom of the armoire and another pair of stockings and soft slippers."

The girl did as she was bid, then stepped back, waiting to see if there was anything else her mistress needed.

"Did Lord Coverdale ask you if you had seen any strangers around the house and grounds, Dora?" Catherine asked.

"No, milady, he didn't, but I heard him asking the others," Dora said.

"Well, he probably thought that I would ask you myself. Have you seen anyone unusual around?" Catherine asked as she bent down to pull on a stocking.

"No, milady, I've not seen anyone I didn't expect to see," the maid replied.

There was something in her tone of voice that did not sound quite right, and Catherine glanced up quickly, just in time to catch the strangest expression on Dora's face—almost a guilty look.

Perhaps the girl had been sneaking out to meet her boy friend, she decided, for, if she recalled correctly, Edwin's mama had chosen her because of her having a friend here, but she could not recall what his position was.

Picking up a gown and murmuring something about pressing it, Dora left the chamber. Meanwhile, Catherine took out a piece of paper and tried to sketch as much as she could recall of the statue. She knew that she would never be able catch the expression on the woman's face, but there was a good chance that the large chunks she had put away could be pieced together.

Once she was satisfied with her sketch, she put it aside and went down to the kitchens to discuss tonight's dinner menu with the chef, and while she was there, Crazy Nell walked in.

It was quite apparent that she was used to having her midday meal here, but it would not be ready for some time, and Nell seemed to have another reason for being here today, for she kept glancing at Catherine, and then looking away again.

As soon as her business with the chef was finished, Catherine went over to Nell, for she had not seen her since the day the foal was found in the quarry.

"How are you, Nell?" Catherine said brightly, and the girl looked at her strangely, then took her by the arm and led her out of the kitchen and through the back door.

"What is it? Do you want to tell me something?" Catherine asked, reluctant to go any further outside when she had promised Edwin that she would not do so.

"I seen 'im," Nell said in a singsong voice. " 'E had a big 'orse that pulled and pulled until the lady came tumbling down."

"What did he look like?" Catherine asked. "Can you remember?"

Nell stared at her for a moment, as though she was looking right through her, then she said. " 'E's smaller than you are." She giggled. " 'E'd come no 'igher than your nose if 'e stood next to you. And 'e's pasty looking, with eyes like currants and big, big ears that 'e tries to cover with 'is mousy 'air."

"Did you see what he was wearing, Nell?" Catherine asked.

The girl nodded, but said nothing for a moment. Then she said, " 'E's wearing a uniform, but 'e's only borrowed it."

"What kind of uniform, Nell? Can you tell me?" She tried to keep the excitement out of her voice, but it was difficult.

"Just a uniform, that's all," the girl said, and then before Catherine could ask her anything more, she slipped away into the garden. Catherine hurried back into the house, for she had broken her promise to Edwin just by being outside the door alone.

Now she had to find him, and let him know what Nell had just told her, for there was only one person she knew who answered Nell's description, and that was her brother's old friend, Gordon Smith.

Thirteen

CATHERINE FOUND that Carlos had come into the kitchen, and was involved in a vociferous conversation with the chef, but she soon realized that they were not quarrelling but discussing the delights of some Spanish dishes, so she stood back a little, waiting until he saw her.

"Did you need me, milady?" Mrs. Lambert asked, coming bustling through from the linen room.

"Not at the moment, Mrs. Lambert," Catherine said, attempting to sound casual. "I was just trying to recall what time Lord Coverdale asked me to meet him."

At the sound of her voice, Carlos quickly ended his discussion and came over to her, but then quite suddenly the strangest idea came to her. Putting a hand on Carlos's arm to detain him, she turned back to Mrs. Lambert.

"Dora's in the ironing room, I believe. Can you tell me which way it is?" she asked.

"It's just along that passageway, milady," Mrs. Lambert said, "but you'll waste your time looking there for her. She said you were sending her on an errand to the village and she left a good fifteen minutes since. It shouldn't be long before she's back."

"Oh, yes," Catherine said thoughtfully. "It was nothing of concern. I'll see her later in the day." Then, as she was turning to leave with Carlos, another thought occurred. "Please don't tell her I was looking for her, Mrs. Lambert," she said quietly. "She's been a little upset lately and I wouldn't like her to think I was checking up on her."

"Very well, milady," Mrs. Lambert agreed, but when her

mistress had left the kitchen she said quietly to Jarvey, "Her ladyship is a little too kind with that one. Upset, indeed! I think perhaps you might like to have a word with that girl, seeing as I can't, having promised. Pull her down a peg or two as only you can, Mr. Jarvey."

"I most certainly will, Mrs. Lambert. I never did like maids who have worked in the city. They're always too uppity for their own good," the old butler said grimly.

Catherine had no notion of what she had started, for she was far too concerned with finding out from Carlos where her husband might be at this hour. She did not want to wait until luncheon to tell him what she had heard from Nell.

"What can I do for you, milady?" Carlos asked. "I am at your service."

"I just wondered if you might know where Lord Coverdale is at the moment," Catherine said. "I would particularly like a word with him before luncheon."

"He's meeting Mr. Jowitt now, instead of earlier, and went to his house, so there would be no more interruptions," Carlos told her. "Can I assist, milady?"

"Yes," Catherine said, firmly resolved not to be put off. "You can take me to him at once, Carlos, if it is not too much trouble."

He looked at her determined face for a moment, then said, "Of course, milady. I'll order a carriage."

Catherine looked startled. "Does the bailiff lie so far away?" she asked.

Carlos looked down at her footwear, and his brown eyes twinkled. "Not far for me, but a long way for you in soft slippers."

"It will only take me a minute to change into something more serviceable," Catherine said briskly. "Wait here, and I'll return in just a moment."

She ran quickly up the back stairs and into her chamber, where she soon found a pair of stronger shoes. She would have liked to have changed into a more sensible gown, as well, but feared that Carlos might give up on her and leave, for he had seemed most reluctant to disturb his master.

To her surprise, however, Carlos was waiting just outside

her door, and she suddenly realized what he was doing there. Though her first instinct was to accuse him of following her, she refrained from doing so, knowing that it must be upon Edwin's instructions, and he was the person to whom she should complain.

She smiled at the muscular little man. "I told you I would not be long," she said, then, as he led her toward the great staircase, asked, "Wouldn't it have been quicker to go the back way?"

He shook his head. "Quicker, perhaps, but this way curious eyes will not see us."

The bailiff's cottage was no more than a five-minute walk away, and Catherine was glad she had changed her shoes, for she would have felt most uncomfortable using a carriage for so short a distance.

Carlos rapped on the door and waited.

When the bailiff opened it, Catherine smiled at him and said, "Good morning, Mr. Jowitt. I was taking a walk and understand my husband is here, so I thought that perhaps he would like to escort me home."

Coverdale was at the door before the bailiff had time to even step back and invite her in. He glanced quickly at the smiling Catherine, raised an eyebrow at Carlos, then said, "Of course, my dear. If you'll come in and wait for just a moment I'll soon be finished here."

The inside of the house was quite clean and cozy, and she graciously accepted the chair Mr. Jowitt drew forward for her. Their discussion meant little to her, so she spent her time assessing the house, doubting that it was Crazy Nell who kept it in such good order.

It seemed no more than a moment before the two men pushed back their chairs. Coverdale offered her his arm, and she thanked Mr. Jowett before stepping outside. Carlos was nowhere in sight, and Catherine could not help but wonder where he had gone to.

"Now, my dear," Coverdale began, "though I am always happy to see you, I know that it must have been something of importance for you to have asked Carlos to bring you here. Has something happened?"

"I saw Crazy Nell quite by chance, in the kitchen, and she drew me out of the house to tell me what she had seen," Catherine said quietly.

She felt his grip on her arm tighten and he stopped and swung her around. "When you gave me your word you wouldn't leave the house without someone with you, I did not mean someone like Nell," he said angrily.

"I know," Catherine said, "but we went no more than twenty yards from the door, and I went back inside as soon as she left."

"That is not the point," Coverdale snapped, but she interrupted him.

"Please listen and scold me later if you wish," she begged. "I don't know whether it was a vision, or if she actually saw him, but she described Gordon Smith perfectly, and said he had a big horse that pulled and pulled until the lady came tumbling down."

"No one heard this but you?" he asked sharply, the scold forgotten for the time being.

When she shook her head, he put his fingers to his mouth and gave a low whistle.

Carlos was beside them in a moment.

"You'd better hear this," Coverdale told him. He asked Catherine to repeat it, and she willingly complied.

"That was all? Was there nothing else?" Carlos asked, and when she shook her head, he said, "Give me her description of the man again."

"She said that he would come no higher than my nose if he stood next to me, which is true, and that he was pasty-looking with eyes like currants and big ears that he tries to cover with his mousy-colored hair," Catherine repeated, "and when I asked what he was wearing she said it was a uniform but that he had only borrowed it."

"What kind of a uniform?" It was Carlos who asked, but they both waited eagerly for her response.

She shook her head. "I asked her, but she said it was just a uniform, that's all, and then slipped away, as is her manner."

"Maybe servants' uniforms," Carlos suggested, then he asked Catherine, "Did you send Dora on an errand this morning, milady?"

She shook her head. "She was supposedly ironing one of my gowns."

"I thought as much," the batman said.

Coverdale put his arm around Catherine in a comforting hug. "Come along, my love, let's go and have luncheon," he said. "I'll see you later, my good friend."

When they were alone once more, Coverdale drew her close and cupped her face in his hands. "I should not have scolded you like that, particularly when I knew Carlos was watching, but I did it only because I was worried. Forgive me, my dear Cathie," he begged.

She nodded. "I'll even forgive you for having Carlos watching me earlier, for I know it was for my own good," she said softly.

He looked quickly around, then bent and dropped a kiss on her parted lips before resuming their stroll back to the house.

"What do you think Dora is doing?" Catherine asked, then suddenly her eyes grew wide with horror. "She could not be the one who told of our changed plans to go to Dover, could she?"

"You know the answer to that, my love, don't you?" he asked, adding, "And to think that it was Mama who gave her to you. We're going to have to watch her every move from now on, and hope that she'll lead us to Smith, if it is he who is behind these "accidents." "

"He must be very close by if she told Mrs. Lambert that she was going to the village. Do you think that's where he might be?" Catherine asked, remembering that delightful shop and the man who had known Edwin since he was a little boy.

Edwin smiled and shook his head. "It's much more likely that she went in quite the opposite direction, for Smith is far too bright to give himself away like that," he said thoughtfully. "My guess would be East Langdon, or somewhere on the way to it. I believe I'll send a note to Lazenby and ask him if he's seen anyone in that vicinity answering to Smith's description. Carlos can take it and fill him in on any details."

When they reached the house, Catherine ran upstairs to her chamber to change her shoes and wash her hands before going in to luncheon. Dora was there, and her eyes were red as though she had been crying.

"Is something wrong?" she asked the girl, wondering if she and Smith had quarreled. He had always seemed to her to be a rather vicious young man, and if he was angry with her he was not likely to treat her gently.

"It's Mr. Jarvey, milady," Dora said. "He says I've been taking too much time off, when all I did was run to the village to get some threads to repair your gowns."

"But I bought threads for my gowns just the other day and gave them to you, Dora," Catherine said. "And when I finally make that trip to Dover I'll get matching ribbons also."

The girl quite obviously realized that she had slipped up and made the wrong excuse, for her cheeks went a deep shade of pink and she started to bluster.

"I don't know where I put them then, for I just couldn't find them when I came to look," she said, adding a little too sharply, "Perhaps you put them somewhere."

"Perhaps I did, and perhaps you had better take a look for them before buying new ones another time," Catherine said, careful not to show her disgust with the girl. "Show me the ones you just got, and I'll endeavor to recall which gowns I bought them for. We may be going to Dover this afternoon, and I would not wish to have more than one of the same shade."

Of course, as Catherine had anticipated, Dora brought out the threads she had given to her the other day, but she had no intention of making her aware that she knew.

"I'm confused," she said, "for I was sure I had bought that particular shade of blue, but then again perhaps I didn't. Give me a fold of paper with one of each of these tied around it, then I'll know not to get more."

"What time are you leaving, milady?" Dora asked, looking more interested in her mistress than she had since she entered the chamber.

"I've no idea. It depends upon what Lord Coverdale has planned, but I'll certainly have to come back for my reticule and bonnet if we do go," she said. "And don't take what Mr. Jarvey says too much to heart. I've heard that his bark is far worse than his bite."

Catherine hurried out of the chamber, pleased with her conversation, and sure that she had not let the girl realize that she knew what was going on. She must remember to tell Coverdale, for he might need to have a word with Jarvey. The girl was their only lead to where Smith might be, and they did not want Jarvey to upset her so much that she ran off. Feeling much like a conspirator, she joined Coverdale in the dining room.

He glanced at her with eyebrows raised and the semblance of a smile, and when they were alone he said, "For one who is usually so prompt, you took a long time to change your shoes, my love."

"Oh, I got involved with Dora," she told him. "She had obviously been crying and so I had to find out what was wrong. Perhaps you'd best have a word with Jarvey, for he just gave her a severe scold for going off so much, and I rather think it's better not to have her suddenly leave us at this time."

"I will, of course, but you can be sure that no matter how upset she may become at Jarvey's scolds, Smith will not allow her to leave here until he no longer has a use for her," Coverdale said wryly.

"She's really not very bright," Catherine remarked, "for she did not expect me to discover that she'd been out at all, and then she had nothing to show for the errand she had been scolded for."

"Proving that she went in another direction, of course," he said with satisfaction.

"It would seem that Smith told her to let him know when we are going somewhere again, for I mentioned that we might go into Dover this afternoon, and she asked at once what time we would be going." Catherine grinned. "Can't we set a trap for them?"

"Not this afternoon, unfortunately, but they're certainly making it easy for us to do so," he agreed. "I suggested to Lazenby that if he was not too busy he might like to have an early dinner with us this evening. If he is free, then we'll bring him into our plans, for he's a good man to have around in a difficult situation."

Catherine felt sorry for the chef, who had gone to a great

deal of trouble to make a most delicious luncheon, for neither of them had paid heed to what they were eating.

Viscount Lionel Lazenby was indeed free for dinner that evening, and over a glass of wine Coverdale gave him the little information they had on Gordon Smith, and their suspicions as to the area in which he was lying low.

"You say that he's just a youngster? He may have secured a position as underfootman at one of the neighboring houses, which would account for the uniform—could even be in my own house, for that matter, for I always leave the hiring to my butler," Lazenby said, frowning. "What does he have against you?"

"I really don't know," Coverdale said, "but we have much against him, or, rather, I do on Catherine's behalf. You see, her brother, Mark, is a lightweight," he said, then looked over to where his wife was glaring at him, and added, "I'm sorry, my love, but he does not have even a fraction of your strength of purpose and character."

"Mama spoiled him atrociously, that's all," Catherine said.

Coverdale shrugged and turned back to his friend.

"Well, young Mark met Smith when he first arrived in London with his own pockets to let and, presumably admiring Smith's capacity for making money, allowed himself to be led into all sorts of crooked schemes. One of them caused Catherine to be blamed for something she had absolutely no knowledge of at all—and it isn't a bit of good looking at me like that, Catherine, for he'll never convince me that when Smith produced a chestnut wig for him to wear with your clothes, he didn't realize he was, in fact, posing as you."

"Viscount Lazenby probably has no idea what you're talking about, Edwin," Catherine remarked.

"Begging your pardon, my lady," Lazenby said, "but I could not possibly have missed the rumors that went around, and if your brother was responsible for them, and let you take the blame, he should have been thrashed."

"My brother should probably have been thrashed daily from the age of about seven, my lord," Catherine said sadly, "but he had a father who was too busy killing Frenchmen, and a mother who thought the best thing she ever did in her life was to finally produce a son and heir. With such a combination, he stood little chance.''

She felt Coverdale's fingers gently stroking her shoulders, and immediately regretted saying so much. ''I do beg your pardon, my lord,'' she said to Lazenby. ''I'm afraid that my wretched tongue sometimes runs away with me. I probably spoiled him as much as everyone else. Mark is young, and will no doubt grow more responsible with time.''

''Gordon Smith is only seventeen or eighteen, but he is extremely bright and up to all the rigs within the limitations of his class,'' Coverdale said. ''After Mark went to Cambridge, I tried to locate this young man, mostly to warn him of the consequences should he pursue the Haywards further, but he must have found out that I was looking for him and simply disappeared. Perhaps because of this, and his consequent loss of income, he decided to try to make me pay in some way.''

''He sounds quite a charming youngster,'' Lazenby said with a grin. ''Now, how can we catch him at one of his pranks?''

There was a knock on the door and Jarvey informed them that dinner was served. Once the servants had left, however, they started to discuss ways in which, by means of Dora, they could tempt Smith to try once more.

Catherine was all for making the postponed trip to Dover, and letting Dora know well ahead of time so that she could pass the information along to Smith. But Coverdale would not hear of her being used to bait the trap, so to speak, and made it clear that though she could drop hints to Dora, to be passed along to Smith, she could take no part in the actual performance of the plan.

''I will not permit you to place yourself in danger, Catherine,'' he said quite sternly. ''Don't forget that this young man had every intention of putting you so far in disgrace that you could never have been accepted in polite society.''

She glared at him mutinously but wisely kept a still tongue in her head.

''Let me first check my own household and see if any new underfootmen have been hired of late,'' Lazenby said, ''and if I have no success we'll go on from there. There is a chance of it, for we use more than anyone else in the entire neighborhood, except, of course, for you.''

"I believe I will excuse myself this evening," Catherine said, "for I am sure you gentlemen have other things you would like to discuss, and I'll have tea in my chamber."

She had hoped that Coverdale would protest, but was disappointed, for he merely smiled and murmured, "Of course, my dear, I'll see you later."

Forcing a smile, she bade them a good night and swept out of the room and up to her chamber, dismissing Dora as soon as she had brought the tea and helped her out of her gown, for she had little patience with the girl this evening, but did not wish her to notice anything amiss.

After brushing out her hair, she sat in a wing chair beside the hearth where a small fire still glowed, for though it was yet summer, when the night winds blew from across the channel it was needed to take off the chill.

Edwin had not wished her a good night, and it puzzled her, for instead he had said he would see her later. Had it been to prevent the conclusions his friend would inevitably draw, or did he really mean to come to her chamber at last?

She knew that until he finally came to her she would never feel completely married, but it was still not even two weeks since their marriage, and he had expressed his determination to wait a month.

She was still sitting there, thinking and sipping her cold tea, when she heard a light tap and glanced toward the dressing room. Edwin was standing in the doorway, clad only in a wine-colored dressing gown, and she felt the heat rise from somewhere below her neck and suffuse her cheeks as he walked toward her and took the opposite chair.

"Did you not care for Lazenby?" he asked.

"I liked him very much, as a matter of fact," she said. "What I disliked was being left out of the plans you are making. You made me feel like a child who could not be trusted."

"That was not at all my intention," he told her with a sigh. "Can't you understand that I want to protect you from this wretched fellow? How do you think I would feel if I allowed you take part and then you were harmed in some way?''

"Much the same way as I would feel if you were harmed because of me," she said quietly. "Your leg is still not fully healed, you know."

"No, it's not yet as good as new," he agreed, "which is why I thought it best to bring my old comrade, Lazenby, into the fray."

He got up and came over to sit on the arm of her chair, then he put his hand beneath her chin and raised it until he could look into her upturned face. "I made a vow to cherish and protect you. I don't take my vows lightly, my dear," he murmured.

"You also vowed to love me and to worship me with your body," she reminded him softly.

"Do you think I don't wish to?" he asked, and when she nodded, he made no further comment but lowered his head. His lips captured hers, gently caressing them until they parted of their own accord and allowed him to sip more deeply.

Catherine was nervous, but she knew that she had brought upon herself anything and everything that was to follow. And if this was just the start, she scarcely knew how she would stand it, for her heart had already begun to beat wildly, and she felt as though she was melting like a candle before a flame.

Her eyes were closed tightly, but she knew he was lifting her and carrying her over to the bed. Then his hands seemed to be everywhere at once, touching her skin and setting it afire until she was lost to all except the most unbelievable sensations sweeping over her, much as the incoming tide had swept over that narrow shore at St. Margaret's Bay, receding, then surging forward again and again.

She heard cries, like the sounds the seagulls had made as they circled overhead, and then a peace more tranquil and serene than she had ever known.

The light touch of a finger circling her cheek brought her back to the present, and Catherine opened her eyes to see Edwin's face just above her, his bright blue eyes smiling with a rueful tenderness.

"I'm afraid that I broke my resolution, my love," he murmured. "You're no longer a virgin and your sheets bear the proof of it, but from the look on your face it was not so very frightening as you had imagined, was it?"

She shook her head. "It was indescribably lovely, exciting and peaceful at the same time," she said in a breathy whisper. "And now I'm truly married, aren't I?"

"Now we're truly married, my love," he agreed, nodding his head slowly, "and there is no turning back."

"I have no wish to turn back, Edwin," Catherine told him happily. "Have you?"

"None whatsoever," he assured her, "but I had a feeling that you were not very much like your mother, and now I know I was right."

"Apparently so," she said, feeling a moment of sadness for what her mama had missed. Then, not knowing what was usual, she asked, "Will you stay here tonight, or do you return to your chamber?"

"If you wish me to, I will stay here," he said, eyeing her with warm approval. "But I must warn you that when we waken I will in all probability make love to you again, just in case the first time was not quite right."

"Is there a chance of that?" she asked in all innocence.

He nodded gravely. "A very big chance," he said, "and we may need a vast amount of practice until it is absolutely perfect."

When she looked puzzled, he laughed, framing her serious face in his hands. "I'm afraid I'm teasing you, my love, for you must know that nothing could have been more perfect."

This was not precisely true, of course, for he had wanted to make love to her so much that had he let himself go he could very easily have frightened her. Instead, he had exercised a restraint he would at one time have thought completely beyond his power.

Now he bent his head and kissed her lips with a tenderness he'd not known he possessed. He smiled softly when he realized she had fallen asleep, and he drew the covers over her, snuffed the candles, and slipped into bed beside her.

When Dora entered the chamber the next morning with her mistress's early morning tea, Coverdale had already returned to his own bedchamber. Had there not been that telltale stain, it would still have been obvious, however, from Lady Coverdale's happy glow that all was now very well indeed between them.

Gordon Smith did not share their happiness when Dora passed along this information a few hours later, for he had hoped that the problems he had created might help to drive a wedge between the newlyweds. It did not, however, affect in any way his plans for the couple's future.

He was secretly gloating, for he knew that his chances of being noticed, let alone recognized, were remote. Garbed in a torn and tattered grenadier's uniform, like so many others seeking work in town and country these days, he blended in completely and looked so different from the well-dressed young cit friend of Mark Hayward that he thought there was little chance of his identity being discovered.

Very soon now he would put into action a plan he had devised, and start to revenge himself on the aristocracy who would never allow him to become one of them no matter how much more intelligent he might be.

He had meant to have Mark Hayward caught and imprisoned, but Coverdale had thwarted that plan. Coverdale himself was a far better target, however, for he had married Catherine Hayward, who had always looked down her aristocratic nose at her brother's low-bred friend. It was Coverdale who had sent one of his thugs into his neighborhood to look for him. And that was a mistake. Now he meant to get even.

"I have word of your father," Coverdale said as he seated Catherine at the luncheon table. "He is much improved and will be brought back to England within a fortnight."

Her sigh of relief seemed to come from the tips of her dainty house slippers. "Can we go to meet the boat and take him to Aunt Genevieve's house?"

"Of course," he said, smiling indulgently, quick to note the attractive flush that had tinged her cheeks when she first saw him. "As soon as they let me know the exact details, we'll make all the arrangements. In the meantime, however, how would you like to take a trip up to Norfolk with me to see what condition your estates are in?''

"Is it wise after all that has been going on here?" she asked, surprised.

He nodded. "After you left us last evening, Lazenby and I decided that it might be the best thing to do, for we would, of course, take Dora with us, so that Smith would have no further contact inside the house and would have to come out into the open if he wanted to attempt anything else."

"But what if he went completely crazy and we came back to a shambles?" she asked.

"I really cannot see that happening, and it might just give him time to cool off a little and realize that what he's doing is childish, to say the least," Edwin said slowly. "And it would give us back the wedding trip he is trying his best to spoil."

Catherine looked a little doubtful. "I'm not sure that a visit to Hayward House will be much of a pleasure for you—or me either—for it's not at all like this, I'm afraid. But I have to admit that I would like the chance to set it in order as best we can before Papa returns there."

Coverdale was reluctant to admit that the idea behind the plan was to get her out of the way of Smith, for there was little doubt that his behavior so far indicated a malice toward her bordering on hatred.

"Did you ever have much to do with him? I mean when you first met," he asked.

"I only met him the once, and though he said nothing at the time, he told Mark to bring me along with him the next day," she told him, an expression of disgust on her face. "I most decidedly told Mark, in the strongest terms, what I thought of his little cit, and made it clear that I wanted nothing whatever to do with him."

Coverdale nodded. "I thought something like that might have happened," he said, "and from my knowledge of your brother I would say that he told the young man what you had said, word for word, meaning to illustrate to his friend what a witch you really were."

"That sounds like Mark," Catherine said, adding, "but, of

course, in all fairness, he had no idea what he was getting involved in at that time.''

"Can you be ready to leave this afternoon, say in a couple of hours?'' he asked. ''If you forget anything we can always stop and pick it up on the way. But make sure that Dora cannot get out to let Smith know where we're going.''

Catherine grinned. ''Of course. Now I see what you're doing. You mean to make him come here looking for her.''

"It might work,'' he said. ''I have set Carlos to watching her to be sure she doesn't try to run off when she's supposed to be ironing gowns or something. And he'll also keep an eye on her on the trip so that she cannot just disappear. You probably didn't miss her, but she slipped away this morning for a short time, so he can't be far away.''

"You think of everything, sir,'' Catherine said, ''and I'm certainly glad that I'm on your side.''

"And I on yours,'' he said, looking at her warmly, and remembering the previous night. ''This will be like a second wedding trip for us.''

Catherine was glad that she was able to hurry out of the room then, for a feeling of shyness came over her, and she knew she could not hide her blushes.

Fourteen

DORA DID, of course, make an attempt to let Smith know of their plans. She deliberately creased the carriage dress Catherine was to wear and scurried out with it to press it before her mistress knew what she was doing.

Ironing the gown quickly and hanging it, she hurried into the kitchen and told Mrs. Lambert that she had to run an errand for my lady.

Carlos stepped forward as if out of nowhere. "Her ladyship sent me down to tell you she needs you at once, Dora," he said. "I'm free for a half hour—perhaps I could run the errand for you?"

He thought for a moment that she was going to take advantage of his offer, then she changed her mind and shook her head.

"If I hurry with the packing, there'll probably be time before we leave," she said, almost to herself, then ran back to the ironing room to get the gown and take it upstairs.

But when she got there she found that her mistress had been busy deciding what to take with her, and by some strange chance half of the clothes she must take with her needed some minor repair. Dora could not understand how she had missed them when she put the things away. She did not for a moment suspect anything, for she put her carelessness down to having to spend time slipping out to see her friend.

Coverdale was ready ten minutes ahead of time, and he knocked on his wife's door to see how she was coming along.

"Are you ready so soon, my dear?" Catherine exclaimed, then turned to Dora and said, "You'd better pack the threads you need and take those things along with us, Dora, for there'll be plenty of time for you to finish them at whatever place we spend the night."

Five minutes later, they were on their way, Coverdale riding inside the traveling carriage with Catherine, while the maid rode with Carlos on the back. An armed outrider on each side of the carriage accompanied them, and an armed guard sat on the box with the coachman. Coverdale was taking no chances.

"She tried to reach Smith," he said as they started down the long driveway. "Did you know?"

"No, but I had an idea that she would," Catherine told him, "for I selected this gown because it was freshly ironed, but somehow it got creased and had to be ironed again. While she was gone I cut off buttons and made small tears in the clothes I was to take with me and insisted she repair them before we leave."

"Good girl, you've got a lot of sound common sense in that pretty head of yours," he said, grinning, and she was sure she felt the head in question swell with pride.

Cook had packed a hamper to the brim with fresh fruit, cold chicken, slices of ham, meat pasties, and the like, and a bottle of cold white wine, and Catherine was quietly dozing when Coverdale opened it up to investigate. The coach was comfortable and well sprung, and it was a splendid surprise, when Catherine opened her eyes at about five o'clock, to find the informal meal set out on the opposite seat.

"I think we'll be able to get as far as Chelmsford tonight," Coverdale told her, "for we're moving along at a good pace, and if we get an early start tomorrow we should reach Bury St. Edmunds for luncheon and be at your home before dark. I'll send one of the outriders ahead when we are a little closer, to secure suitable apartments for tonight."

"I'd rather not sleep in the same room as my maid this time," Catherine said firmly.

He laughed. "I would rather you didn't also, but not, perhaps, for quite the same reason," he told her, then put his fingers to her flushed cheek. "I suppose that eventually you will stop doing this, but I shall be sorry when you do, for it is quite delightful. I cannot remember when I saw a young lady over the age of eighteen blush.''

He held out a chicken drumstick, and she reached for it but kept her eyes averted, then she delicately nibbled on the succulent meat before carefully wiping her mouth and dropping the bone into the empty container.

''I trust your method of testing for blushes is not practiced on every young lady you see,'' Catherine said dryly.

He chuckled. ''Only the ones I marry, my love,'' he said, bending down to drop a kiss on her slightly parted lips.

It was some fifteen minutes before either one of them felt the need to resume their discussion, and then Catherine asked, ''What will happen if Gordon Smith decides to do something else to Westcliffe House while we're gone? I was surprised that you were willing to go away and leave the house just now.''

''Didn't I tell you that Lionel Lazenby is staying there until we get back?'' He was at first puzzled as to why he had omitted to tell her something of such importance, then he remembered and his smile held tenderness. ''I must have forgotten because I had much better things to talk about when I came upstairs last night, but, anyway, he will be there, and keeping a careful watch on everything for us.''

''Were you in the army with him?''

He nodded. ''Right up until this last brush with Napoleon, and he'll never stop regretting that he missed it, but his father was dangerously ill at the time, and he simply could not go and leave him.''

''Gordon Smith may just wait until we return, for he won't have Dora to tell him where we'll be at a given time,'' Catherine said bitterly. ''I feel chagrined at not having realized what she was doing. But I assumed, I suppose, that she was an old and trusted servant.''

''She is—or, rather, was,'' he said sadly. ''My mama will be quite shocked when this whole thing is over and I finally tell her what the girl was doing. Particularly when she finds that her favorite statue was destroyed by Dora's accomplice.''

Changing the subject, Catherine said, ''I'll count us fortunate if we find aired beds to sleep in at Hayward House, for before he left, Papa laid everyone off save the housekeeper and butler, for he said he could not afford to pay them to sit around doing nothing while he was gone.''

"That's what I thought, and why I suggested making this trip, for I'd hate him to return after his recovery and find the place in a shambles,'' Coverdale said, "when we could spend a few days there and get things started for him.''

Catherine hesitated. She hated to say it, but it had to be said some time, so better now than later. She bit her lower lip, wondering how to put it.

Finally, she blurted out, "You do realize that any money you spend you may very well not see again, don't you, Edwin?''

He smiled. "Is that what has been worrying you, my love? It needn't have, for I am fully aware that Sir John may not be in a position to pay me. But he is now my father-in-law, and I feel bound to do what I can to help him.''

Catherine sighed. If that was how he felt, so be it. She had done everything possible to warn him of the vast amount of work needed on their much neglected estates, and now it was up to him.

They arrived late the following evening, Catherine having insisted that they stop for supper at an inn before proceeding to Hayward House. Though Coverdale had sent a note ahead of time to let the butler and housekeeper know they were coming, they found the house in complete darkness.

"Did you not say that the two servants live in?'' Edwin asked.

"They have done so for as long as I can recall, and were certainly here when we left. Berkett has been our butler since Papa was a young boy. One of them must surely be about,'' Catherine said a little anxiously.

There was the sound of a derisive snort and Lord Coverdale turned slowly around, looked sternly at Dora, then asked, icily, "Did you say something, my girl?''

Catherine could not at all fault the girl for appearing terrified, for she might quite easily have felt the same way herself had Coverdale addressed her in such a tone.

"N-No, milord,'' the maid stammered. "I was just coughing.''

He turned his attention back to the door, and then from inside the house there came the faint sound of footsteps approaching.

"Who is it? There's nobody home, whoever you are." The voice sounded old and gravelly.

Catherine looked at Coverdale and suddenly started to laugh. She put up a hand, "Let me," she whispered.

"Berkett, you just open the door this minute. What do you mean by keeping us standing waiting on the doorstep?" she called loudly.

There came the noise of banging, fumbling and scraping as locks and bolts were carefully withdrawn and then the great door slowly opened to reveal a bent old man, holding a candle in one hand and a cudgel in the other. "Miss Catherine?" he croaked.

Pointing to the cudgel, Catherine said, "You can put that down at once, Berkett, for you'll not be needing it." Then, as he dropped it to the floor, narrowly missing Coverdale's foot, she flung her arms around the old man and gave him a big hug.

Mrs. Berkett must have been lurking close by in case it really was burglars, for she gave a shriek, dropped something heavy onto the floor, and then hurried forward with arms outstretched.

"Oh, lovey, we thought you were never coming home, and that the master must surely have been killed," she said, holding Catherine close.

The group had stepped into the great hall, and over Mrs. Berkett's shoulder Catherine looked at Coverdale and was relieved to see his warm smile.

"Papa wasn't killed, but he was wounded worse than ever before," she told the housekeeper. "And I'm no longer Miss Hayward, but Lady Coverdale. This is my husband, Lord Coverdale, who helped Papa after he was wounded."

Mrs. Berkett looked amazed, then she sank into a deep curtsy before Coverdale, who took her wrinkled old hand in his and helped her up.

"I'm very pleased to meet you, Mrs. Berkett," he said quietly, "and you, too, Berkett. The first thing we need to know is if there are any bedchambers that can be prepared for us, or should we retire to an inn for the night and come back in the morning?"

While the old couple were being introduced, Carlos had

quietly taken Dora on one side, lighted a couple of candles, and started off on a tour of inspection of the ground floor.

"I've kept the bedchambers clean and the beds aired, milord," Mrs. Berkett said, "and it won't take a minute to put warmers in. And our Billy's been sleeping above the stable and looking after the horses. I could give you a cold supper, but that's all, for we've been buying only food enough for ourselves."

"Of course you have, Mrs. Berkett," Catherine said soothingly, "but didn't you get my letters?"

The old lady looked embarrassed. "Two letters did come, Miss Catherine, but we were waiting until our Mabel came back for a visit. You see, neither one of us, nor Billy either, ever learned to read."

"I never knew that," Catherine said in surprise. "If I had known I would have taught you myself. But never mind, we'll manage. We've already had supper, so you needn't worry about that. Do you have enough food for breakfast in the morning?"

"There's plenty of home-cured ham, and the hens are laying. I'm always up with the sun, and can bake fresh bread and some scones and such," Mrs. Berkett began.

Coverdale interrupted. "That's probably much better than we would ever get in an inn," he told her, "so it's settled, we'll stay here. Then in the morning we'll hire some extra help and get all the supplies we'll need."

He was not at all upset by their not being expected, for he was seeing a new side of Catherine which amazed and delighted him. They might be only servants, but she quite obviously had such a deep feeling for them that she did not want them to be upset. Her arms had gone around them so caringly and protectively that for the first time he could see her as she would be with their children when they came along.

It was also quite obvious that she really had run this house for many years, and must have been very young when she first started to do so.

Carlos came back, a frightened-looking Dora with him. "We'll be all right here, milor'," he said quietly, "for there's a good master suite you can use, all clean and dusted, and I found several chambers in the servants quarters where we can sleep. The Berketts are not lazy, you can see that, they're just too old to be able to do much."

Coverdale nodded. "Take a look in the stables. There's a fellow there who sees to what horses they've got. If he doesn't have facilities for our carriage and horses, see if he knows an inn where they can be kept for the night."

"Yes, milor', and what shall we do with that one," he pointed to where Dora was standing, "who thinks herself too good to dirty her hands?"

"Come here, girl," Coverdale ordered, and she came up, almost trembling with fear of him. "As you can see, there's no one here to wait on you, for you happen to rank lower than a housekeeper and a butler, whether you like it or not. Either you stir yourself and help with what's needed, or you can go out of that door right now and not show your face in any house of mine again. Is that clear?"

"Yes, milord," she whispered. "I'll do whatever you say."

"Whatever I or anyone else here says," he thundered.

"Yes, sir," she said, close to tears.

"Then go and ask her ladyship what she needs done first, and be quick about it," he said sternly.

As she scurried away, Carlos murmured, "You think perhaps your rank is showing just a teeny, little bit, colonel, sir?"

Coverdale turned and glared at him, then grinned. "I've little patience with shirkers, as you know only too well," he said.

He looked across to where Catherine was directing Dora as to what she should do, and as soon as the girl had left, he joined his wife.

"My goodness, Edwin, what did you say to Dora to make her so eager to help me?" she asked, her eyes sparkling with hidden laughter.

"It's not what I said, but the way that I said it, my love, and I believe you have to be either a sergeant major or a colonel in the army to acquire the knack," he told her, smiling and adding, "Do you know that you have a speck of dust on your nose?"

"Would you like to take it off?" she asked, tempting him.

He looked at her for a long moment, a smile still playing around the corners of his mouth while he thought of what he would really like to take off of her. Then he said, "I'd be delighted, my lady," and took a large kerchief from his pocket to perform the simple operation.

"Do you know about a dozen reliable servants we could hire at short notice?" he asked. "Because that's what I estimate we will need for starters."

"Yes," she said brightly.

"Yes, what?" he asked, wondering if they were not all, perhaps, going a little mad in this great, empty mansion.

"Yes, I do know about a dozen reliable servants," she said, "and as they're most of them the ones Papa laid off when we left for London, I think they will still be available and glad to come back right away. They're used to working well with the Berketts."

"You really don't know how extraordinary you are, do you?" he asked thoughtfully. "I would be willing to hazard a guess that you have never carried a vinaigrette of smelling salts. You just step right in and start to work on the problem, don't you? I had no idea, when I saw you striding along that first day, how very much different you were from the usual miss, but I count myself fortunate that I had the opportunity to find out—and that I took advantage of it."

"I'm glad, also," she told him, softly, "for despite that wretched Smith, I feel happier now than I have ever been in my life. And with Papa coming home, and Mark back at Cambridge, things really are working out well, don't you agree?"

He was about to tell her just how much he agreed when he saw Carlos hurrying toward him, so he reached for her hand and squeezed it before going to see what his man wanted.

"There's plenty of room in the stables to keep twice as many horses as we have and a couple of carriages, milor'," he said, "and there's room enough for the men, but they've not been used for some time and the smell is not good. Perhaps we should send them back to the inn on horseback and they can stay the night, it will leave enough oats for the rest of the cattle and they can bring more back with them in the morning."

"Sounds good to me, but tell them that they'd better be here early," Coverdale warned, "for there's much to be done."

He went in search of Berkett, and ran him to earth at the top of the steps leading to the cellars.

"I was just going down to see if we can produce a bottle of port for you, milord," the old man said. "Would you like to come with me and see what there is?"

"Certainly," Coverdale said. "You go ahead and I'll be right behind you."

He lit a second candle, to take down with him, then followed Berkett into the cellars, which proved remarkably dry and held, besides a goodly supply of wines, a couple of sides of bacon, several rounds of cheeses, and barrels of pickles and of ale.

"Your master will be staying in London with his sister until he is better able to travel," Coverdale said, "and then I would doubt very much if he'll be quite as active as he used to be, for his injuries were very severe and it will still take some time for them to heal. He is most fortunate to be alive."

"We are very grateful, milord," the old man said sincerely. He was holding a bottle of port and one of sherry, and lifted them so that Coverdale could read the labels. "Will these be suitable?"

"Eminently," Coverdale said, "and I'll carry them so that you can light the way."

When they got back to the kitchen, they found their ladies already there.

"I think we've done all that we can for tonight, my lord," Catherine said. "All that remains is for me to thank the Berketts and wish them a good night."

She kissed each of them on the cheek. "I'll see you both in the morning. Now don't worry about anything, for there's no need. By noon tomorrow all will be as it used to."

"Would you like this in the library, milord, or in your chamber?" Berkett asked, for he had opened the bottle of sherry and put it on a tray with glasses.

Coverdale looked at his wife and raised his eyebrows. "My dear?"

"Our chamber, I think, but while we're still informal, I think we can take it up ourselves," she said. Handing the bottle of wine to her husband and picking up the tray herself, she preceded him out of the room, calling over her shoulder, "I'll lead the way, Edwin, for I don't know if you've been upstairs as yet."

"I haven't," he told her, "but I must admit that I'm glad to do so. It's been a long day, and I can think of nothing pleasanter just now than to sip a glass of wine with you before retiring."

As they went up the stairs and then along a wide corridor, Coverdale could not help but notice that the upper floor was in no better state of repair than was the one below. Carpets were, to all intents and purposes, quite threadbare, and though some of the furniture was handsome, this was due more to the craftsmanship and to the enduring quality of the wood than to its lesser years.

As Catherine paused before a door, he stepped in front of her, saying, "Allow me," and stood aside for her to enter a good-sized bedchamber with a sitting area in front of a large fireplace. The fire that blazed there had not been lit very long, but its dancing flames were still a cheerfully welcoming sight.

She placed the tray on a side table and Edwin went over to pour the golden sherry into the glasses. Then he handed one to her and, touching it with his own, said, "A toast, my love. To your father's return to health and strength here."

She drank, then raised her glass again. "And to my brother's return with a willingness to work, and the knowledge of how to restore this place to its former glory."

He touched her glass once more, and drank gladly, though he knew it would take a lot more than willingness. Mark's marrying a rich heiress would be a better cure for what ailed Hayward House.

The next morning, Catherine's tea was brought by Carlos, for, as he told them with a grin, Dora was terrified to come near the earl. But once he had gone into his dressing room, Catherine rang for the girl and set out what her day's duties would be, the least of which was assisting her with her gown.

But once the additional staff had been rehired, and the supply cupboards filled as befitted a staff of that size, things returned to normal.

An interview with the bailiff proved the point that he was too old for his position, and once the new man Coverdale had in mind was hired, the former bailiff was induced to retire on a small pension.

By the time word came of Sir John's impending arrival in England, the old place was running smoothly, and at a much faster pace then before, leaving the Coverdales free to depart for the London dock where they were to meet him.

"You do realize, I hope, that your father will not look at all the way he did when you saw him last," Edwin warned Catherine. "He's been through a great deal, and you'll have to bear that in mind. In a month or two, however, with your aunt's careful nursing, he'll start to look as he used to."

"I know," she told him, but when she saw the dreadfully pale, painfully thin officer who walked slowly off the boat, with a nun supporting him on each side, she could not help but clutch Edwin's arm tightly in order to maintain her self-control.

Coverdale watched her as she forced her lips into a smile, then stepped forward to put her arms around her papa and hug him as tightly as she dared, for she was afraid of hurting him.

Then, when they were settled comfortably in the carriage on the way to Kennington Lane, she quietly told Sir John that she and Edwin had married just a month ago.

His face broke into the first smile they had seen, and he said, his voice barely a whisper, "That's the best news you could have given me. He's a good man and just right for you, Cathie."

When they reached his sister's house, Carlos and one of the outriders made a chair with their linked hands and carried him up the stairs, for the journey had tired him considerably. Soon after that they said good-bye so that he could get some rest, promising to return the next day to see how he felt after a good night's sleep.

It was not until Catherine was in the carriage with Edwin at her side that she finally gave way, and then she wept in his arms until at last there were no more tears left. Borrowing his handkerchief, she blew her nose hard, and then looked up at him.

"I didn't mean to be a watering pot, Edwin," she said sadly, "but I just couldn't hold it back any longer."

"You didn't let your father see it," he said gently, "which

was the thing that mattered most. I tried to warn you, for I knew how it would be, but I think you were extremely brave not to break down in front of him. And each time you see him after this will be a little less trying.''

He found a dry handkerchief for her, smoothed back her hair, and then she lay in the crook of his arm with her head on his shoulder the rest of the way to Grosvenor Square.

They had the place to themselves, for his mother had removed herself to Bath for a few weeks. It was a relief to find that, because the Season was finally over and the Little Season was not yet begun, they need pay no calls except to her aunt's house. The knocker was off the door, and remained that way, for Catherine had a difficult enough time adjusting to seeing her father in such a weak state, without receiving curiosity seekers. She had seen him wounded many times in the past, but he'd never looked like this, just a shadow of his former self.

However, just being back on English soil seemed to have a beneficial effect upon Sir John, and by the time he had been in London a week, he looked a great deal better, and had even started chafing against spending so much of his time in bed.

The day he began to berate his sister for not yet permitting him to go up and down the stairs was when Catherine and Edwin decided he was well enough for them to go back to Kent and see what, if anything, was happening there. Reports from Lazenby were not helpful for, with Dora away, nothing seemed to have occurred, and it was impossible to find out whether Smith was still in the area or not.

They spent their last day in London replenishing stocks of a number of things they could not get in the country, such as Coverdale's favorite blends of tobacco and snuff from Fribourg & Treyer.

Catherine had at first professed to be in need of nothing, but Edwin quickly realized that she was reluctant to go out attended by only a maid, lest she meet any of the ladies of the *ton* who might remember and cut her. When he offered to take her with him in the afternoon, she readily accepted and begged him to stop at Fortnum & Mason's for some delicacies unobtainable in Kent. She would not, however, buy any fripperies for herself, for she still felt that the vast quantities her mama-in-law bought before her marriage should last for several years.

The following morning they made an early start, but though they maintained a fast pace, stops to change horses and to partake of luncheon and supper took more time than they expected and they did not reach Westcliffe House until quite late, leaving Catherine time for little else but much needed sleep. Despite the hour, Coverdale and Lazenby retired to the study to discuss the happenings, or lack of them, in the last weeks, and the possibilities now that they had returned.

When Catherine awoke the next morning and rang for Dora, there was no response. She bathed quickly in the cold water remaining from the previous night, and was just about to don a gown when Mrs. Lambert came bustling in with a tray and a pot of tea.

"I've just sent one of the girls up to see where Dora can have got to, milady," she began, but Catherine stopped her.

"I'm afraid she has probably departed, Mrs. Lambert," she said, "so if you could just fasten up my gown for me before you leave, I would appreciate it."

"Left without notice or her pay or anything?" the housekeeper asked. "Begging your pardon, milady, but I can't believe that."

Catherine smiled, for if her guess should prove correct, she would not be at all sorry.

When Mrs. Lambert had fastened the last hook, she told her, "If you find that she really has gone, see if any of your girls is suitable to help me for a few days. Then I'll send for my own maid, who has been visiting her sick mother."

Coverdale was already in the breakfast room when Catherine went down, and he had, of course, heard the news.

"You just missed Lionel Lazenby," he said, "but he'll be back later and I asked him to join us for dinner. So Dora took French leave, did she?"

Catherine nodded. "I can't say that I'm sorry to see her go, but I was wondering if perhaps there had been a note waiting for her when we got back."

"I thought of that too late, also," he admitted. "But I doubt that Smith would have given his location away. I'm afraid it leaves you in the difficult position of having to use someone untrained.''

She shrugged. ''I've done it before, and Dora has been such a misery since you made her do work she did not wish to do at Hayward House, that it's frankly a relief not to have her around.''

He grinned. ''If I can be of service, you know, you only have to knock on the door and I'll be there in a minute.''

''Thank you, kind sir,'' she said, her eyes twinkling, ''and I'll most likely take you up on that offer—at least at night before I go to bed.''

''That was what I had in mind, of course,'' he told her, ''but, teasing aside, I know that it is a nuisance and you've put up with so much lately, I hate you to have one more inconvenience.''

There was a light tap on the door and Carlos came in.

''Sorry to disturb you, milor', milady,'' he said, ''but there was note for Dora, left with one of the other maids who already spent the coin that came with it.''

''Did she happen to say good-bye to anybody when she left?'' Coverdale asked.

It seems she did not know she was staying away, for her clothes are all here, even the bag she had with her on the trip. So she must have thought she'd be back.'' Carlos paused, adding, ''I'm sure we have the same idea about this.''

''It's too early for guesses,'' Coverdale said grimly. ''Let's wait the day out and see if she returns.''

Fifteen

When Dora had not returned by noon, Catherine decided to take a look at the girl's chamber, which, though somewhat larger than a pantry, still had not room enough to swing a cat. She did not care to think what size chamber a tweeny might have, and frankly felt it a shame, for it was such a very large house.

It was impossible to tell whether the girl was normally so tidy, for she had obviously come in and put her travel bag upon the neatly made bed, meaning to unpack it later. And it seemed safe to assume that only after performing her final duties for the night had she received the letter Carlos had spoken of.

There was a small chest with four drawers, and Catherine opened each in turn, checking through the uniforms, petticoats, and stockings for any letters that might be hidden beneath them, but finding none. Then she looked under the bed, but all that could be seen was an unused chamber pot and an extra pair of shoes.

She saw a small box on the bedside table, and tipped its contents onto the bed and to her complete surprise found, among other trinkets, a small pearl and ruby brooch that her mama had given her on her sixteenth birthday. She had missed it just after she had arrived in London to stay with her aunt, and had assumed that she had left it in Norfolk. Now she realized that Mark must have taken it for some reason and given it to Smith, who in turn had given it to the maid.

She pinned it onto her gown, welcoming it back like a lost friend.

Then, as she started to look through the travel bag, her hand slipped inside a tear in the lining and she heard the faint crinkle of paper. She withdrew it slowly, hoping it would not be just a letter from the girl's mother, and she was not disappointed.

Catherine had no compunctions about taking the letter out of its envelope and reading it, for the girl was missing and had probably gone to wherever Gordon Smith was presently hiding, to help him make more mischief.

It was unsigned, but there was no doubt that it was from Smith, and that he had written it in a fury because Dora had failed to let him know that the Coverdales were going away.

He told her that if she was not at their usual meeting place by twelve o'clock on the night they returned, he would see to it that she never worked again, either in London or outside of it.

Catherine wondered if the threat was intended merely to frighten the girl, or whether he meant to injure her in such a way that she would be unable to work again. The only thing to do was take the letter to Edwin at once.

She found him in the library still going through the correspondence, bills and the like, that had accumulated in their absence.

"What is it, my love?" Edwin asked, getting up at once and coming toward her.

She held out the letter she had found. "I went to Dora's room to look through her things, and found this tucked in the lining of her bag. I fear that something may have happened to her."

He read it quickly, then looked up. "Either that or he realizes we know the part she has played, and now means to use her by his side. It also means that he is still in this vicinity."

"You don't think . . ?" Catherine began.

Edwin placed his arm around her shoulders and steered her toward the door. "I don't know what to think at this moment, except that we should go and have some luncheon and talk about it later. The less the other servants know, the better."

Her fingers were unconsciously playing with the pearl and ruby brooch she had recovered, and Edwin could not help but notice.

"That's pretty. I don't recall having seen it before," he remarked, then raised his eyebrows as he saw her almost guilty flush.

"It was Mama's," she said quietly. "She gave it to me on my sixteenth birthday."

He knew there was more to it than that, so he paused and leaned against the corner of a bookcase, waiting with the utmost patience for her to continue.

"I missed it after we arrived in London," she said unhappily, "and I found it just now in Dora's room."

He had no difficulty in filling in the rest. "If that's where it was, it must have passed through at least two pairs of hands to get there," he said lightly, adding, "Would you mind very much if I thrash that young brother of yours when next I see him?"

"I believe it's a little too late for that," she said sadly, "but if he took it, it was a particularly nasty thing to do, for this was the only piece of jewelry I owned."

"Despicable is a better word, my love," he told her. "Please allow me to deal with it."

"Not by thrashing him," she said softly, shaking her head. "In any case, I believe your previous scolds have been far more effective."

"I can but try, and only hope you're not out on your reckoning, for he should not be permitted to get away with something of this sort," Edwin said grimly.

They went into the dining room then, and had almost finished luncheon when they heard the doorbell, followed by the sound of voices in the hall.

Coverdale raised an eyebrow. "Are we expecting anyone so soon after our return?" he asked, just as the door opened and his mama came in. He rose at once and went toward her.

"I'll not disturb you," she said quickly, kissing Catherine's cheek and then allowing her son to help her into a chair. "I must lie down for a while, for the journey was exhausting, but before doing so I just wanted to make sure that you're both all right."

"If you just came from Bath, I'm not surprised that it was exhausting," Coverdale said, "but we only got back ourselves last night, from London, and of course we are all right. Why should we not be?"

"Oh, Edwin, I was so worried about you both, for I had a

letter from old Lady Witherspoon first, hinting about some accidents happening here. Thank you, my dear,'' she said to Catherine, who had poured her a cup of tea. "I know Eliza likes nothing better than to exaggerate, so I took little heed. But then I heard from Lady Summerskill that someone had tried to run you off the road, and I thought I'd best come and see what is going on.''

"You shouldn't have cut short your stay in Bath, Mama,'' Coverdale said gently. "We've been away for the last month, first at Hayward House, and then in London, for Catherine's father was brought back two weeks ago.''

"Oh, what a relief that must be for you, Catherine. You should have let me know and I would have returned to London to help in any way I could. How is he feeling?'' she asked.

It was Coverdale who answered. "He's coming along slowly, but he's got a long way to go yet. Why don't you let me help you upstairs, and we can talk about all these things when you've had a rest, Mama?'' he suggested.

She took the arm he held out, and as they reached the door he turned around to Catherine and murmured, "I'll be back in just a moment, my love.''

From his last words, it was obvious that Edwin wished to talk further, so Catherine stayed where she was, but as she sipped her tea something she had forgotten suddenly came clearly to mind, and she could hardly wait until he got back to tell him.

"You remember we passed some ex-soldiers on our way home yesterday, Edwin,'' she began as he came in and closed the door behind him. "Well, I think I know what uniform Smith is wearing.''

"You mean an army uniform?'' he asked. "What makes you think that?''

"Because I know now that I saw him the day after the foal was killed,'' she said. "I was looking toward the woods, and saw a figure disappear into the trees and though something seemed familiar about it, I couldn't think what it was. Now I know that it was Smith, and he was wearing a red jacket but with something gray below, which to me did not seem like army uniform. But that's what a couple of those men wore yesterday.''

"It would be gray service-overalls, which are often worn in battle, or when doing something dirty," he said. "Are you sure it was him?"

She nodded. "It's a certain way he walks, for though I only met him once, I saw him several times walking on the street with Mark."

"That's useful," Coverdale said, "for now, at least we know what to look for. And it makes an excellent disguise. What I wanted to ask you was if you mind Mama having come back so soon, my love?"

"No, of course not," Catherine said in surprise. "Why should I?"

"No reason except that we're not getting quite as much time alone together as I had hoped," he said, grinning ruefully.

"I don't need babying, Edwin, and as long as we're together every night, as we have been for the past month, that's all that really matters, isn't it?" she suggested softly.

He bent to drop a kiss on her upturned face, then warned her, "Don't forget, you're not to go out of the house alone for now, not even with Mama, and I'll explain it to her this evening."

"She's not going to care for it very much, I'm sure, and may even wish she had not returned," she told him, "and I've no doubt that Carlos will be hovering over us. But what about you? You are in just as much danger as we are, and I worry also, you know."

"Do you, my love?" he said softly. "You needn't, for I'm much more capable of taking care of myself than you are. My leg is practically as good as new now."

"Perhaps I should take another look at it, and make sure you are not trying to cozen me, sir," she murmured, her eyes sparkling with fun. "Should I bring my medicine case to your chamber this evening?"

He suddenly frowned. "If there is any cozening going on, you are the culprit I believe, young lady, for I distinctly recall a promise you made that I might check you out for bruises after our accident."

She gazed at him seriously, but her eyes sparkled with fun. "I had thought you made that check each night, my lord. And, if not, what have you been doing all this time, may I ask?"

He smiled. "A rhetorical question, I hope, my dear. But what was it you said to me once, in such a disgruntled tone? That I had vowed to worship you with my body, but done nothing about it, I believe. Do you still have complaints?"

"None at all," she murmured. "I've learned so very much in such a comparatively short time. It won't change, Edwin, will it?"

As he firmly shook his head, Catherine recalled his mother's words on her wedding day. Now it seemed they had that little piece of love, and she meant to tend it very carefully indeed.

The dowager Lady Coverdale quite sensibly rested in her bed-chamber all afternoon, and when she came down early for a glass of wine before dinner, she was much like her old self.

Lionel Lazenby had been closeted in the library with Coverdale most of the afternoon, and was staying for dinner, so the three of them, without trying to frighten her, told the dowager some of the things that had been happening at West-cliffe House before their departure to Norfolk. She was quite shocked, to say the least.

"I've known Dora since she was a little girl, for her mama worked for us, you know," she said sadly, "and I would never have thought she could have been so easily led by that young man."

"Her whole disposition changed," Catherine told her, "for she was most unwilling to help when we went to Hayward House, but then Gordon Smith did just the same thing to my brother, until he went back to Cambridge and escaped his clutches."

"And it breaks my heart to think of my husband's beautiful statue being smashed to pieces," Lady Coverdale said. "Was everything thrown away?"

Edwin looked across at Catherine with eyebrows raised, and Catherine shook her head. "We picked up all the pieces, putting the bigger ones in separate baskets, and they're in one of the spare rooms, I believe."

"Bless you, my dear," the dowager said, giving Catherine a hug. "I'd like to see them tomorrow, if I may."

In sonorous tones, Jarvey announced that dinner was about

to be served, and they went into the dining room, Catherine on Lazenby's arm and the dowager on her son's.

They had just finished one of the dowager's favorite dishes, a delicate cream of asparagus soup, when Jarvey and a footman came in with the next course. The door was open or they might not have heard so clearly the sound of a crash and then the tinkling of glass coming from the direction of the portrait gallery.

Lazenby was on his feet in a moment and heading for the door, while Coverdale stopped just long enough to grab hold of Catherine's arm to prevent her from leaving the room.

"No, my dear, I cannot go after him if I think you are in danger. Promise me you'll not move from this room." In his urgency he shook her a little and she quickly nodded.

"I promise," she said, adding, "but I don't think it at all fair."

The younger footmen joined their master but when Catherine saw Jarvey about to leave also, she called, "If I cannot go, then you cannot either, Jarvey. You may bring us a pot of coffee while we are waiting, but you know quite well that Lord Coverdale would not wish you to be outdoors."

He sighed heavily, then went slowly from the room, returning a few minutes later with a freshly brewed pot. For the first time that she could recall, he glared at her as he placed the pot upon the table, and then stalked from the room.

Catherine had just reached for the pot and was pouring a cup for Lady Coverdale when she heard a grunt and the sound of someone falling. Before she could do more than get to her feet, however, Gordon Smith, dressed just as she had described earlier, came rushing into the dining room and straight toward her.

She heard Lady Coverdale's stiffled scream and, not even thinking but acting purely on instinct, she flung the scalding coffee in his face, then bent down and snatched up a poker from the nearby hearth. Grasping it firmly in both hands, she hit him on the head as hard as she could.

Coverdale, who had seen Smith knock out the old butler, then dash into the dining room, came running in just in time to see his wife's actions, as did Lazenby, who was right behind him.

Without so much as a glance at the unconscious Smith, Edwin went over to Catherine and removed the poker from her shaking hands, then led her carefully past his friend, who was taking a look at Smith, and into the library. Lady Coverdale went with them, holding Catherine's other hand.

"We could have used you at Waterloo," Edwin murmured as he poured a glass of brandy for his wife.

"Is he going to be all right? I didn't kill him, did I?" she asked anxiously.

Lazenby came in just at that moment. He looked with admiration at Catherine, then, smiling a little, said, "He'll have a sore head, but he'll be fit to stand trial, and I've no doubt that enterprising young man will do very well for himself in Australia."

There was a hesitant tap on the door, and one of the footmen Catherine had occasionally seen at work came in, pulling after him a reluctant, red-eyed Dora. After explaining how Smith had used her, then threatened to expose her if she said anything, the footman begged them not to send her to prison.

"So you think you can handle her?" Coverdale asked.

"I know I can," the young man said earnestly. "She'll never do anything like this again, for we're going to be married, and I'll soon see that she's too much to do looking after me and the family to get into trouble any more."

Coverdale looked at Catherine, eyebrows raised.

"Let them go, my lord," she said. "I'd not wish to see her imprisoned."

"Jarvey will give you any pay owed," Coverdale told the footman. "Just see that you live up to your promises, and you'll have no problems here."

When the door closed behind them, Coverdale said, "I don't know about you people, but I'm still hungry. Shall we go back and finish our dinner? I believe they've had time to put the dining room to rights again."

He was greeted first with surprise, then the others realized that he was right. He allowed his mama and Lazenby to go ahead, then, when they were alone at last, Catherine went into his arms—and into his heart forever.